Earl of Belmore

Certain matters relating to the College of the Holy and Undivided Trinity of Queen Elizabeth, near Dublin : report, minutes of evidence and appendix

Earl of Belmore

Certain matters relating to the College of the Holy and Undivided Trinity of Queen Elizabeth, near Dublin : report, minutes of evidence and appendix

ISBN/EAN: 9783742812766

Manufactured in Europe, USA, Canada, Australia, Japa

Cover: Foto ©Andreas Hilbeck / pixelio.de

Manufactured and distributed by brebook publishing software (www.brebook.com)

Earl of Belmore

Certain matters relating to the College of the Holy and Undivided Trinity of Queen Elizabeth, near Dublin : report, minutes of evidence and appendix

DUBLIN UNIVERSITY COMMISSION.

REPORT

OF

HER MAJESTY'S COMMISSIONERS,

APPOINTED

TO INQUIRE INTO CERTAIN MATTERS RELATING TO THE COLLEGE OF THE HOLY AND UNDIVIDED TRINITY OF QUEEN ELIZABETH, NEAR DUBLIN,

WITH

MINUTES OF EVIDENCE AND APPENDIX.

Presented to both Houses of Parliament by Command of H:

DUBLIN:
PRINTED BY ALEXANDER THOM, 87 & 88, ABBEY-STREET,
PRINTER TO THE QUEEN'S MOST EXCELLENT MAJESTY.
FOR HER MAJESTY'S STATIONERY OFFICE.

TABLE OF CONTENTS.

COMMISSION.

Victoria R.

(L.S.)

Victoria, by the Grace of God, of the United Kingdom of Great Britain and Ireland Queen, Defender of the Faith, To Our Right Trusty and Right Well-beloved Cousin and Councillor, Somerset Richard Earl of Belmore, Our Right Trusty and Well-beloved Councillor, Mountifort Longfield, Esquire, Doctor of Laws, Our Right Trusty and Well-beloved Councillor, Stephen Woulfe Flanagan, Esquire, Judge of the Landed Estates Court in that part of Our United Kingdom of Great Britain and Ireland called Ireland, Our Trusty and Well-beloved Andrew Marshall Porter, Esquire, one of Our Counsel Learned in the Law in Ireland, Our Trusty and Well-beloved Joseph Allen Galbraith, Clerk, Master of Arts, Fellow of Trinity College, and Our Trusty and Well-beloved John Mulholland, Esquire, Greeting.

Whereas Our College of the Holy and Undivided Trinity, near Dublin, has recently in pursuance of provisions in that behalf in the Irish Church Act, One Thousand Eight Hundred and Sixty-nine contained, received certain sums of money in compensation for the advowsons and rights of presentation, which previous to the said Act were vested in, and the property of, Our said College; And whereas the loss of patronage connected with such advowsons and rights of presentation will, by rendering less frequent the occurrence of vacancies, delay and prevent the election of Fellows in Our said College, and may thereby injuriously affect the interests of learning in Our said College; And whereas, by the Dublin University Tests Act One Thousand Eight Hundred and Seventy-three, the position of Our said College of the Holy and Undivided Trinity and of the University of Dublin as regards the teaching and granting Degrees in the Faculty of Theology, has been in some respects modified; And whereas, by reason of the premises, We have deemed it expedient that a Commission should forthwith issue for the purpose of inquiring into the several matters hereinafter mentioned, Recitals.

NOW KNOW YE, that We reposing great Trust and Confidence in your Knowledge, Ability, and Discretion, have authorized and appointed, and do, by these presents, authorize and appoint you, the said Somerset Richard, Earl of Belmore, Mountifort Longfield, Stephen Woulfe Flanagan, Andrew Marshall Porter, Joseph Allen Galbraith, and John Mulholland to be Our Commissioners for inquiring into the amount received by Our said College as Compensation aforesaid, and the remedies proper to be provided for any injurious consequences arising from such loss of Patronage as aforesaid, and whether the said compensation is affected by any equitable claim arising out of the said recited Acts, or from any changes recently made in the condition or constitution of Our said College and University, and also into the Offices of Professors and Lecturers in Divinity in

Appointment of Commissioners

Subjects of Inquiry:—

1. Amount received as compensation and remedies for consequences of loss of Patronage.

Whether such sums are affected by any equities.

2. Divinity School: Its Offices and Endowments.

Our said College and University, the endowments and emoluments either of private or public foundation connected with the same respectively, and into the mode of conferring degrees in the Faculty of Theology in Our said University; and into the expenditure of Our said College and University in connexion with the Divinity School, and whether it would be proper that the same respectively should be continued or other provision made in lieu thereof; and having regard to the several inquiries aforesaid and other the premises, also to inquire into the mode in which the said several sums of money so received as Compensation, and the income to arise from the same, respectively, may most properly be applied, and generally to inquire and report in the premises as to you shall seem expedient. And for the better enabling you to carry these Our Royal Intentions into effect, We do, by these Presents, authorise and empower you, or any three or more of you, to call before you, or any three or more of you, such persons as you may judge necessary, by whom you may be the better informed on the matters herein submitted for your consideration; also to call for and examine all such Books, Documents, Papers, and Records, as you shall judge likely to afford you the fullest information on the subject of this Our Commission, and to inquire of and concerning the premises by all lawful ways and means whatsoever.

Mode of conferring Degrees in Theology.

Expenditure of College and University on Divinity School.

Propriety of change therein.

Proper application of Advowson Fund.

General power of Inquiry in the premises.

Power to summon and examine Witnesses.

Three to form a Quorum.

Power to call for and examine Books and Documents.

And it is Our further Will and Pleasure that you, or any three or more of you, do report to Us in writing, under your hands and seals, within the space of twelve months from the date of these Presents, or sooner, if the same can be reasonably done, your several proceedings by virtue of this Our Commission, together with your opinions touching and concerning the several matters hereby referred for your consideration.

Report to be made within Twelve Months.

AND WE WILL and Command, and by these Presents ordain, that this Our Commission shall continue in full force, and virtue, and that you, Our said Commissioners, or any three or more of you, may from time to time, proceed in the execution thereof, and of every matter and thing therein contained, although the same be not continued from time to time by adjournment.

And for your further assistance in the execution of these Presents, We do hereby appoint Our Trusty and Well-beloved Henry Brougham Leech, Esquire, Secretary to this Our Commission, whose service and assistance We require you to use from time to time, as occasion may require.

Given at Our Court, at Saint James's the Fifteenth day of March, 1877, in the Fortieth Year of Our Reign.

By Her Majesty's Command,

R. Assheton Cross.

COMMISSION,

Extending the duration of the Commission of Enquiry into various matters relating to the position of the College of the Holy and Undivided Trinity and of the University of Dublin.

VICTORIA R.

(L.S.)

VICTORIA, by the Grace of God, of the United Kingdom of Great Britain and Ireland Queen, Defender of the Faith, To Our Right Trusty and Right Well-beloved Cousin and Councillor, SOMERSET RICHARD Earl of Belmore, Our Right Trusty and Well-beloved Councillor MOUNTIFORT LONGFIELD, Doctor of Laws, Our Right Trusty and Well-beloved Councillor, STEPHEN WOULFE FLANAGAN, Judge of the Landed Estates Court in that part of Our United Kingdom of Great Britain and Ireland called Ireland, Our Trusty and Well-beloved ANDREW MARSHALL PORTER, Esquire, one of Our Counsel Learned in the Law in Ireland, Our Trusty and Well-beloved JOSEPH ALLEN GALBRAITH, Clerk, Master of Arts, Fellow of Trinity College, and Our Trusty and Well-beloved JOHN MULHOLLAND, Esquire, Greeting.

Whereas We did, by Our Commission under Our Royal Sign Manual, bearing date the Fifteenth day of March One Thousand Eight Hundred and Seventy-seven, in the Fortieth year of Our Reign, appoint you to be Our Commissioners to inquire into various matters relating to the position of the College of the Holy and Undivided Trinity, and of the University of Dublin.

And Whereas We did by Our said Commission declare Our Will and Pleasure to be that you Our said Commissioners, or any three or more of you, should report to Us in writing, under your Hands and Seals, within the space of twelve months from the date of the said Commission, or sooner if the same could be reasonably done, your several proceedings by virtue of Our said Commission, together with your opinions touching and concerning the several matters thereby referred for your consideration.

And Whereas it has been humbly represented unto Us, that it would be expedient to extend the period in which you, Our said Commissioners, were therein required to make your Report.

NOW KNOW YE that We have extended, and by these Presents do extend the duration of Our said Commission, for the term of three months, for the purpose of enabling you, Our said Commissioners, to complete the inquiries thereby required to be made.

And Our further Will and Pleasure is that upon due examination of the Premises therein mentioned, you do within the space of three months from the date of the expiration of the said Commission, report to Us under the Hands and Seals of you, or any three or more of you, what you shall have done in the Premises.

Given at Our Court, at Saint James's the Eleventh day of February, 1878, in the Forty-first Year of Our Reign.

By Her Majesty's Command,

DUBLIN UNIVERSITY COMMISSION.

REPORT.

TO THE QUEEN'S MOST EXCELLENT MAJESTY.

May it please Your Majesty,

We, your Majesty's Commissioners appointed to inquire into certain matters relating to the College of the Holy and Undivided Trinity of Queen Elizabeth, near Dublin, consequent upon the passing of the Irish Church Act, 1869, and of the Dublin University Tests Act, 1873, do most humbly submit to your Majesty the following Report:—

Part I.

The first matter into which we were commanded to inquire was the amount of compensation received by Trinity College for the loss of patronage connected with certain advowsons and rights of presentation which it had enjoyed previously to the passing of the Irish Church Act, and of which it was, by that Act, deprived; which "loss of patronage will by rendering less frequent the occurrence of vacancies, delay and prevent the election of Fellows in the said College, and may thereby injuriously affect the interests of learning" therein; also into the remedies proper to be provided for any injurious consequences arising from such loss of patronage as aforesaid; and whether the said compensation is affected by any equitable claim arising out of the said recited Acts, or from any changes recently made in the condition or constitution of the College and University.

We have invited certain bodies and persons whom we thought to be affected, to submit to us statements in writing, and have examined witnesses upon this subject, as well as with regard to the other matters referred to us. We have accordingly received statements from the Provost and Senior Fellows, who form the Governing Body of Trinity College, commonly called the Board; from the Junior Fellows; from certain of the Fellows in Holy Orders; from a committee appointed by the General Synod of the Church of Ireland with respect to the Divinity School of Trinity College; from some of the Fellows of Trinity College, with respect to the proposed separation of the Divinity School from Trinity College; and from the Professors of Trinity College, who are not Fellows. We have also received separate statements from the Provost, the Vice-Provost, the Registrar, and from the Archdeacon of Dublin, who at present fills the office of Archbishop King's Lecturer in Divinity. A copy of a letter addressed by the Rev. Dr. Salmon, Regius Professor of Divinity, to the Registrar, upon the subject of the Divinity School, dated December 29th, 1876, has been laid before us. We have, further, addressed certain queries to the Board, upon subjects as to which we required information, and have received answers from them. All these statements we have placed in the Appendix to this Report.

We find that the total amount of compensation received by the College, for the loss of its patronage, was £121,908 1s. 7d. The livings which were twenty-one in all, with aggregate incomes awarded as annuities under the Irish Church Act to the Incumbents, of £17,287, were of two classes. The first class consisted of eighteen livings, which were App. No.
granted to the College by the Patent Roll, 8 James I. (1610). The following table gives xviii.
their names, and the particulars relating to them:—

App. No. XIV.

TABLE.

[illegible]	Diocese in which situated.	Amount of Annuities awarded to the Incumbents.			Compensation.		
		£	s.	d.	£	s.	d.
Arboe,	Armagh,	6[illegible]	13	4	2,[illegible]	1[illegible]	[illegible]
Ardtrea,		5[illegible]	[illegible]	2	[illegible]	[illegible]	[illegible]
Clonfeacle,		[illegible]	7	3	[illegible]	7	[illegible]
Clonoe,		3[illegible]	4	6	[illegible]	1	[illegible]
Desertcreight,		637	3	9	[illegible]	10	[illegible]
Aghalurcher,	Clogher,	7[illegible]	[illegible]	[illegible]	8,141	16	5
[illegible]		[illegible]	4	[illegible]	6,[illegible]	[illegible]	3
Derryvullen,		[illegible]	[illegible]	[illegible]	8,101	[illegible]	11
[illegible]		[illegible]	3	[illegible]	5,[illegible]	1[illegible]	1
Ardstraw,	Derry,	1,[illegible]	4	9	9,[illegible]01	11	1
Cappagh,		1,[illegible]	14	[illegible]	7,[illegible]	15	4
Drumragh,		1,[illegible]	[illegible]	[illegible]	9,413	8	7
Clondahorky,	Raphoe,	3[illegible]	4	1	[illegible]	[illegible]	[illegible]
Clondavaddog,		431	16	7	[illegible]	[illegible]	[illegible]
Conwall,		7[illegible]	1[illegible]	[illegible]	[illegible]	16	[illegible]
Kilmacrenan,		591	[illegible]	0	[illegible]	[illegible]	1[illegible]
Raymunterdoney,		8[illegible]	13	0	[illegible]	[illegible]	[illegible]
Tullyaughnish,		1,14[illegible]	3	8	[illegible]	5	[illegible]
		14,[illegible]67	[illegible]	[illegible]	[illegible]	[illegible]	11

App. No. XVI.

App. No. XIX.

The second class consisted of three livings, the advowsons of which were purchased by the College—viz. (1), Killyleagh, which was purchased in 1757 by virtue of the King's Licence, dated 12th April, 1757, 30 Geo. II., the price paid being £1,500, of which £500 was a bequest by the Rev. Claudius Gilbert, D.D., Senior Fellow; (2) Killeshandra, which was purchased in 1763 under the authority of a Patent of 23rd March, 1763, 3 Geo. III., the price paid being £2,108 5s.; and (3) Clogherny, which was purchased in 1823 under the authority of the same Patent as Killeshandra. The price paid for the advowson of Clogherny was £14,000. The following table gives the particulars with regard to the livings in this class:—

Names of Benefices.	Diocese in which situated.	Amount of the Annuities awarded to the Incumbents.			Compensation.		
		£	s.	d.	£	s.	d.
Clogherny,	Armagh,	1,463	14	7	11,701	2	5
Killyleagh,	Down,	418	13	6	4,231	[illegible]	6
Killeshandra,	Kilmore,	1,037	8	2	9,7[illegible]	7	7
		3,318	15	[illegible]	25,700	19	[illegible]

We find that the compensation money derived from the three livings purchased by the College, with accumulated interest upon the whole fund, was, after having taken Counsel's opinion, applied by the Board, together with a further sum taken out of the general funds of the College, in redeeming tithe rentcharges on the estates amounting to a gross annual sum of £2,571 13s. 3d. Rev. Dr. Carson, Q. 180.

We have been furnished with the following particulars by the Senior Bursar of Trinity College, as to the disposal of the Advowson Fund:— App. No. xiv.

	£ s. d.	£ s. d.
I. The amount of Rentcharges redeemed by the College,	2,571 13 3	
Deduct Poor Rates,	143 [illegible]	
		2,437 12 2
II. The amount of Redemption Money, distinguishing the accumulated interest of the whole Advowson Fund from the proportion of capital which consisted of the Compensation Money of the three purchased Livings.		
Total amount of Redemption Money,	—	54,631 2 10
This amount was thus provided:—		
(a.) Received from the Church Temporalities Commissioners for the three Livings,	25,700 19 8	
(b.) Received from do., Interest on the whole Advowson Fund, £17,098 8 4; Deduct Income Tax, 343 16 5	16,754 [illegible] 11	
Interest on Deposit Receipts for Advowson Fund, received from Bank of Ireland, December 31, 1872, to March 26, 1873,	110 13 10	
Half-year's Interest on £83,080 13s., being part of the old Crown Advowson Fund invested in Government Stock, due 5th October, 1873, net,	1,819 15 0	
	44,452 14 [illegible]	
(c) Taken from the General College Funds,	10,167 [illegible]	
	54,631 2 10	54,631 2 10

III. Amount of New Three per Cents, and of Interest thereon, which represents the balance of the Compensation Money, being the proceeds of the 16 Crown Livings.

	£	s.	d.
Received for the 16 Livings granted by the Crown,	96,307	5	8
This sum purchased New Three per Cents,	104,560	0	3

Under the old system, each Tutor, who was necessarily a Junior Fellow, received all the tuition fees that were paid by his own pupils. These fees were eight guineas a year for a Pensioner, and sixteen guineas for a Fellow Commoner. The great mass of the Students were Pensioners. The chief income of a Junior Fellow was derived from the tuition fees, and thus it frequently happened that one Junior Fellow received a much larger income than another Junior Fellow his senior by several years. This income, depending on the number of his pupils, was precarious, and therefore of much less value than a certain income of the same average amount. Under the present system, which originated in a voluntary agreement entered into by the Junior Fellows, and which came into full operation in 1839, each Tutor receives directly only one-eighth of the fees paid by his own pupils. The remaining seven-eighths are divided in the following manner:— The Tutors are divided into three grades, according to their standing among the Fellows —the five Junior form the junior grade, the five Senior Tutors form the senior grade— all the Tutors of intermediate standing (of whom there are at present nine) form the middle grade. The divisible seven-eighths are divided into as many equal parts as there are Tutors; each Junior Tutor receives two-thirds of one of such parts or shares. Each Tutor of the senior grade receives a share and a third of a share, and those in the middle grade receive each one share. From all these payments there is a deduction of 6*d.* in the pound, which is paid to one of the Junior Fellows, who is called the Junior Bursar, and is elected by the Tutors to receive all the fees and distribute them among the Tutors, according to their several rights. Thus a Tutor's income, which largely consists of his share of the tutorial fund is now to a great extent independent of his success as a Tutor.

Dr. Stubbs, Qs. 103 *seq.*

Mr. Gray, Q. 255.

This system, coupled with the liberty to marry, with perhaps some other causes, has made the College livings much less attractive to the Junior Fellows than formerly. According to a calculation made by the Provost, one-third only of the livings given away after 1840 were accepted by Junior Fellows. It is long since a Senior Fellow has thought it worth his while to retire upon a College living; there has been no instance in the last fifty years. Latterly the livings may be said to have had the effect of producing circulation only at the bottom of the body. At the time of the passing of the Irish Church Act, there were (as is shown by the following table) in fact only eight out of the twenty-one livings held by ex-Fellows; of these, it will be seen, some were of but short standing as Fellows, and not one of them had been a Senior Fellow.

The Provost, Q. 35.

App. No. XIV.

Names.	Date of obtaining Fellowship.	Date of Appointment to Livings.	Annuity as passed by Commissioners.		
			£	*s.*	*d.*
Robert V. Dixon (Clogherny),	June 11, 1838	Feb. 26, 1853	1,063	14	7
(*a*) Wm. A. Willock (Cloonish),	June 6, 1845	June 14, 1851	905	5	10
James MacIvor (Ardstraw),	June 3, 1841	May 19, 1847	1,136	4	0
(*b*) James Byrne (Cappagh),	June 15, 1818	Oct. 8, 1849	1,234	11	3
(*c*) Geo. Sidney Smith (Drumragh),	May 30, 1831	April 20, 1867	1,089	3	0
(*d*) John C. Martin (Killeshandra),	June 15, 1871	May 30, 1851	1,037	8	3
(*e*) Henry Kingsmill (Cavan),	June 2, 1828	Dec. 7, 1836	767	19	6
(*f*) John Gwynne (Tullyaghnish),	May 23, 1833	Oct. 17, 1863	1,140	2	5

* In December, 18[illegible], the Rev. James Byrne accepted the Living of [illegible], with an option which he exercised by accepting Cappagh.

† In the year 18[illegible] the Rev. George Sidney Smith accepted the Living of Aghalurcher, and he was promoted to Drumragh, on its being refused by all the Fellows in the year 1867.

In addition to these there were two Ex-Fellows living who had retired upon College livings, but had by arrangement with the Fellows been permitted to exchange them. One of these exchanges took place so long ago as March, 1824, when the Rev. Thomas Romney Robinson, D.D. (who still survives), exchanged Enniskillen for Carrickmacross. He was elected a Fellow in 1814, and retired upon Enniskillen in 1823.

Enniskillen has since been twice vacant. Once in 1860 by the death of the Honorable and Rev. Charles Maude, and the second time in 1868 by the promotion of the Rev. W. C. Magee, D.D. (now Bishop of Peterborough), to the Deanery of Cork. On both occasions it was refused by all the clerical Fellows. The annuity awarded to its Incumbent was £583 8*s.* 2*d.*

The other living, Derryvullen, upon which the late Rev. John Rutledge, D.D., who was elected a Fellow in 1830, had retired in 1837, and which he had exchanged for Armagh, was still occupied at the passing of the Irish Church Act by the Rector who had been appointed under an arrangement made between the Lord Primate, Patron of the Rectory of Armagh, and the Board.

Mr. Gray, Q. 218.

Had it become vacant it might possibly, but not certainly, have "taken out" a Fellow. The same observation applies to Clonfeacle, which had been filled by the Crown on the occasion of the promotion of the Rev. H. Griffin, D.D., an Ex-Fellow, to the Bishopric of Limerick. The annuities awarded to their Incumbents were respectively £880 5s. 11d. and £936 7s. 2d.

When we come further on in our report to deal with the proper application of the Advowson Compensation Fund, we shall have occasion to return to the question of stagnation, and we believe that what we shall then recommend will provide a sufficient remedy for any injurious consequences, so far as they may arise from the loss of patronage.

We were further to inquire whether the compensation received by the College is affected by any equitable claim arising out of the before recited Acts, or from any changes recently made in the condition or constitution of the College and University.

A statement was submitted to us by some of the Fellows in Holy Orders claiming compensation out of the Advowson Fund for the loss of their right of succession to the livings formerly in the gift of Trinity College. Two of them, representing the larger number, appeared before us and gave evidence upon the subject. App. No. 1. QQ. [illegible]-311

We are of opinion that the compensation received by Trinity College for the loss of patronage is not affected by any equitable claim arising out of the said recited Acts. It is only necessary to consider the case of the Fellows who had been elected before the passing of the Irish Church Act, 1869. They had all refused at least one living of greater value than any of those which have fallen vacant since the passing of the Act; and judging of the future by the past it is highly improbable that any of those Fellows would ever accept any of the old crown livings, or would derive any advantage from the existence of that patronage, if that Act had not been passed. As long as the patronage existed the Board was obliged by custom to offer each vacant living to the Fellows in succession, but that custom would not create an equity to prevent the purchased advowsons from being sold for the purpose of procuring other property more valuable to the College as an educational institution. If any loss was thereby sustained by the Junior Fellows it will be much more than compensated if the suggestion which we shall make hereafter, for an increase in the number of Senior Fellows, be adopted. Mr. Mahaffy, Q. [illegible]. Mr. Gray, Q. [illegible]. Mr. Gray, Q. [illegible].

No compensation was awarded to the College on the ground of a right of succession on the part of the Fellows in Holy Orders. Rt. Hon. M. Longfield, Q. [illegible].

No equitable claim arises from any changes recently made in the condition or constitution of the College or University. Dr. Traill, Q. [illegible].

Part II.

The next branch of our inquiry is into the offices of Professors and Lecturers in Divinity in the College and University, the endowments and emoluments either of private or public foundation connected with the same respectively; and into the mode of conferring Degrees in the Faculty of Theology in the University.

With regard to the offices of Professors and Lecturers in Divinity, we requested the Board to furnish a list of such Professors and Lecturers; stating—

The modes of their appointment.
The tenure of their offices.
The duties which they perform; and
The salaries and other emoluments which they receive.

"The duties are, to lecture in two of the three terms of each year in subjects to be appointed by the Board, and to assist at the Divinity Examinations held by the Professor of Divinity, and by Archbishop King's Lecturer. The salary is £100 per annum.

"The Professor of Ecclesiastical History, appointed by the Provost and Senior Fellows. The tenure of the office is for five years.

"The duties are, to lecture twice a week during two of the three terms in each year for all Students requiring the testimonial of the Professor of Divinity, to hold an examination in each year for prizes in Ecclesiastical History, and to examine in Ecclesiastical History at the Divinity Professor's Prize Examination. The salary is £100 per annum.

"Four Assistants to the Professor of Divinity, appointed by the Provost and Senior Fellows.

"The Assistants appointed before the year 1876 hold the office usually during the continuance of their Junior Fellowship. The tenure of those subsequently appointed is fixed by the Provost and Senior Fellows at the time of their appointment.

"The duties are, to lecture Students twice a week during each term in the second year of their Divinity Course, and to assist the Professor in the Divinity Examinations. The salary of each Assistant is £50 per annum.

"Five Assistants to Archbishop King's Lecturer in Divinity, appointed by the Provost and Senior Fellows.

"The duties are, to lecture Students twice a week during each term in the first year of their Divinity Course, and to assist Archbishop King's Lecturer in the Divinity Examinations. The tenure of office and the salary are the same as those of the Assistants to the Professor.

"N.B.—The Senior of the nine Assistants receives £60 per annum.

"Note.—The list given above does not include Catechetical Lecturers, or other persons appointed to give religious instruction to all classes of Students, as it was assumed that the questions were intended to refer solely to the Divinity School."

We also further inquired as to the dates of the creation of the several offices mentioned in our preceding questions. We have been unable to find the exact date of the creation of the Professorship of Divinity; we have been informed, however, that the first

Mr. Pilkington, Q. 231. Professor was Luke Challoner, who was one of the three Fellows named in the original Charter of the College in 1591, and that Archbishop Usher was appointed to succeed him in the office in 1607.

App. No. XIV. Archbishop King's Lecture was founded in 1718.

The Professorship of Biblical Greek was founded in 1838.

The Professorship of Ecclesiastical History was founded in 1850.

The first Assistant Divinity Lecturer was appointed in 1783.

The first Assistant to Archbishop King's Lecturer was appointed in 1833.

We also inquired the nature and dates of change (if any) made in the salaries, emoluments, or duties of the several offices before mentioned, during the last twenty-five years.

We learn from the Registrar that the following changes have taken place in the salary

App. No. XVI. and emoluments of the Regius Professor :—

	£
(1) By King's Letter, Car. II., the salary named was	[illegible]
(2) " " 1 Geo. III., the salary was raised to	300
(3) " " 30 Geo. III., the salary was raised to	700
(4) " " 41 Geo. III., the salary was raised to £1,200 Irish, equal to £1,100 British currency.	
Twelve pounds were added as compensation for degree fees by Decree dated 18th December, 1855, pursuant to statute of 18 Vic., making the salary	1,112

No change appears to have been made in his duties during the last twenty-five years.

There have been in the same period no changes in the salary, emoluments, or duties of either

Archbishop King's Lecturer,
The Professor of Biblical Greek, or
The Professor of Ecclesiastical History.

In June, 1867, the salary of the Senior Assistant-Lecturer was raised from £36 18s. 8d. to £60 per annum; and the salaries of the Junior Assistants were raised from £27 14s. to £50 per annum each. There does not appear to have been any change in their duties.

As regards the endowments or emoluments of either private or public foundation connected with the study of Divinity in the College, we find that there have been no public grants made either by the Crown or Parliament for the purposes of the Divinity School.

The private endowments are as follows:—

1. In 1718 £500 late Irish currency was given by Archbishop King towards founding a Divinity Lecture for the use of the Bachelors of the College.

In 1729 a further sum of £500, being a bequest by the Archbishop, was paid to the College for the further endowment of the Divinity Lecturer.

These endowments were invested in the purchase of £388 17s. 8d. Bank of Ireland Stock in 1869.

The income arising therefrom has varied from £85 to £39 9s. 11d. per annum, and has been applied in part payment of the salary of the Divinity Lecturer.

The salary since 1833 has been £700 a year—the increase having in that year been granted by the Board as a charge on the Decrements.*

	£	s.	d.
6. Theologiæ Baccalaureus, ...	13	15	0
8. Theologiæ Doctor, ...	26	0	0

PART III.

The third branch of our inquiry is into the expenditure of the College and University in connexion with the Divinity School, and whether it would be proper that the same respectively should be continued or other provision made in lieu thereof. This expenditure would include Scholarships, Exhibitions, and Prizes in addition to what is paid to Professors, Lecturers, and Examiners. We put queries to the Board as to the Number of Scholarships, &c., &c., in Divinity, their value, and the trusts affecting any that may be of private endowment. We find that those of private endowment are as follows :— App. No. XV.

Scholarships.

	Annual Value. £	s.	d.
Two "Bedell" Scholarships of £30, ...	60	0	0
Exhibitions.			
An annuity of £50, late Irish currency, for the foundation of 6 "Downes'" Exhibitions of £[illegible] [illegible]s. [illegible]d. each, ...	46	3	1
Prizes.			
Prizes founded by Nicholas Foster, Bishop of Raphoe (with accumulation), to the two best answerers at the *Final Examination* of the Junior Divinity Class, .	16	0	0
Prizes founded in 1797, by the Rev. W. Downes, D.D., as follows :—			
"Downes'" Divinity Premiums for Written Composition, . . .	18	8	3
And	9	4	7
"Downes'" Premiums for Extempore Speaking, ...	11	1	6
And	7	7	8
"Downes'" Premiums for reading the Liturgy, ...	7	7	8
And	3	18	10
The "Bedell" prize, ...	10	0	0
The "Kyle" prize, ...	8	10	6
"The Church Formularies" prize (founded by Judge Warren), . . .	10	0	0

App. No. XVII.

The following prizes are paid out of the funds of the College, viz. :—

	Annual Value.		
	£	s.	d.
Archbishop King's Divinity Prizes,	20	0	0
	10	0	0
Biblical Greek Prizes,	5	0	0
And			
Ecclesiastical History Prizes,	10	0	0
	5	0	0
And			
Divinity Composition Prizes, of £3 each,	Varying in total amount.		

There are six Theological Exhibitions founded by the Board with the consent of the Visitors; three of £60 each and three of £40 each, amounting to £300 per annum.

The total average expenditure of Trinity College on the Divinity School during the three years ending November 20, 1877, was £2,867 16s., as shown by the following return, dated 14th January, 1878, and signed by the Bursar :—

Particulars.	1875.			1876.			1877.		
	£	s.	d.	£	s.	d.	£	s.	d.
1. Salary of Regius Professor,	1,313	0	0	1,313	0	0	1,313	0	0
2. Pure salary of Archbishop King's Lecturer, over and above endowment,*.	655	6	8	653	0	8	635	3	7
3. Assistant Lecturers,	460	0	0	400	0	0	472	10	0
4. Salary of Professor of Biblical Greek,	100	0	0	100	0	0	100	0	0
5. Payments to Examiners in Divinity,	88	5	0	60	3	0	90	13	8
6. Prizes and Exhibitions, viz. :—									
Archbishop King's Prizes,	30	0	0	—			10	0	0
Biblical Greek do.,	20	0	0	15	0	0	15	0	0
Ecclesiastical History do.,	15	0	0	15	0	0	15	0	0
Divinity Composition do.,	13	0	0	13	0	0	13	0	0
Theological Exhibitions, and Prizes granted at that Examination,	300	0	0	200	0	0	200	0	0
	2,901	11	8	2,653	8	8	2,848	7	7
1875,	2,901	11	8						
1876,	2,653	8	8						
1877,	2,848	7	7						
	3)8,603	7	11						
	£2,867	16	0						

* [illegible]

App. Nos. VII. & XII. Rev. Dr. [illegible], Qq. 591–596.

The question as to whether the present expenditure should be continued, or other provision be made in lieu thereof, and if so what other, has occupied a good deal of our attention. There has been a strong opinion expressed that the Divinity School should remain within the walls of Trinity College.

At the same time it is generally (though not quite unanimously), felt that it cannot remain on its present footing. The time may possibly arrive when there will not be a single clergyman upon the Board of Trinity College: several members of it may after a long interval not even be members of the Irish Church. Should that state of affairs

Compensation Fund as a convenient source from which the capital sum required may be obtained, the equivalent annual income now expended by the College on the Divinity School being transferred to the general purposes of the College.

II. From the Board, who give us the text of certain resolutions passed on 3rd November, 1874, to the effect that (1) they are willing to allow the continued use of their lecture rooms to Students in Divinity, provided the lecturers are subjected to collegiate discipline, and accommodate their hours to the requirements of secular instruction in Trinity College; (2) that they are willing to confer a similar privilege on any other religious body desiring it; and (3) that in fixing the qualifications for Theological degrees they are willing to accept the certificate of any of the Theological Schools so placed in connexion with Trinity College. App. No. III.

They also give us the text of two other resolutions of the 15th January, 1876 :—

1. That the control and management of the Divinity School of the Church of Ireland be transferred to a council appointed by the Church of Ireland, reserving the statutable rights of the existing Professors and Lecturers, and

2. That on the vacancy of any Professorship or Lectureship a sum equal to the salary and payment made to such person be paid annually to the Representative Body for the maintenance of the Divinity School, on condition that the Students of Trinity College shall continue to receive instruction in the School as hitherto without charge.

These two last resolutions were carried at the Board by 5 votes to 3.

The resolutions were communicated by the Board to the Divinity School Committee, who in turn communicated two resolutions to the Board—(1) accepting the offer with thanks, and asking for steps to be taken to secure the legal permanence of the arrangement; and (2) requesting that the income might be capitalized and handed over to the Representative Body.

The Board on May 31, 1876, agreed to the first of these resolutions, but were evenly divided on the second. On a subsequent occasion, however (April 26, 1877), the second of these resolutions was negatived by a majority of 5 to 3. Rev. Dr. Carson, Q. 889.

The Board submitted this plan as well as another suggested by Dr. Salmon (the Regius Professor of Divinity), to be presently noticed, to their legal adviser, who was of opinion that either plan would require an Act of Parliament to carry it out. App. No. III.

We were informed that the above were the views of the Board collectively, but that individual members were understood to entertain special views in reference to certain points, which might be more conveniently brought before us in separate communications. The Provost in his separate paper, whilst making further suggestions, strongly supported the plan of the Board (including the adoption of the resolution submitted by the Divinity School Committee that the income should be capitalised and handed over to the Representative Body). The Vice-Provost also expressed his agreement, and we have received no separate communication in a contrary sense. App. No. IX. App. No. X.

III. Some of the Fellows, both Senior and Junior, have submitted a statement which we shall further notice presently, deprecating the proposed separation of the Divinity School from the College, and from the control of the Board. App. No. VIII.

IV. The present Regius Professor, the Rev. Dr. Salmon, in December, 1876, proposed a scheme in a letter which has been put in, addressed to Mr. Stack, the Registrar of the College. Dr. Salmon was unwilling that there should be a separation between the Divinity School and the College, and in order to meet the present altered state of affairs, suggested the appointment of a special Council (similar to the new University Council), consisting of members of the Church exclusively, and composed of— App. No. XIII.

(1.) Members appointed by the Board ;
(2.) Members appointed by the Teachers in the School; leaving it a question whether the Regius Professor and Archbishop King's Lecturer should not be members *ex-officio* ;
(3.) Members nominated by the Bishops ;
(4.) Members nominated by the clerical and lay members of the Synod, or else by members of the Senate who are also members of the Church.

Amongst some other suggestions made by Dr. Salmon, perhaps the most important was the removal of the restriction of the Regius Professorship to Fellows (or ex-Fellows).

Dr. Salmon, however, stated to us in evidence that when the Commission was appointed he withdrew his proposal of a special Council, as he did not wish to create any difficulty. Rev. Dr. Salmon, Q. 191.

These are the main proposals which have been made to us ; and they have been further explained, as to matters of detail, by some of the witnesses who have appeared before us.

Mr. Mahaffy, Q. Rev. Dr. Hampton, Q.

Two points have been pressed upon our attention which deserve particular notice. One is, that if the Divinity School were to be entirely removed from within the walls of Trinity College, the probability is that a considerable number of Students who are now attracted to the College by its Divinity School, intending to take holy orders not merely in Ireland but also in the Church of England, would be lost to it; whilst the College would be, at the same time, the loser by the amount of compensation which might have been paid out of its funds to the Church of Ireland on account of its Divinity School.

The second point, which indeed is not altogether dependent upon the retention or non-retention of the Divinity School within the College buildings, but would arise if the suggestions which have been made either by the Board or by Dr. Salmon should be carried out, is this:—By the proposed changes, two outlets which have hitherto helped to relieve the stagnation in the flow of promotion amongst the Fellows, will be closed.

Mr. Gray, Q.

Originally, only a Senior Fellow was eligible for the Regius Professorship; afterwards the eligibility was extended to Junior Fellows, and finally to ex-Fellows; it was considered probable, however, that the Regius Professorship would "take out" a Senior Fellow, and Archbishop King's Lectureship a Junior Fellow.

App. No. VII.

Our attention has been directed by some of the Fellows in their statement before alluded to (III.) to the fact that Trinity College was not established or endowed specially or mainly for the education of the clergy of Ireland. They urge that the object was that the youth of Ireland should be piously and liberally educated, and that in order to carry this out the Students were granted the right of obtaining degrees in all Arts and Faculties, including Theology.

They say that the Dublin University Tests Act declares that the benefits of the College and of the Schools, as places of religion and learning, shall be freely accessible to the nation; and they maintain that as long as the present Charter remains in force the University must continue to grant degrees in Theology.

They further remark that Trinity College has always given instruction in all the Faculties in which it grants degrees (except perhaps Music).

Whilst they admit that the obligation is removed from Fellows of taking holy orders they think that the circumstances of the case will induce many Fellows voluntarily to do so in the future.

Coll. Stat. Vol. i. p. 117.

They show that the Divinity Lectures were from the earliest period given to all Students and especially to Bachelors of Arts; and they lay stress upon the following words in the Statute 1 Geo. III., which regulates the present Professorship of Divinity:—"Cum vero permultum refert ut *juventus academica*, illi praesertim qui sacris ordinibus destinantur, in sacris literis et religionis Christianae doctrina diligentius erudiantur, in quem praecipue finem fundatum fuit hoc Collegium." They then go on to tell us that at the time of the foundation of Archbishop King's Lecture, in 1718, there does not appear to have been any special school for the instruction of the clergy.

They show that the first apparent connexion between the Church and the Divinity School was in 1790, when the Irish Bishops drew up a list of books in which they decided to examine candidates for holy orders, which list they sent to the Board of Trinity College. The Board recommended the Professors and Lecturers in the Divinity School to prepare the Students in these books. On this occasion eleven out of the twenty-two Bishops signed an agreement that they would not ordain any graduate who had not attended one course of lectures by the Assistant Divinity Lecturer, the Divinity Lecturer, and the Regius Professor, respectively. They show further that the School was placed on its present footing so late as 1833. That Presbyterian Ministers not unfrequently have received part of their Theological training in it, and so have in some instances ministers of other Protestant denominations. They fear that if the School were removed from the control of an independent body like Trinity College it might reflect the Theological views of one party in the Church, and sink to the level of one of the English Theological Colleges.

They think it important that some of the Junior Fellows should be clergymen, and that, should the disposal of the offices in the Divinity School be removed from the control of the Board of Trinity College, a Junior Fellow, having small chance of obtaining one of these appointments, would have little or no inducement to make Theology the study of his life, or to take Holy Orders; and that the College might thus be left without a sufficient number of Clerical Fellows to give religious instruction to the Students, or to carry on the services in the College Chapel.

For these reasons the only change which they recommend is this, that if in course of time a member of the Board should not be a member of the Church of Ireland, in cases where any question connected with the Divinity School should come before the Board.

his place should pro hâc vice be taken by the next Junior Fellow, in the order of seniority, who should be a Churchman.

We have asked for and received returns of the attendance at Divinity Lectures and of the number of Divinity Testimoniums in different years. It will be seen that the number of Students attending these Lectures fell off largely after the passing of the Irish Church Act. The lowest point as regards Students attending Lectures was reached in 1871–2 when the number was only 75. Immediately before the passing of the Act the number was 140, in itself a considerable falling off from what it had been in the years from 1856–7 to 1859–60, when the attendances were respectively 175, 169, 179 and 172. In 1876–7 the number had risen to 118. In 1867–8 the Divinity Testimoniums issued were 50, in 1873–4 they had fallen to 21. In 1876–7 they rose to 30. App. No. XVII. Tables I–VII.

We find that the Regius Professor and Archbishop King's Lecturer deliver prælections. The Professor takes the senior, the Lecturer the Junior Students. The assistant Lecturers, four of whom are attached to the Regius Professor and five to Archbishop King's Lecturer, lecture Students twice in each week during term, and assist the Professors in the Divinity Examinations. Students now begin to attend Lectures in the Junior Sophister year, and it has been considered desirable to limit the number of Students in each of the classes to fifteen. Rev. Dr. Salmon, Q. 172. The Provost, Q. 101. Mr. Gray, Q. 297.

Having carefully considered the matter we are of opinion that it is desirable that for the future the present system of "expenditure should be discontinued, and other provision made in lieu thereof." We think that a liberal provision for the future support of the Divinity School of the Church of Ireland should be secured and paid to the Representative Church Body. The average amount of annual expenditure of the College on the Divinity School we have shown above to be £2,867 16s.

The Regius Professor has told us that the expenses of the School are not likely to decrease, and we think it should be placed in as good a financial position after as before the proposed changes take place. Rev. Dr. Salmon, Qs. 168–173.

We think that the offer of the Board to allow the continued use of Lecture Rooms in the College, on the conditions that the Lecturers should be subject to ordinary Collegiate discipline and accommodate their time to the requirements of secular instruction should be accepted, and that the Students of Trinity College should continue to receive instruction in the School as hitherto without charge. This would meet the wishes of the Board and would be in accordance with their resolution of 15th January, 1876, on the subject.

It has been suggested that the Divinity School in the event of its being entirely severed from Trinity College, and so being deprived of the use of the Lecture Rooms and Examination Halls which it has hitherto enjoyed, would become entitled to further compensation upon that account. As we have reported against the proposal for complete severance in this sense, we do not think it necessary to express any opinion upon this question.

We recommend that the Board of Trinity College should cease to be the Governing Body of the Divinity School, and a Council should be appointed on behalf of the Church of Ireland.

The position of the present Regius Professor and Archbishop King's Lecturer must remain unaltered, unless with the consent of the Board they voluntarily submit

ancient power of conferring degrees in Divinity should fall into abeyance, and as also the Clerical Graduates of Trinity College might consider themselves aggrieved were they to be debarred from the privilege of proceeding to the degrees of B.D. and D.D. in future in their own University, we suggest that whenever a Candidate for either of these degrees presents himself the best solution of the difficulty might be to give power to each religious body to appoint an Examiner, to be approved of by the Board, by whom the examination should be held or the thesis approved of, as the case might be. The examiner might receive his remuneration out of the fees payable by the Candidate.

Part IV.

We now come to the last branch of our inquiry, viz., the "mode in which, having regard to the several inquiries aforesaid and other the premises, the several sums of money so received as compensation, and the income to arise from the same respectively, may most properly be applied, and generally to inquire and report in the premises."

The sum paid by the Commissioners to the College for its advowsons, together with interest paid at the same time, amounted to £140,060 16s. 4d.

We have now to deal with the disposal of the income arising from this sum, which, if the College invest it at 3½ per cent., will produce an annual income of, in round numbers, £4,900. It would appear at first sight that the College had invested a portion of the Compensation Fund in the redemption of tithe-rentcharge at such a price as would probably secure on the entire fund a greater annual return than 3½ per cent., but as this redemption could have been effected by conversion into an annuity slightly larger and terminating in 52 years, we have considered that the profit of this transaction ought not to be rated so high as would materially alter the average return of 3½ per cent.

Rev. Dr. Carson, Q. 380. App. No. xiii.

In the first place we recommend that in addition to the Private Endowments, so much of the interest of the Compensation Fund as may be requisite shall be applied in payment to the Representative Church Body for the purposes of the Divinity School of the future. The Board of Trinity College and the Representative Body should have power by agreement to substitute for this annuity the payment of a capital sum.

In the earlier part of our Report we have stated that we are of opinion that the stagnation which exists in the flow of promotion amongst the Fellows, and in the occurrence of vacancies, has been caused only in a minor degree by the loss to the College of the patronage of its former livings; and this opinion is mainly based upon the frequency with which valuable livings were refused of late years by the majority of, and in one remarkable instance (in 1867) by all the Clerical Fellows. Still there is no doubt as to the fact of the stagnation, and as to its injurious consequences not only to the members of the present corporation, but to the interests of learning; and as regards the last, in two ways—first by retaining men for an excessive number of years in the position of teachers, when at least much of their interest in their work is abated; and secondly by making the occurrence of vacancies so infrequent, that some young men are discouraged from competing for Fellowships and in some instances go away to Oxford or Cambridge; whilst others spend some of the best years of their lives in repeatedly preparing for examinations, which can only be held at uncertain and perhaps at considerable intervals, and at which usually only one candidate can hope to be successful. The last examination was held after an interval of four years from the preceding one.

Mr. Mahaffy Q. 536. Mr. Gray, Q. 983. App. No. II.

Mr. Mahaffy Q. 237. The Provost, Q. 18. Mr. Williamson, Q. 311.

The income to arise from the Advowson Compensation Fund, it appears to us, affords a remedy which may properly be applied to giving relief for this state of things.

App. No. IV.

The question has been pressed upon our notice in a statement which we have received from the Junior Fellows, and which has been explained to us in considerable detail by Dr. Traill, one of their number, who with Mr. Williamson attended to give evidence upon it. The Junior Fellows show that the average length of time which it has taken a Junior Fellow to reach the Board since 1637, when Fellowships first became tenable for life, has gone on gradually increasing. The average duration of Junior Fellowships from 1637 to 1696 was five years. From 1696 to 1740 ten years, from 1740 to 1790, fifteen years, and from 1790 to 1841, (the year after the repeal of the Celibacy Statute), twenty-three years. We may remark upon this in passing that it also appears from their statement, that whilst the number of the Senior Fellows has remained constant at seven, that of the Junior Fellows, which was in 1637 only nine, had by gradual additions risen in the year 1808 to eighteen. After the repeal of the Celibacy Statute it was increased as we have before shown, by elections in ten successive years (1840–1849), to twenty-eight; since which time the Board have reduced the number, in accordance with powers vested in them by Letters Patent, to twenty-six.

Dr. Traill, Qq. 830 sqq.

The last Fellow co-opted to the Board was elected in 1841 and co-opted in 1876. He was therefore upwards of thirty-four years a Junior Fellow. But the Junior Fellows anticipate that if no relief be given, a still worse state of things will arise.

Dr. Traill went into a calculation with a view of showing that it will probably take the present Junior Fellows (excluding the one elected last year), periods of time ranging from thirty-eight to forty-five, and then gradually falling to thirty-four years, giving an average of thirty-nine years, from the date of their respective elections to the period of their probable co-option to the Board. Dr. Traill, Q. 321.

The Junior Fellows give in their statement the numbers of Fellows who have become Bishops in the four periods before alluded to by them. There were eighteen in the first, six in the second, seven in the third, and seven in the fourth, i.e., between 1760 and 1841. They argue that the Disestablishment of the Church must produce a serious effect upon the vacancies. Admitting the fact that of late years Fellows have not accepted livings as freely as formerly, they say that since 1841 thirteen vacancies have occurred owing to Ecclesiastical preferment, viz., ten owing to College livings and three to Professorships in Divinity, during which time only thirty-five Fellows have been elected, including the ten on the new foundation. They compare the number of acceptances of College livings by Fellows between the years 1760 and 1800, which were twenty-eight, and of elections to Fellowships which in that period were fifty, with the number of acceptances of livings between 1800 and 1841 which were twenty-four, and of Fellowship elections which, between those years, were forty-nine, and they say that it thus appears that the proportion of the vacancies caused by Church preferment to the total number of vacancies, did not much alter during the century previous to the Disestablishment of the Church.

They further say that all the avenues of exit and retirement from Collegiate work which have hitherto depended on College livings and promotion to Bishoprics have been closed for ever by the Act of 1869; and as the result of this and of the repeal of the Celibacy Statute together with the creation of the ten Fellowships on the New Foundation, it can be shown that if the body of Fellows be maintained at its present number, and without any provision for retirement, no present or future Junior Fellow could hope to reach the Board till after his sixtieth year, and that half the Board at any time must be over seventy years of age. They think that during all the period between 1877 and 1898, there would be on an average five Junior Fellows between the ages of sixty and seventy, and very probably some beyond the latter age, in addition to the Members of the Board whose ages could not be more favorably circumstanced although they might reach higher limits. This state of things they consider would be fraught with danger to the College as a teaching institution and would involve grave considerations in relation to the progress of higher education in Ireland. They think that a scheme of retirement is required not only to provide for the case of persons of advanced age, but also for those who may sooner become incapacitated by mental or bodily infirmity. They point to the Advowson Fund as the source from which a remedy may be procured; and they maintain that every trace of Church property has been eliminated from it.

Dr. Traill thinks there is even a much more serious consideration than the length of time it will take to reach the Board, and that is the number of years each Fellow will remain in each grade of Tutors. It is more serious "because as a Fellow in the senior grade of Tutors has a competence on which he can live comfortably at any rate, it does not matter so much to him peculiarly to be delayed in reaching the Board as it does to a Fellow in a lower grade to be delayed in reaching a higher one." Dr. Traill, Q. 334.

We think that what we have stated above is sufficient justification for our proposal to apply the income to arise from the Advowson Fund so as to afford some relief for the state of stagnation which does exist and is for some time likely to continue to exist. We now come to the consideration of the best way in which to do this. The Board submitted to us an extract from a proposal for a new statute, which was laid before the Government in December, 1876, with the consent of all the Junior Fellows. This provided that if a Senior Fellow should become permanently incapacitated he should be permitted by the Visitors of the College to resign his Fellowship, and to become an Honorary Fellow, upon certain terms therein specified. A similar provision was made for the case of a Junior Fellow, being either Junior Bursar or Senior Tutor, a Tutor, or a non-Tutor Fellow. The Advowson Fund was to meet the expense of these retirements, and it was therefore provided that the number of Honorary Fellows should not exceed the means of the fund to meet their salaries, excepting only that when once retired they should have their incomes secured out of the general funds of the College, if at any time the income of the Advowson Fund should run short. It also proposed that until the number of Junior Fellows should reach twenty-eight, one new Fellow should be elected in each year; that unless the number of Junior Fellows should be less than twenty-three, one Fellow only App. No. 17

should be elected in each year: if it fell below twenty-three, two and two only should be elected in each year; and lastly, that the number of Tutor Fellows now existing should not be increased. The Junior Fellows added to this, in their statement, a suggestion that any Fellow at or after seventy years of age should be allowed to retire upon one of the places provided for in the scheme. They also made some further suggestions with regard to the retiring salaries and to the application of any balance of the income of the Advowson Fund.

The Provost suggested that, in addition to the scheme of the Board, two additional
App. No. ii. Senior Fellows should be added to the Board, the two Senior Tutorships being at the same time abolished; that the number of Junior Fellows should be reduced to eighteen, and that instead of the present Studentships, which are worth £100 a year, and are held for seven years, two temporary Fellowships, tenable for seven years, should be created; and for these there should be an election every year. This would make fourteen temporary Fellows, and he proposed that they should receive £200 a year each. It may be remarked at this point that a Junior Fellow as such only receives £40 a year, late Irish currency, and his income is made up from the tutorial fund (if a Tutor), and other sources such as
The Provost, Q. 12. examination fees, Readerships in Chapel, &c. The Provost thinks that the temporary Fellows would be almost certain to set aside other candidates for permanent Fellowships.

App. No. i. The Vice-Provost appears to prefer the plan of the Board; the Registrar, on the
App. No. ii. contrary, supports the Provost's plan of terminable Fellowships, but would not add to
App. No. iii. the numbers on the Board; whilst Archdeacon Lee would create twenty decennial Fellowships, would reduce the number of permanent Fellows to eighteen, and fill up vacancies from amongst the decennial, or in cases of exceptional eminence, ex-decennial Fellows, without examination; and would abolish the fourteen Studentships; he would also reduce the number of Tutors.

Having thus drawn attention to the principal proposals which have been made, we now proceed to state our own conclusions. We are averse to the creation of honorary or retiring Fellowships; the retirements would be only voluntary, and the cases of permanent incapacity might be exceeding rare. At present there are but two such cases. One incapacitated Fellow is a member of the Board; the other a Junior Fellow. The Provost has stated that in all his long experience he has known only one other member of the Board to be permanently incapacitated. We recommend, as a more effectual measure of relief, that the number of Senior Fellows should be increased to nine, and that the quorum of the Board should be six, of whom the Provost or Vice-Provost should always be one. This would allow for the absence of any incapacitated member, and would probably quicken promotion to the Board, by about five years. If this be done, we recommend that (unless a quorum could not be otherwise secured) the practice of calling up a Junior Fellow to take the place of an absent Senior should be discontinued. A Junior Fellow has not the same rank, nor can he have the same influence, as a Senior Fellow, who is more fully acquainted with College affairs.

In addition to this, we think that an election for one Fellowship, and one only, should be held every year irrespective of vacancies. Assuming the average age of a newly elected Fellow to be twenty-six, the expectation of the duration of life at that age being 35·41 years, according to the Government Tables, the average number of Fellows would remain as at present, but the average number of Junior Fellows would be reduced by two. There would, in general, be two ex-Fellows who had retired on appointment to Professorships of Law. The cost of two new Senior Fellows would be £2,900 a year. That of the Junior Fellows, if above the present number, would of course vary with the numbers.
App. No. xviii. The calculations which appear in the Appendix, will show that under this system the number of Fellows existing at any period will never be so great as to cause any serious strain on the funds of the College.

Putting the income to arise from the Advowson Fund at £4,900 a year, there would be still a balance to dispose of.*

We do not recommend the creation of terminable Fellowships. Hitherto every person who has competed for a Fellowship has done so with the expectation that he would have to devote himself, if successful, to taking part in the teaching of the College, for the greater part of his career as a Fellow. Temporary Fellows on the other hand, having no certainty of ever obtaining permanent Fellowships, would in many instances be more anxious to devote themselves to some other profession by which they might gain a livelihood in after years. They would only be the present Students with another name and a larger income.

App. No. viii. With regard to the claims made upon the Advowson Fund by the Professors who are not

*By the application of a part of the interest of the Advowson Compensation Fund in payment of the expenses of the Divinity School an equivalent amount of the general funds of the College now applied to that

Fellows, although we thought it right to hear and report the evidence, which they wished some of their body to give to us, yet we consider that their suggestions do not come within the scope of our Commission. We therefore refrain from offering any opinion concerning them. Professors Dowden, Atkinson, and Wright, Qs. 313–340.

In conclusion we recommend generally that any balance of income from the Advowson Fund be left at the disposal of the Provost and Senior Fellows, to be applied to such purposes as they shall at their discretion consider to be most calculated to advance the interests of learning in Trinity College.

All which we humbly submit unto Your Majesty.

BELMORE.	(L.S.)
MOUNTIFORT LONGFIELD, LL.D.	(L.S.)
JOHN MULHOLLAND.	(L.S.)
JOSEPH A. GALBRAITH.	(L.S.)
* S. WOULFE FLANAGAN.	(L.S.)
* A. M. PORTER.	(L.S.)

H. Brougham Leech,
Secretary.

* Signed by us subject to the following remarks.

We desire to qualify as follows our adoption of the conclusions in the foregoing Report.

We are of opinion :—

(1) That there should be an entire separation of the Divinity School and Trinity College, and that no special privileges in relation to the College, its buildings or discipline, should be preserved or established in favour of the members of any particular Church.

(2) That sufficient time has not elapsed since the passing of the Church Act to enable us to form a correct estimate of the probable future average number of students in the Divinity School. But we find that there has been a sensible diminution of the number since the passing of the Church Act.

(3) That we have not therefore sufficient data to enable us to decide what sum should be allotted for the maintenance of the school in as efficient a condition as before the passing of the Church Act.

We are, however, of opinion that the sum proposed in the foregoing Report is in excess of a liberal provision for its future support, and more particularly should be reduced by the portion of the salary (£653 19s. 8d.) paid to Archbishop King's Lecturer out of the "Decrements." We further think that the salary of the future Regius Professor of Divinity is in excess of what under the altered circumstances of the Church, and the proposed separation of the School from the College would probably be necessary, and also that the number of the assistant lecturers might be reduced.

S. WOULFE FLANAGAN.	(L.S.)
A. M. PORTER.	(L.S.)

LIST OF WITNESSES.

Rev. H. Lloyd, D.D., Provost,

A. S. Hart, Esq., LL.D., Vice-Provost,

Rev. G. Salmon, D.D., the Ven. Archdeacon Stopford, and H. Pilkington, Esq., Q.C.,

Rev. T. T. Gray, F.T.C.D., and Rev. J. P. Mahaffy, F.T.C.D.,

Professor E. Dowden, Professor R. Atkinson, and Professor E. P. Wright,

A. Palmer, Esq., F.T.C.D.,

Rev. J. Carson, D.D., S.F.T.C.D., Bursar,

The Right Hon. M. Longfield, LL.D.,

Rev. J. W. Stubbs, D.D., F.T.C.D.,

Rev. Samuel Haughton, M.D., F.T.C.D.,

Rev. H. R. Poole, F.T.C.D.,

A. Traill, Esq., M.D., F.T.C.D., and B. Williamson, Esq., F.T.C.D.,

Rev. J. A. Galbraith, F.T.C.D.,

MINUTES OF EVIDENCE.

FRIDAY, NOVEMBER 2, 1877.

PRESENT.—Right Hon. the EARL OF BELMORE, K.C.M.G., in the Chair; Right Hon. MOUNTIFORT LONGFIELD, LL.D.; Right Hon. S. W. FLANAGAN; A. M. PORTER, Esq., Q.C.; JOHN MULHOLLAND, Esq., M.P., D.L.

between [illegible] and 1834, I found the mean duration of a Fellow's life after election to be thirty-eight years. That result is confirmed also by the tables of mortality. It is generally considered that the average age of election to Fellowship in Trinity College is twenty-six. The Carlisle Tables give 37·1 as the expectation of life of a person of twenty-six years of age; and the tables of the insurance offices give 37·3 years. Assuming the number 38 to be correct, it follows that the future average rate of succession to Fellowships is obtained by dividing the actual number of Fellows by 38. For the existing number of Fellows (35) therefore, the average annual number of vacancies is the fraction 0·92; or, if the Provostship be regarded as an office which will be filled by Fellows only, 0·95, or nine in every ten years. The chief objection to the present state of things is the variability of the times. There may be two or three years without a vacancy, and afterwards two or three vacancies in a single year. A remedy has been suggested by the Board, and included in the draft of the proposed statute which they forwarded to the Government. The remedy is to vary the number of Fellows, keeping the number of vacancies as constant as possible. I believe this would be a very great improvement.

63. Lord Belmore.—Then instead of there being a fixed number of Fellows you would have one elected every year?—Yes; within certain limits.

64. Sometimes there would be more, sometimes less, sometimes twenty-three, sometimes twenty-eight?—Yes, precisely.

65. Judge Longfield.—You remember the creation of the new Fellowships—when ten were added?—Yes.

66. What effect had that on the time of coming to the Board?—It increased considerably that time, and in a very objectionable way. The statute which created the ten new Fellowships ordered that the appointments to them should be irrespective of actual vacancies. That was expressly contrary to the provisions of the statute of George III., by which the preceding addition to the body of the Fellows was made. The result of that mistake has been to bring ten men into the body of nearly the same age, and who may consequently be expected to become superannuated about the same time.

67. Judge Flanagan.—How were these elections made?—In ten successive years.

68. Judge Longfield.—Was there not a reservation that no more than two should be elected in each year?—Yes. But that was after the whole addition had been made.

69. Lord Belmore.—Do you anticipate the probability that in a certain number of years when these ten men become superannuated there will be a sort of reaction, and the vacancies will occur more quickly?—Certainly.

70. I think the Board stated in their paper that they had been advised that the Fellows in priests' orders have no special claim for compensation on account of the loss of the advowsons?—Yes, we have had legal advice on that question from two eminent lawyers.

71. Mr. Mulholland.—In the answers to the Queries (p. 10), I find that "In the year 1833 the Rev. Geo. Sidney Smith accepted the living of Aghalurcher, and he was presented to Drumragh on its being refused by all the Fellows in the year 1837?"—That is true.

72. Lord Belmore.—The Board, I think, from what I see in these papers have made a proposal to the Divinity School Committee?—Yes, to hand over an annual sum to the Church Body equal to that at present expended on the Divinity School.

June 4, 1877. — Rev. H. Lloyd, D.D.

with Trinity College, as a sufficient testimonial of the candidate's theological acquirements." Do you agree in that resolution?—I do.

82. What test would you, or could you, apply for the exercise of any control that should be vested in the College?—I do not think that it would be advisable to grant such privilege to a religious body of minor importance. Indeed, such a case could hardly arise, because the proposition is that the body should itself be able to constitute professorships in the College.

83. That is, that they should be able to pay professors?—To pay professors for the religious instruction of their own members.

84. Then, with regard to the question of the application of part of the Advowson money asked for by the Divinity School Committee, the plan proposed was, I think, that a capital sum equivalent to what may be ascertained to be spent by the College on the Divinity School should be handed over in trust to the Representative Body of the Church, and in return for the money the students of Trinity College should continue to receive instruction in the School as hitherto without charge—was not that the plan?—It was.

85. Are you in favour of that plan?—I am; I think it preferable to the plan of the Board.

86. The original plan was that an annual sum should be handed over to the Church Representative Body?—Yes.

87. Judge Longfield.—You would take the certificate of the Divinity Professors as a sufficient qualification?—Yes, for a Divinity degree.

88. That is, in addition to the candidate being a graduate of the University of a certain standing?—Certainly.

89. Lord Belmore.—You would admit to the lectures but not to the degrees?—By the statutes of the University, Degrees in Divinity cannot be granted except to graduates of Oxford, Cambridge, or Dublin, of a certain standing.

90. Judge Longfield.—The candidate should have a certificate from the College to obtain a University degree?—Certainly.

91. That is, a certificate of being a B.D. for the degree of D.D., and a certificate of being a B.A. of a certain standing for the degree of B.D., besides the certificate of the Professor?—Yes; and thus the secular education of the candidate would be conducted in the College with other students.

92. Lord Belmore.—Would you be satisfied that the College should confer the degree of B.D. on a person over whom the College had no control, or who might not be a member of the University at all?—No.

93. Would you be willing to confer it if he should be a member of another University?—Yes, if he were admitted ad eundem gradum here.

94. Mr. Porter.—Are ad eundem degrees conferred on graduates of other Universities?—Yes; on graduates of Oxford and Cambridge.

95. Lord Belmore.—Are ad eundem degrees conferred without any examination?—Without further examination. A graduate of Oxford or Cambridge is admitted ad eundem gradum here on the production of his University certificate.

96. Judge Flanagan.—That is limited to Oxford and Cambridge?—It is.

97. It does not extend to the Queen's Colleges?—

Divinity testimonium, but before he got his degree. We do not acknowledge, as yet, the degrees of the Queen's Colleges. We could not give a Divinity degree to a graduate of one of the Queen's Colleges, although he might have gone through the Divinity course.

101. Would the practical course be that no person could go through the Divinity School unless he has gone through the ordinary college course?—No; students are now permitted to join the Divinity School after a preliminary examination, and without passing through the arts course, or any portion of it.

102. Lord Belmore.—I think your plan proposes two things: one, that the students should get the advantage of the Divinity School, with a view to their becoming clergymen, and the other, that they should get the regular education to qualify them for a degree?—Yes.

103. You would allow students outside the College to go through what would be necessary to qualify them to be clergymen, but would limit the granting of degrees to persons who were either students of the College or ad eundem graduates?—Precisely.

104. Mr. Porter.—But, as I understand, then Divinity School would be under the control of the Church Body?—It was so proposed, in reference to the existing Divinity School, but it was not contemplated that any body external to the University should interfere with the degrees.

105. I understand you to say that the only point the College would stipulate for was, that the students of the College should be admitted to the Divinity School gratis?—Yes, precisely.

106. As regards bodies, other than the Church of Ireland, any religious body might have a Divinity School in connexion with Trinity College?—Yes, if the number of their students was so large as to make it desirable.

107. Do you think it likely that any other religious body would avail itself of the privilege?—I think it not improbable that the Presbyterian body would. They might found one or two professorships in connexion with their own Church, and require their Divinity students to attend besides the lectures of our professors. I know that Presbyterians have frequently attended the lectures of the two Professors of Divinity.

108. In order to get degrees?—Not necessarily for the purpose of graduation; but for the certificate of the Divinity Professor.

109. Lord Belmore.—As I understand the plan of the Board, the Professors of the Church of Ireland would not be Professors of the College?—Not necessarily.

110. They would not be recognised as Professors of the College?—No. But inasmuch as it was proposed that they should lecture in College they would, to a very limited extent, be under College control.

111. Judge Longfield.—I think the Professors of Spanish and Italian are not under the control of the College?—They were formerly paid and appointed by the Crown. They are now paid and appointed by the College. I do not know whether I might venture to offer a suggestion as to the compensation of the Church of Ireland for her Divinity School. It is simply, that the Church of Ireland should receive a sum for the support of her Divinity School which

115. Judge FLANAGAN.—Since the Act of 1869 has there been an increase or diminution of Divinity students?—There was a considerable diminution after the time of the passing of the Act. But the number is now recovering again.

116. Lord BELMORE.—What is the average number of Divinity students in Trinity College?—For some years before the passing of the Church Act it was about 130 in the two classes.

117. Do you happen to know how many students there are at Maynooth?—I believe upwards of 600. But the duration of the course is much greater than ours.

118. Judge FLANAGAN.—I believe there are a good many assistant Lecturers in Divinity?—There are nine.

119. Are they not Junior Fellows?—Until lately they have been so; at present two of them are not Fellows.

120. Do you think that the same number would be necessary if the Divinity School was separated from the College?—I do not think so. At present the Divinity Assistants lecture twice a week. A Divinity Lecturer who had not the same engagements as the Junior Fellows might readily lecture four times a week. I dare say that if the plan suggested were adopted the work could be done by four or five assistant Lecturers.

121. Lord BELMORE.—Are the classes small?—The Lecturers do not like to have more than fifteen or sixteen in a class. The lectures are mainly tutorial.

122. Judge LONGFIELD.—What do the Assistant Lecturers get?—£50 a year.

123. Do you think you would get them for that if they were not Fellows?—Not easily. There are, however, now two Assistant Lecturers who are not Fellows.

124. Judge FLANAGAN.—Would the Junior Fellows have more time for other work if they ceased to be Assistant Lecturers?—It would certainly diminish their work, for, though much time is not taken up in the act of lecturing, the preparation for lecture is not inconsiderable.

125. Lord BELMORE.—When you said that the compensation to the Church of Ireland ought to be in proportion to what was given to Maynooth, did you point to any source from which the compensation was to come outside the revenues of the College or the Advowson Fund?—I think it should be taken, as in the case of Maynooth, from the Funds in the hands of the Church Commissioners, at least so far as it exceeded the amount at present expended by the College.

126. Mr. PORTER.—I suppose that the vast majority of the students who take holy orders take them in Ireland?—Yes.

127. Some in England?—There are some, but the proportion is smaller than is often publicly stated.

128. Has that proportion been altered by the Church Act?—That I am unable to answer. There are always some going to England. There is a class of men who obtain holy orders in the Church of England without passing through a University. Such men frequently enter the University of Dublin and graduate there, because they can get a degree without residence.

129. Lord BELMORE.—Dr. Salmon states in his letter (p. 7) "I find that out of 213 students who became qualified by standing to join the Divinity School this year, seventy actually did so"—do you agree with that?—I have no doubt that Dr. Salmon's statement is exact.

130. How long does the Divinity course last?—Two years. They join in the Junior Sophister year, not in the Senior Sophister year as formerly.

131. Mr. PORTER.—Seventy is the average of those who join the Divinity School?—That is about the average of the years preceding the disestablishment of the Irish Church; but it is above the average of later years.

Nov. 2, 1877.

A. A. Hart, Esq., LL.D.

142. Have you ever known the Bursarship to be given to a Junior Fellow?—No; a Junior Fellow would not conveniently discharge the duty.

143. There is but a small number of Senior Fellows sitting on the Board?—Only six at present.

144. How many Senior Fellows have held the office of Bursar?—Two of them. The provisions of the statute 22 Victoria is intended to meet the case of one or two more being disabled. One of the Junior Fellows would be made a member of the Board for the time being. The advantage of that system over that of having nine Senior Fellows is that it only comes into operation when the occasion requires it. Ten years ago some of the Senior Fellows were disabled. At that time to add to the number of Senior Fellows would have been a waste of money. At present the case is different. But if a temporary remedy is to be applied, the temporary system of substitution would be effectual.

145. Would you make it compulsory to retire?—To make it compulsory would require an Act of Parliament.

146. You were elected Fellow in 1850?—Yes.

147. Mr. William Roberts was elected in 1841?—Yes.

148. So that every one of the present Senior Fellows was elected in those years?—Yes. It was after 1850 that a large number of Fellows came in.

149. Lord Belmore.—Now, as to the Divinity School?—In your suggestion to the Board three years ago that the qualification for theological degrees should be the residence of the particular denomination to which the candidate belonged. Since then the public has been brought before the Senate of the University, and they have adopted the system. According to the new rule a person may get a theological degree without belonging to any particular religious sect. No declaration of opinion is required. All that is required is to pass an examination before the Regius Professor of Divinity. The Senate clearly supposed that the Regius Professor should be a member of the University. If the Professor should be appointed by the Church of Ireland, it would be necessary to have a new Professor appointed by the University. The new rule of the Senate seems to modify the proposal of the Board with regard to this particular.

150. Would it be possible under the present system for a Jew to get a degree?—It would.

151. Judge Flanagan.—What particular doctrines would the Regius Professor teach him?—That is left entirely to the Professor of Theology. The course should be under the authority of the College. I presume it would be a course intended for a Christian, but a Jew might make himself acquainted with that course.

152. Judge Longfield.—There are two difficulties—one that the examination might be by a person not bound by the rules of the College; the other that the examination might be by a person of a different faith from that of the candidate?—Yes.

153. Do you not think that those difficulties might be provided against?—I believe the system carried on in the Scotch Universities and on the Continent, is to have the examination in theological works without inquiring into the religious belief of the candidate. The University would settle the course.

154. Lord Belmore.—Would there not be this difficulty, that the Professor would have to inquire into the religious profession of the candidate?—I presume the questions would be as to what were the opinions of such and such an author, and the candidate should give the answer correctly. Suppose a member of the Church of Ireland was examined in a work written by a Roman Catholic author, he would be required to state what the arguments of the author to support his views were, without stating whether he agreed with him or not.

155. Mr. Mulholland.—What is your opinion as to the proposed plan of a Joint Board consisting of members appointed partly by the College, partly by the Irish Church?—It would get over the temporary difficulty. But I am speaking now not of the Divinity School but of the mode of examination for degrees.

156. Mr. Pearson.—The Regius Professor is appointed by the Board?—Yes. The only function of the Regius Professor would be to examine for degrees.

157. Is there more than one examination for degrees?—Only one.

158. Judge Longfield.—As it stands at present the Regius Professor of Divinity must be a member of the Church of Ireland?—Certainly.

159. No matter who elects him?—Yes.

Nov. 3, 1877.

Saturday, November 3, 1877.

Present:—Right Hon. the Earl of Belmore, K.C.M.G., in the Chair; Right Hon. Mountifort Longfield, LL.D.; Right Hon. S. W. Flanagan; Rev. J. A. Galbraith, F.T.C.D.; John Mulholland, Esq., M.P., D.L.

[illegible] to continue as at present to its exercise of the [illegible] [illegible] to Trinity College for theological instruction, provided that the lecturers are subject to ordinary collegiate discipline, and that they [illegible] their [illegible] by the [illegible] of regular [illegible] in Trinity College.

"[illegible]. That the Board of Trinity College are willing to [illegible] [illegible] privileges on any other religious body, [illegible] that its candidates for [illegible] should be instructed in Trinity College."

The committee accordingly had a conference with the Board in which they expressed their approval of these resolutions, except that in reference to the [illegible] [illegible] they suggested the advisability of [illegible] the [illegible] of the [illegible] part of the arrangement by capitalizing the proposed annual payments, and handing [illegible] such capital sum to the Representative Body in trust for the purposes of the Divinity School. The Board informed the scheme to their legal advisers, who stated that an Act of Parliament would be necessary in order to give effect to the plan.

[illegible] The control and management of the Divinity School was, in the first instance, to be in the College, but was to be handed over to the council appointed by the Church after vacancy in the professorships and lectureships. We may take it for granted that an Act of Parliament can be obtained, and that the Government will be prepared to take any steps to carry out the recommendations of the Commissioners provided they agree with them?—Yes. The Divinity School Committee would prefer a capital sum.

Mr. [illegible].—It has been thought that the Church made a direct claim on the Advowson Fund, and accordingly the Provost and Senior Fellows say in their statement, p. 3:—

"It has been suggested that the advowsons were granted to the college for the good of the Church, and that therefore the Church has an equitable claim on the money which was given as compensation for these advowsons."

But you will find that our suggestion was that the Advowson Fund afforded an opportunity to capitalize what may be claimed by the Church, and that would not conflict with the claim of the Junior Fellows because the income of the Divinity School would be there to recoup them.

The passage to which I refer in our statement is on page 5:—

"Whatever may be thought of the direct claim of the Church on this fund, its existence will facilitate the redemption of her claims on the general funds of the college, for it will be eminently expedient, for many reasons, to capitalize whatever may be fairly claimed from the college for the purposes of the Divinity School and the possession of the Advowson Fund makes it easy for the college to do so."

of assistants without injury to the teaching?—Yes, I think the present staff of assistants is as small as it could be—but I think the payments to them would in all probability require to be increased. The present Junior Fellows have undertaken the work in addition to their position. They think their Fellowships were not [illegible] to [illegible] [illegible] [illegible] part of their work as Fellows, was the work of the Divinity School. But if we have to employ other gentlemen as assistants we must pay them properly. It is quite possible that [illegible] the salaries of the professors might be reduced and those of the assistants increased.

[illegible]. What salaries would you think would procure efficient men as professors?—It is hard to say until we know with what success [illegible] [illegible] in the Church of Ireland will be provided on our new system, for this will regulate the standard of payments to Professors. It will [illegible] be necessary to provide [illegible] and scholarships for the school. Hitherto the College Scholarships were confined to members of the Established Church, and a large proportion of those entered Holy Orders, all being obliged to attend the Divinity Lectures. Now it will be necessary to make other provision for poor Students. I am sure there would be no saving, but absolutely the reverse.

[illegible]. You do not agree in opinion with the Provost, who stated yesterday that in case of an alteration in the Divinity School the number of assistants might be reduced to four or five?—There would certainly be no economy in that. The [illegible] [illegible]—There are at present several Fellows who give part of their time to the Divinity School, receiving £[illegible] a year each. If you get one man to give up his whole time and give him the whole work of two, you must give him the salaries of two men. Perhaps a man could be got to do the double work for £[illegible], but I doubt it. I do not think that by getting two [illegible] [illegible] [illegible] you would get a man to do the work of them for £[illegible].

[illegible]. What number of students are there now in the Divinity School?—About [illegible]. Lately the numbers have been constantly increasing. The Divinity School got a great blow by the disestablishment of the Church, but the number of students has been increasing every year since. At the time of the disestablishment my class was at once reduced to about half what it had been before. It has not got up to its former numbers, but it is not near so low as it was in [illegible]. Every year it is increasing as the prospects of the Church improve, and it may get up to its former number.

[illegible]. Will you tell us the system on which you proceed in the Divinity School. For example, what part do you yourself take in it, and what part of the work do

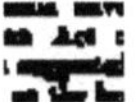

June 5, 1871.

Dr. Salmon, Archdeacon Stevens, and Mr. Pilkington.

be entitled to attend the Divinity lectures as before. Other persons who are divinity students should be charged.

205. That would not be for the purpose of their having secular instruction, but merely because the fund was originally intended to work for the benefit of Trinity College and not for the benefit of the Divinity Students?—Yes.

206. In reference to degree examinations is there at present a serious examination for Divinity Degrees or is the production of a testimonial by the student sufficient to enable him to obtain the first degree—as the production of the degree of B.A. for the degree of M.A.?—That is a thing we have made a change in. In former times the exercises for a Divinity Degree were merely formal. But six or seven years ago the Board made a change. The University of Cambridge introduced a serious examination as a qualification for a Divinity Degree, and we followed the example and the test for a Divinity Degree became a severe one. The consequence of working that out has been exceedingly good. Candidates now present themselves for a degree in a way they did not come before. The best class of young men have presented themselves for two or three years as candidates for Divinity Degrees; and I expect a very good result from the change.

207. So that in future Divinity Degrees will not be as they were, merely formal?—They will imply that a man who gets them has more knowledge than a clergyman ordinarily has.

208. Orthodox knowledge in connexion with the Church of Ireland?—Yes.

209. So far as compliance with recent legislation?—That is to provide for religious equality, and with that view we should confer them in one or other of the two ways, which I have already mentioned. I think it is not creditable for a university to abandon so extensive field of study.

210. Mr. Mulholland.—When you say that [illegible] proposed to go through the statements to show to what extent they conflict with our claim. But the course pursued has been so satisfactory, and the Commissioners have shown so much knowledge of these statements, that I do not think it necessary to go through them. I will only add that we shall be at all times most anxious to furnish the Commissioners with any information they may require.

211. Do the other statements conflict with yours?—The statement of the Provost and the Board does not, but that of three of the Senior and six of the Junior Fellows does.

212. In respect of the suggestion that the Divinity School should continue under the exclusive control of the College?—Exactly.

213. Does that conflict with the statement which you sent in?—It does. It claims that the control of the Divinity School should be committed to the College. We ask that the Divinity School should not be altogether under the control of the College.

214. Mr. Galbraith.—I suppose this is the passage in the statement which you refer to:—

"It may be said that the government of the College may in future years be vested in a body some of whose members may not be of the religious views of the Irish Church. This will be a distant contingency, and it may be easily met by a Royal Statute, which will enact that, in cases where any question connected with the Divinity School shall come before the board, the place of any senior fellow who is not a member of the Church, shall pro hac vice, be taken by the next junior fellow, in the order of seniority, who is a churchman."

Mr. Pilkington.—The statement of the three Senior and six Junior Fellows commences by submitting reasons, which in their opinion render it inadvisable that the School of Divinity should be severed from its present connection with the College, and that is in reference to our statement which suggests a certain amount of severance. I do not mean to advocate a severance as to the residence of the students or the

Mr. Pilkington.—I do not think the first reason would influence me. I believe that it is essential to the education of the future clergymen of the Church of Ireland that they should be educated in the company of secular students. I think an exclusive education would be most objectionable.

223. I notice that Ethics and Moral Philosophy are taught in the Divinity School, and they are important branches of a clergyman's education. Is there anything to prevent that course of study being altered?—I do not know that there is, but I am certain that if it was altered it would be supplemented if we had the control of the School.

Dr. Salmon.—Even if the Board of Trinity College were all of religious opinions different from the Church of Ireland and prescribed in the ordinary course books which conflicted with our teaching, we should still wish our clergymen to be taught everything that it was considered good for laymen to learn. We should, of course, try independent means to correct what we thought erroneous or defective in such teaching.

224. In the former University Commission there was a proposition, which was strongly objected to by the Board of Trinity College, that graduates of the Queen's University should be admitted at once into the Divinity School without having gone through a course in Arts in Trinity College?—I think Trinity College can only claim that we shall admit their students to the Divinity School free of charge; but we ought to be permitted, if we pleased, to allow other persons who paid us fees to attend the lectures of the Divinity School and get a testimonium with regard to that. We would object that Trinity College should make a rule prohibiting us from taking students of the Queen's Colleges.

225. *Mr. Galbraith.*—Do you not think that there is a general desire that there should not be a severance of the Divinity School from the College. I will read in connexion with the passage which I have already referred to the following passage from the letter of Doctor Salmon:—"I believe that one of the reasons of the failure of the attempts that have been made to arrange an immediate separation between the Divinity School and Trinity College is, that nobody really wishes for such a separation." Is it not plain that there is a manifest desire that the connexion should not be severed?

Mr. Pilkington.—There is a manifest desire that there should be no actual severance, but there is a very great desire that the Divinity School from which our clergy shall be hereafter taken shall not be under the control of a purely secular body.

226. *Judge Flanagan.*—That would be an important in itself; professors in connexion with Trinity College, but independent of it.

Mr. Pilkington.—The proposition of the Board is that the school should be entirely under college discipline, but that the appointment of the professors should be vested in us.

Dr. Salmon.—The only power in the government of the school that the Board would lose would be the appointment of the course of study. And, practically, at present the Board does not interfere in the matter, but leaves the choice of text-books to the professors. So that practically under the system proposed things would be exactly as they are.

227. *Mr. Mulholland.*—Was the Divinity School regulated by statute or by Royal letter?

Dr. Salmon.—The professors were established by Royal letter.

Mr. Pilkington.—The letter of 1st George III. c. 1, recites the Royal letter of the 36 Car. II., by which provision was made for the Professor of Divinity. The 1st George III. c. 1, establishes the Regius Professorship, and contains the statement that instruction in divinity, especially of those intended for Holy Orders, was one of the objects of the foundation.

perpetuam valent, ut juventus academica, illi promotius qui eterni ecclesiae dominantur, in curis literis, et religionis Christianae doctrinis, diligentius erudiantur, in quem praecipue finem fundatum fuit hoc collegium."

228. *Mr. Mulholland.*—Is there any condition annexed to the grant of the advowsons of any obligation on the College to maintain a Divinity School? The Divinity School appears to have been established from the earliest period of the foundation, so far as having Professors of Divinity who taught Divinity. The statute 36 Car. II., imposed the obligation of maintaining a Divinity Professor as did the statute 1 Geo. III.

229. *Mr. Galbraith.*—Is it not the fact that at the period of the foundation of the College, when no religion was recognised but one, a religious education was enforced on all the students, and that the charter of Elizabeth states that the object of the foundation was "Pro eo modo, quam de juventute regni nostri Hiberniae pie et liberaliter instituenda singularem habemus?"

Dr. Salmon.—I believe all the students were instructed in Divinity. It is on the failure of a legal obligation on the College to maintain a Divinity School that our claim arises. If the Board are legally bound to go on spending the money on the Divinity School in our sense we need not care. We can compel them to continue it, and the Church will have the benefit of it. But on the failure of a legal obligation we rest on our moral claim to compensation. We point to the passage in the Royal letter establishing the Regius Professor to show that, as a matter-of-fact, theological education was then believed by everyone to have been one of the main objects of the foundation of the College—"In quem finem fundatum fuit hoc collegium." We have evidence that for 150 years no one has had a doubt. We have evidence as strong as can be desired that that was the general opinion, and in fact the true opinion. I am not a lawyer, and I cannot say what constitutes a legal obligation, but it seems to me that there is a high moral claim on the part of the Church.

230. *Lord Belmore.*—The only machinery provided for the divinity school would seem to have been the appointment of the Regius Professor?

As long as there were Fellows in the College bound to take Holy Orders they were bound to teach in it; it was a part of their work.

231. From the information we have received from the Board it would appear that the creation of the Professor of Divinity is lost in antiquity?—The royal letter of Charles the Second states that "there hath been for these many years and still is a Professor of Divinity in that our University and Colledge of the Holy and Undivided Trinity near Dublin." So far as I can see that was the only machinery for instruction which existed for many years, until the appointment of Archbishop King's Lecturer in 1718. The first appointment of an Assistant Divinity Lecturer was in 1762. Then came the Royal Letter of 1st George III. by which every student was obliged to receive instruction in Divinity.

Mr. Pilkington.—I find that Luke Chaloner was the first Divinity Lecturer. I cannot give the date of his appointment. In 1607 James Usher succeeded him.

Mr. Galbraith.—It is so stated in the statement of some of the Fellows.

232. *Lord Belmore.*—The first connexion between the Church of Ireland and the Divinity School was in 1790?

Dr. Salmon.—The Bishops then made a rule that they would not ordain any Graduate of Trinity College who had not attended one course of lectures by the Assistant Divinity Lecturer, by the Divinity Lecturer, and by the Regius Professor of Divinity respectively.

233. I find this statement in the statement of "Some

Jan. 8, 1877.

Dr. Salmon, Archdeacon Stopford, and Mr. Pilkington.

MONDAY, NOVEMBER 5, 1877.

Nov. 5, 1877.

PRESENT:—Right Hon. the EARL of BELMORE, K.C.M.G., in the Chair; Right Hon. MOUNTIFORT LONGFIELD, LL.D.; Right Hon. H. W. FLANAGAN; A. M. PORTER, Esq., Q.C.; Rev. J. A. GALBRAITH, F.T.C.D.; JOHN MULHOLLAND, Esq., M.P., D.L.

Rev. T. T. Gray, M.A., F.T.C.D., and Rev. J. P. Mahaffy, M.A., F.T.C.D.

The Rev. THOMAS T. GRAY, M.A., F.T.C.D., and the Rev. JOHN P. MAHAFFY, M.A., F.T.C.D., presented themselves before the Commissioners in support of the statement of the claim of certain of the Fellows of Trinity College in Holy Orders for compensation for the loss of their right of succession to the livings formerly in the gift of Trinity College.

[illegible]. LORD BELMORE.—I believe you wish to make some remarks to the Commissioners with regard to the right of the Fellows in Holy Orders to succession to the livings which formerly belonged to Trinity College?

Mr. Mahaffy.—Yes, my lord. We propose to take the several subjects in the order mentioned in our statement:—First, as to the right of succession to the livings; secondly, as to the Divinity School, and thirdly, as to the [illegible] question.

Mr. Gray.—We submit that the clerical Fellows had a right of succession to the livings formerly in the gift of the College, which has been taken away by the Church Act. The number of Fellows who were promoted to these livings, not only junior Fellows but senior Fellows, of Trinity College, appears in the College Calendar. Now, in reference to the claim which we put forward in this document, Dr Steele, Mr. Mahaffy, and I, on the 31st of December, 1871, made an application to the Commissioners of Church Temporalities under sec. 15 of the Irish Church Act, 1869. The case was argued before Mr. Justice Lawson and Lord Monck, on the 1st of February, 1872, by Mr. Pilkington. Nothing was done in it then, and judgment was reserved. In May, 1873, we received a letter from the secretary of the Commissioners, stating that they wished to hear the case reargued before the Master of the Rolls, Judge Lawson, and Lord Monck. On the 3rd of June, 1873, the case was accordingly re-argued, but judgment was not delivered until the 20th of December, 1873—two years after we made the application to the Commissioners. In the meantime, the Board of Trinity College had sent in an application to the Commissioners of Church Temporalities claiming compensation for the loss of the College Advowsons, under the 16th section of the Irish Church Act. Their application was acceded to, and payment of the compensation awarded to them was made between the dates which I have mentioned of our application and the final refusal of it by the Church Commissioners. When our case was first argued before Lord Monck and Judge Lawson, Mr. Pilkington appeared for us and pressed two points on the Commissioners—our right of succession to the appropriated benefices, and that we were Ecclesiastical persons within the meaning of that to the appropriated benefices. Afterwards, however, when the case was reargued, he and the Master of the Rolls and Lord Monck disallowed the claims of the Fellows on the grounds that the Fellows were not ecclesiastical persons within the meaning of the Act, and that the right of succession provided by the 46th section was a right incident to an ecclesiastical status. But they were clearly of opinion that the Fellows had proved a right of succession. The Master of the Rolls says (p. 8),—

"Under ancient patents or grants from the Crown, the Corporation of Trinity College was, at the passing of the Irish Church Act in 1869, the owner of a considerable number of advowsons, the next presentation to each of which, upon avoidance, would be tendered to the Fellows of the College in rotation according to seniority, in conformity with a usage of such ancient standing, and such uniform observance, that we may take it to have the force of law."

And in p. 4 the Master of the Rolls again says—

"We are disposed to think that this right, though one somewhat difficult of exhaustion, is a right of succession within the true meaning of that term, and therefore the question is, whether the Irish Church Act has given the right of claiming compensation for the loss thereof."

Again, in p. 16—

"The Act of Parliament, by its 16th section, gives to the Corporation itself the fullest measure of compensation for the entire advowson, which, of course, covers the very same property, the right of succession to which compensation is claimed by individual members of the Corporation. It seems to me that the Fellows of Trinity College, though in Holy Orders, are not entitled to claim compensation under the Act; in other words, that the claim for compensation by the individual members of the Corporation cannot be made good against the property vested in the Church Commissioners, but is, if it at all exists, a matter of adjustment between them and the Corporation itself. But it would appear more just and equitable that where the entire advowson vested in the Corporation is compensated for by payment in full to the Corporation, a right to a next presentation vested in a member of that Corporation should be adjusted by the Corporation out of the fund it has got for compensation, rather than that the same thing should be doubly paid for, an intention which it is most difficult to impute to the Legislature."

the very thing upon which the appellants, members of the Corporation, and claiming as such, base their rights, and it does not happen to the Legislature the novel conception of awarding double compensation for the same thing."

Mr. Justice LAWSON says, p. 16:—

"The status of Trinity College and its Fellows is not affected by the provisions of the Church Act; but the College, like any other person, lost its advowsons, and has been compensated for the loss, and the individual members of the Corporation, who have subordinate rights against the Corporation, must assert them against the sum paid to the Corporation in respect of those advowsons. I am very far from saying that the Fellows have not such a right. I only decide that they have them not against the Commissioners, for that would be to make them pay for the same thing twice."

It would appear from the passages of their judgments which I have read that the Master of the Rolls and the Commissioners of Church Temporalities agreed that we had established a right of succession to these suppressed benefices. In support of this claim to a right of succession, we would refer more particularly to the Statute of Celibacy, 52nd Geo. III., from which we have quoted a sentence in our statement.

237. Lord [illegible].—The Statute of Celibacy was passed in 1811?—In 1811. By that statute, if a Fellow married he should, within three calendar months, serve notice declaring that he was married, and a Fellow so giving such notice should continue to be a Fellow, and enjoy all the rights, privileges, and emoluments of his Fellowship during one year from the time of his marriage, and, in particular, his right to be co-opted to the Board, and of being nominated to a living.

238. Suppose a Fellow married before 1811, and did not give notice of his marriage, had the Fellows junior to him any power to call attention to the fact that he was married?—It would appear that they either had not, or had not acted on it, because that is the ground assigned for passing the statute. But my object in referring to that statute is to show that the right of the Fellows to succession to the livings is admitted in the clause which gives a Fellow who has served notice that he is married one year's enjoyment of his Fellowship. The preamble of the statute recites—

"Whereas, it hath been reported to us that an opinion had many years prevailed in our said College, that the said [illegible] clause in the said statute (13 Car. I, c. 7) did not ipso facto, on the marriage of a Fellow of the said College, avoid his Fellowship in the said College, but that it was lawful for such Fellow, notwithstanding his marriage, to continue to hold his Fellowship in the said College, until the fact of his said marriage should be made known to the Provost and Senior Fellows of the said College, or to the [illegible] thereof, and proved before them, and until such Fellow shall be removed from his said Fellowship for such cause by the order or sentence of the Provost and the major part of the Senior Fellows of the said College, or the Visitors thereof; and whereas it hath also been reported to us that many persons, who have formerly been Fellows of the said College, but have long since left it, have in consequence of such opinion married during the time in which they were Fellows of the said College, and nevertheless continued for several years after their respective marriages to hold and enjoy their Fellowships in our said College, no proceedings having been taken for removing them from their said Fellowships, either by or before the Provost and Senior Fellows or by or before the Visitors of our said College; and whereas the true sense of the said recited clause, and the intention thereof was that no Fellow of the College should continue to hold his Fellowship after his marriage, but that his Fellowship should upon his marriage become ipso facto vacant. Therefore know ye that we do hereby declare that the true intent and meaning of the said clause, in the said statute hereinbefore recited, was, and that henceforth the same shall be deemed, taken, and construed to be, that no Fellow of the said College should continue to hold his Fellowship in the said College after his marriage, but that his Fellowship should, upon his marriage, become ipso facto vacant; and [illegible] mentioned, *if any Fellow of our said College shall marry* (save in the case hereinafter mentioned), *his Fellowship in the said College shall become ipso facto vacant upon such marriage. Provided always, and our will and pleasure is,* that any Fellow of our said College shall, within three calendar months after he shall have married, by notice in writing signed by such Fellow, and delivered to the Provost, or, in case of his absence or the vacancy of his office, to the Vice-Provost of the said College, declare that he is married, and the true day his marriage shall have taken place, (of which said notice the Provost, or, in his absence, the Vice-Provost shall, within one week after the same shall have been delivered, cause an entry to be made in the registry book of the said College), then and in all such cases, such Fellow, so giving such notice, shall and may continue to be a Fellow of the said College, and enjoy all the *rights,* privileges, and emoluments of his Fellowship thereon, for and during the term of one whole year from the day on which such marriage shall have taken place, and no longer, and shall and may during such year be capable (if otherwise under the statutes of the said College entitled to the same), of being co-opted into the place of Senior Fellow of the said College, in like manner as if he had remained unmarried; but if he shall be so co-opted, he shall hold such Senior Fellowship no longer than the expiration of one year from the day of his marriage as aforesaid; *and our will and pleasure further is, that during such year, such Fellow so marrying, and giving such notice as aforesaid, shall be entitled to such choice or option of ecclesiastical benefices in the gift of the Provost, Fellows, and Scholars of the said College, as he would have been during such year entitled to have had if he had remained unmarried.*"

The clause I lay stress on is, the declaration that during that one year the Fellow who had married would have been entitled to such choice or option of ecclesiastical benefices in the gift of the College as he would *have been entitled to have had* if he had remained unmarried. That was an admission of the right of the Fellows to any benefice which might become vacant. The statute left no alternative to the Board. On this point I may mention a case with regard to myself. In 1857 the Rev. W. Atkins held Tullyagnish, which was worth £1,148 2s. 6d. a year. He was made Dean of Ferns, and the living thus becoming vacant was offered to the Fellows according to the usual course. All the clerical Fellows attended at the Boardroom. The Provost said he would not take it, and he offered it to the Vice-Provost, and the Vice-Provost having refused it, the Provost went down all the clerical Fellows in order of seniority. The living was refused by all until it came to Mr. Leslie. The last three were Mr. Leslie, Mr. Ferrar, and myself. Mr. Leslie accepted the living, and was accordingly, under the statutes, bound to resign his Fellowship within a year. He afterwards changed his mind, and applied to the Board for leave to get a Queen's Letter to allow him to withdraw his resignation, and retain his place among the Fellows. I was the only person concerned. I considered that the living would come to me, as I was told by members of the Board that if Mr. Leslie got the Queen's Letter the vacancy would be looked upon as not a new one, but as the same vacancy. Delays occurred. The Vice-Provost told me that the living would be offered down the body of Fellows, commencing where they had left off on the former occasion. As Mr. Ferrar would not have it, I looked upon it as utterly certain that I would get the living. Delays occurred in procuring the Queen's Letter, and it became necessary, to prevent the right of presentation lapsing to the Bishop of the diocese, that Mr. Leslie should be formally instituted and inducted, which was done. This was in July, at the beginning of the long vacation. When we returned to College in October, notice was given that the living would be offered down the body of Fellows, as it was considered a new vacancy. I memorialed the Board, and represented to them that it was hard on me, as Mr. Leslie, by changing his mind, had deprived me of a step among the Tutors, which [illegible]

Jan. 2, 1871.

Rev. T. T. Gray, M.A., F.T.C.D., and Rev. J. P. Mahaffy, M.A., F.T.C.D.

the body of Fellows. I
a body, were sorry to
were placed in, and the
to me; but Dr. Carson
and satisfied them that
ralis had been instituted
vacancy, and that they

When the living was
r. Gwyn accepted it, and
d the step. As regards
ld observe that there are
Junior grade, the middle
al the proportion of three
case of a Junior Fellow;
al the rest of my lineage
I stood as a Tutor of the
He coming back into his
ation, he got into the
a half before me. He
pelow, or within a few
g those two years and a
ration. That made a dif-
h I had from that parti-

In what year was that ?—
... ago—and it was March,
Mr. Ferran became entitl

... the Letters Patent of
... III., which authorized
... vowson, and which con-
—

... and Scholars of the Col-
Trinity of Queen Elizabeth,
... presented to our right
... cousin, &c., have humbly
Royal licence to purchase
... And whereas our said
... Governor of our said
represented to us that the
will cause a more frequent
said College, and by that
encouragement of learning in
."

... that readily comes to the
... were purchased for
... given to the Fellows;
... exclusively that this was
... up to that time (1763),
... there in the gift of
... the Lord Lieutenant
... dealing of the advowsons
... succession of Fellowships,
... inference, for the Letters
... that a memorial had
to the Lord Lieutenant,
... contained the reasons
... consideration. I have
College for that memorial,

... to the Fellows in Priest's Orders in succession (with the exceptions hereafter mentioned), has prevailed at least as far back as the year 1798. The entries in the Register previously to that year are merely of the fact of a presentation of a person to one of these benefices. On some occasions, a Fellow who accepted a living was allowed an option of taking a living subsequently becoming vacant, if declined by all the Fellows then of senior standing to him; and in a few cases an exchange of a living was allowed."

I went to the Register to-day and looked at the particular case which is said to have occurred first in 1789. The case was this. The living of Clondevaddock in Donegal, was vacant for a considerable time, awaiting the issue of a negotiation for an exchange in which Mr. Hall, one of the Senior Fellows, was engaged, the Bishop of Raphoe having given an assurance that he would in case of lapse give the living to the person whom the Board should propose to him. The negotiation failed, and at last on the 17th of December, 1789, the Provost offered the living to the Rev. William Hamilton, all the Fellows senior to Mr. Hamilton declining to accept it—precisely what would occur in the present day. Mr. Hamilton said that it would take £800 or £1,000 to have a Glebe House built, and if the Board would lend him £800 he would accept the living. The Board refused to lend the money, and Mr. Hamilton thereupon declined the living. The Provost then asked Mr. Elrington, Mr. Hamilton's immediate junior whether he (Mr. Elrington) would accept the living. He said "allow me an interview of a few moments with Mr. Hamilton." They retired, and when they returned, Mr. Hamilton said he would take the living. On the following day a paper was read to the Board by the Rev. J. Stack, who was junior to both Mr. Hamilton and Mr. Elrington, in which he prayed that Mr. Hamilton's retractation of his refusal to accept the living might not be admitted, and upon the ground that such retractation was procured unwarrantably by a pecuniary consideration offered to him on the part of some of his juniors without his (Mr. Stack's) consent, and therefore in violation of his right. This case would go to show that in 1789 the same right of succession was asserted by Mr. Stack as we assert now, viz., that there was a custom that every living should be offered down the body of Fellows according to seniority.

Now, as regards another point—in connexion with the dealing of the Fellows with these livings, I may mention that there are two exceptions mentioned by the Board in their answer to query 5:—

"It appears from the Register of the College, that the custom of offering benefices to the Fellows in Priest's Orders in succession (with the exceptions hereafter mentioned), has prevailed at least as far back as the year 1798. On some occasions a Fellow who accepted a living was allowed an option of taking a living subsequently becoming vacant, if declined by all the Fellows then of senior standing to him; and in a few cases an exchange of a living was allowed."

then offered a second time down the Fellows, with an option, and came to Mr. Willock, who accepted it, and held it with an option until the living of Clonmany became vacant. Clonmany, when offered, came down to him, and he accepted it. He need not have exercised his right when Clonmany became vacant.

212. No Fellow who still continued such, who was junior to him, had a right to claim the living before him?—No. The first consequence of all this is, that the case of option is not an exception to the general custom. On the contrary, it shows the uncontrolled power which the Fellows exercised over the livings as their own property. What they say is this, "We are anxious to get a man to take this living. If you take it we agree that you shall hold it with an option. We prefer to give up the living and get immediate promotion, rather than let you stay on."

213. How long has the custom of option existed?—I cannot say.

214. Is there any case in which a Fellow junior to the man who has the right of option has attempted to assert his right of succession?—No. It is generally taken to be an honourable understanding between the Fellows not to do so.

215. Suppose the retiring Fellow waited for a number of years without exercising his right of option, would that understanding bind new Fellows who had come in since the Fellow had entered on the living?—As a general rule new Fellows abide by the rule of their predecessors.

216. Judge LONGFIELD.—I think the first case of option was the case of Mr. Phelan. He went out on a living with a promise of the next living from the College? He got the Board to obtain a written promise from the Fellows, that they would not accept the next living that became vacant. The point we want to establish is that the Fellows exercised uncontrolled power over these livings, and that they could not be offered to any one else until all the Fellows had refused them. The Fellows had the entire disposal of them. There was no living held with an option at the date of the passing of the Church Act.

217. Suppose the case of one of the smaller livings, supposing it passed all down the Fellows, would the Board be at liberty to present it to anybody who was not a Fellow?—It would be first offered to the Fellows by itself, and afterwards with an option, and if they refused, the Board, as the governing body of the College, might present it to any one they thought fit.

218. The present Rector of Enniskillen, the Rev. Samuel Greer, was never a Fellow?—No. There was an exchange between Dr. Robinson and the Hon. C. Maude. Mr. Greer was not a Fellow, nor was Dr. Magee, the present Bishop of Peterborough. The livings after being refused by the Fellows are generally given to distinguished graduates of the College. There is another case more in point still, relating to the living of Raymochy, the income of which is £810 13s. That case occurred within my own time. Archdeacon Gould was appointed to the living by Lord Eglinton on Dr. Singer being made a Bishop. Dr. Gould was not strong and he was never able to reside there, and he left the Rev. James Irwin, his curate, in charge of the living, and he gave him all the proceeds of the living. In 1865, Archdeacon Gould proposed to resign on condition Mr. Irwin were appointed in his place. Accordingly, the Fellows agreed

of the claimant; and
, F.T.C.D., as umpire.
this arbitration, that a
to the claimant for the
himself, in addition to

have a right, on the death of the curate, to have an addition made to his salary equal to the curate's deduction.

Lord Belmore.—Supposing there had been no deduction for a curate, Derryvullen would have been

get compensation from some source outside the

. . . missioners said that they . . . for both claims—both . . . the right of succession. . . . of the Rolls says in his . . . enacted by its 15th section, . . . fullest measure of compensation—which of course . . . sion—to the right of succession, is claimed by individual . . . It seems to me that the . . . people in Holy Orders, are . . . ations. A claim by the in- . . . poration cannot be made . . . Church Commissioners, . . . matter of adjustment operation itself." The real . . . The compensation is . . . pensation to the College . . . and compensation to . . . the right of succession. . . . Judge Lawson thought . . . the Corporation. They . . . did. I think they paid . . . Lord Dunraven, or any . . . The College should have . . . enjoyed Benefices, including . . . the care, deducting only . . . when holding them, but . . . so long as any living . . . could hold it.

In your paper, referring . . . "It will be seen by the . . . considerable sum was . . . the loss of his right of . . . tion to the sum already . . . gh Temporalities Commissioners, Patron of the Advowson

. . . missioners rated the value . . . at £3,000, but, on . . . sum, in addition, to . . . his right of presenting

. . . about that sum, the Com-

claim a capital sum, or a sum in the shape of income? We ask for compensation simply. There is no use in going into details until the principle is established.

Mr. Gray.—This question appears to be within the scope of the commission which authorizes you "to inquire into the amount received by our said College as compensation aforesaid, and the remedies proper to be provided for any injurious consequences arising from such loss of patronage as aforesaid, and whether the said compensation is affected by any equitable claims arising out of the said recited Acts, or from any changes recently made in the condition or constitution of our said College and University."

Lord Dunraven.—What was meant was that we should inquire what was the sum that was paid to the College.

Mr. Gray.—It occurred to me that the words might also include the additional meaning of "ascertain whether the proper amount has been received." However, as the Commissioners might suggest to the Board to go back to the Commissioners, the Church Commissioners have power, under a clause in the Church Act, to deal with such an application, if the Board should go back to them.

291. Mr. Foster.—Do you know as a matter of fact, whether the College accepted a sum, or whether there was an arbitration?—There was no arbitration. In December, 1871, we made our application, and between that time and June, 1873, the Board applied for and got their compensation. We might have appealed then.

Mr. Mahaffy.—But that would have prejudiced their case.

292. Lord Dunraven.—You are acquainted with the paper sent in to us by the Provost and Senior Fellows? There is a paragraph in it on which I should like your opinion. It is this:—

"The Advowson was no doubt subject to the condition that the Patron should appoint persons qualified to perform the parochial duties, and the commercial value was therefore less than if no such condition had existed. Accordingly, when the condition was abolished by the operation of the Church Act, a sum equal to the estimated value of the relief thus given to the Patron was deducted from the value of the Advowson, and the balance only (amounting to little more than one-half the value) was given to the Patron, the right of the Church having been recognised by Act of Parliament."

June 4, 1873.

Rev. T. T. Gray, M.A., F.T.C.D., and Rev. J. P. Mahaffy, M.A., F.T.C.D.

[illegible]

Rev. T. T. Gray, M.A., F.T.C.D., and Rev. J. P. Mahaffy, M.A., F.T.C.D.

Mr. *Mahaffy*.—The Professors give prelections?

Mr. *Gray*.—It is an object that the classes attending each Lecturer should not be too large.

292. Are the classes large?—I think it is not desirable to have more than fifteen in a class.

293. Judge Lenvfield.—When did it become customary for Senior Fellows to cease taking pupils?—Before my time.

294. Lord Belmore.—Are there not a number of the under graduates who do not attend lectures?

Mr. *Mahaffy*.—A good many.

295. Can a person get a degree without attending lectures?

Mr. *Gray*.—Yes. But it is difficult to answer well at an examination without having attended lectures. An Examiner can tell at once whether a student has attended lectures or not.

Mr. *Mahaffy*.—I find that there are seventy-five per cent. among the senior sophisters attending lectures.

[illegible] Mr. *Gray*.—In the scheme of retirement sent in by the Board, it is stated that "If a Junior Fellow not holding either of said offices," i.e., the office of Junior Bursar or Senior Tutor, "or a Junior Fellow, holding an office in lieu of a Tutorship, for which an income equal to that of a Tutor has been provided, a sum equal to his salary as Junior Fellow, together with an amount equal to the share of the Tutorial Fund to which a Tutor in the grade of such Junior Fellow was entitled for the year preceding such retirement." That must be taken to mean the sum to which he is entitled in the grade to which he belongs if he has no pupils. And so the Tutor who has pupils would get no more than the Tutor who has no pupils. In my own case that would make a difference of £140 a year. For example, Mr. Barlow has no pupils. I have always had a large number of pupils. According to the Board's scheme, if we both retired we would both receive the same retiring annuity; whereas, if the Tutor's pupils were taken into account, Mr. Barlow would get £400 a year—I would get £540 a year. Again, take two Fellows who were elected about the same time—one of them becomes Senior Tutor, and as such he gets a fixed salary of £900 a year. The other, who still remains a Tutor, got his Fellowship, say a year, after him, yet the Senior Tutor goes out at £900 a year; the other goes out on only £800 a year. I would therefore suggest that, in the case of a Tutor Fellow, his whole income as Tutor should be taken into consideration.

296. Lord Belmore.—Are your pupils instructed by yourselves?—The Tutor is the patron of his pupils. He represents his pupils in their dealings with the Board.

297. But it is not necessary that he should deliver lectures to them?—Not necessary. But such of his own pupils as belong to the classes he lectures are always sent to him.

298. Mr. *Mahaffy*.—I have only a very few remarks to make to the Commissioners as to the Divinity School. As to the proposed separation of the Divinity School from the College, it is said to be better that the separation should take place, while the College is favourable to the Church than afterwards. The fallacy in that is that at present there would be a certain injury to the College and the Church from such separation—and that is a more important consideration than the mere probability of an injury fifty years hence. The actual injury which would result from such a separation is the disappearance of the clerical tutors. We find that at present they are the most popular tutors. The public appear to have a fancy for clerical tutors. If the College and the Divinity School were to be separated, there would be no inducement to Fellows to take orders, and the clerical tutors would disappear. A large number of men come over from England here, to be taught Divinity. They would not come over then. The College would then lose the payment. I therefore think that any separation at the present time is not advisable. If there is to be a change in the governing body of the Divinity School, Dr. Salmon's plan might be adopted. There is another plan before the Commissioners, that members of the Church of Ireland should be co-opted to the Divinity Board. If the Divinity School were to be separated from the College and placed under a different governing body, the present Professors and Lecturers who have freeholds in their offices, might not choose to accept such governing body. The only safe plan would be, that the College should pay a capitation fee. The principle of a capitation fee is, that the College should only pay for the number who are taught Divinity.

299. Mr. Mulholland.—Suppose the number should increase?—Then I think, that for every Divinity student, the College should pay.

300. Mr. Fottrell.—Does not the College pay a fixed sum per annum for the Divinity School?—It is not fixed in this way: the number of the teachers may be diminished; it is in the power of the Board to suppress any Divinity lectureship.

301. Mr. Mulholland.—How many students are there in the Divinity School?—Sixty or seventy per annum.

302. Lord Belmore. There are also assistant lecturers, eight of whom receive £50 and one £60, altogether £460?—Yes. If you reduce the number it would only make a difference of £300 or £200 a year. That is only a fraction of the expenditure.

Mr. *Gray*.—One remark I wish to make with regard to the Divinity School. If it be necessary to make any change in the Divinity School, I would prefer a board on Dr. Salmon's plan; but for the present I would let matters remain as they are. For thirty or forty years we shall have the present men on the Board in succession. That succession is not to be interfered with by Mr. Fawcett's Act, and we shall have the same men for thirty-five years, as if Mr. Fawcett's Act had not passed. During that time many circumstances will arise, and men of that day will form a better plan than we could strike out now. One of the effects of separating the Divinity School from the College would be the loss to the College of two offices, Dr. Salmon's and Dr. Lee's, one of £1,313 and the other of £700 a year. Dr. Salmon's professorship can only be filled up from fellows or ex-fellows who are doctors of Divinity. It was only from 1855 that the Board was enabled to elect an ex-fellow; from 1761 to 1814 they could only elect a senior fellow; from 1814 to 1855 they could elect any fellow. The transfer of that office to an outside body would be equivalent to the suppression of a fellowship. In the same way the salary of Dr. Lee's professorship is £700 a year, and the rule is to elect to that office one of the body of junior fellows, and the transferring of that office outside would be equivalent to the suppression of another fellowship.

303. Judge Lenvfield.—Has it been admitted by the Board that they have a freehold in their offices?—It has.

304. Lord Belmore.—In the paper sent in by some of the fellows with respect to the proposed separation, and which is signed by you, it is stated that:—

"In 17[illegible], the Irish bishops drew up a list of books in which they decided to examine candidates for orders, and they sent it to the Board of Trinity College. The Board sent a copy of this list to the Professor of Divinity, the Lecturer, and his assistants, and recommended them to prepare the students of Divinity who attended their lectures in these books. At the same time eleven of the twenty-two Irish bishops signed an agreement that they would not ordain any graduate of Trinity College who had not attended the course of lectures by the Assistant Divinity Lecturer, by the Divinity Lecturer, and by the Regius Professor of Divinity, respectively."

was not recognised by the Bishops as a sine qua non for ordination until that period.

305. From 1718 there were two Professors of Divinity in the College, and the contention is that because from time immemorial there was an obligation on the fellows of the College to take holy orders, Divinity was always taught in the College in connexion with the Church?

Mr. Mahaffy.—On the contrary, we can show from the registry the first appointment of catechetical lecturers, I think in 1763. We have always had catechetical lectures, but I do not consider that that proves anything as to there having been a Divinity School.

306. Do you draw a distinction between the College and the University?—No, we do not separate the College and the University.

307. Judge Flanagan.—In the event of a separation you would lose the English parish?—Yes; because the bishops in England would not recognise a Divinity school outside the College.

308. Suppose there was a separation, and sufficient funds were transferred to establish a school and lecturers, why should not the bishops in England recognise the lecturers of that school?—So far as I know the bishops of the Church of England, they are jealous of any change, and if the Divinity School fell into the hands of the Church Synod, some things would be introduced of which they might not approve. I should hope that no such difficulties would arise; but if they did, I should be bound to stand by the doctrine of the Church as taught in the College.

309. The interests of the College would [illegible] the Divinity School?

Mr. Craig.—My object would be to prevent any separation, in the interest both of the College and of the Church.

310. Suppose a number of Fellows were elected who were not members of the Church of Ireland, how would it be supposed that the nomination of the Regius Professor of the Divinity School should be in the Board?—That would suppose that there would be no Fellows in the body who would be members of the Church of Ireland; I would accept the position as it is, and [illegible]. It can hardly be supposed that no man who will get Fellowship will take holy orders.

312. Judge Lawson.—If any of the existing Fellows should change their religious opinions, would they be deprived of their Fellowship?—I suppose not.

313. Suppose a man who is now a member of the Church, but [illegible] in the efficacy of [illegible]?—There would be nothing in such a case to prevent him holding his Fellowship.

TUESDAY, NOVEMBER 6, 1877.

Present:—Right Hon. the EARL of BELMORE, K.C.M.G., in the Chair; Right Hon. MOUNTIFORT LONGFIELD, LL.D.; Right Hon. S. W. FLANAGAN; A. M. PORTER, Esq., Q.C.; Rev. J. A. GALBRAITH, F.T.C.D.; JOHN MULHOLLAND, Esq., M.P., D.L.

Professors DOWDEN, LL.D., ATKINSON, LL.D., and WRIGHT, M.D., presented themselves to the Commissioners.

314. Lord BELMORE.—I believe you appear on behalf of the Professors of Trinity College who are not Fellows. Do you wish to make any statement?

Professor Dowden.—First, as to our bringing a statement before you at all, it strikes us in this light: If the things for which compensation has been awarded in the Advowson Fund were given to or obtained by the Fellows merely as bearing the name of *Fellows*, we can have no voice in its appropriation, but if they obtained this property as being the guardians of education in the University, then we are concerned in its disposal equally with the Fellows, both by virtue of our numbers and our duties. The chief statement of the Professors has been already sent in to the Commissioners. Their views are set forth in that statement, and as regards their own position four points are insisted on, viz.: "That in order that a teacher should devote his best energies to College duties he should feel his personal interests bound up with his work, and himself an integral part of the institution, and to that end he should have—1st, an assured position; 2nd, a direct interest in the success of his work; 3rd, an expectation of promotion; 4th, a provision for retirement when incapacitated through age or infirmity." We, of course, feel the importance of finding some remedy for the evil of stagnation among the Fellows, but we feel that this is not the sole or chief evil that requires to be dealt with if the fund is to be applied to the general interests of the University. [illegible] tended as to prevent of *Fellowships* being obtained by distinguished students, not only in classics and mathematics, but in the several subjects of importance taught in the University; and that out of the body of temporary *Fellows* should be co-opted permanent *Fellows*, having regard to proved capacity as teachers, and in conformity with the wants of the different departments. The work of *Fellows* incapacitated through age or infirmity might, I think, be performed by deputies.

315. When you say co-opted, do you propose that life Fellowships should be obtained by election from the temporary *Fellows*, or that there should be a particular examination for them?—My opinion is that temporary Fellowships should be given as the result of an examination, but that the permanent Fellows should be co-opted from among the temporary Fellows without further examination.

316. Therefore, every permanent Fellow should be a temporary Fellow at first?—Yes; but with regard to this scheme I only express my own opinion.

317. Would you propose that the temporary Fellows should take part in teaching?—They should take part in teaching, but not become tutors.

318. Judge FLANAGAN.—Do you consider that the teaching staff of the College is at present insufficient?—I do not know that it is at present insufficient for the absolute requirements of the College.

319. Do you propose that deputies should be employed only to provide for cases of incapacity or in-

Jan. 8, 1878. — Professors Dowden, Atkinson, and Wright.

—Not if they were chosen from among the Fellows or Professors.

312. In the event of infirmity or incapacity is there not an efficient staff for the teaching without deputies?—I think there may be at present, that is, without deputies drawn from outside the body of Fellows and Professors.

313. If any particular Fellow, e.g., a lecturer in Greek or ancient history, was incapacitated at present, would not another of the Junior Fellows take his place?—I suppose so.

314. Suppose a Fellow was absent for a year or more from illness, and that the appointment of a deputy became necessary should not some one of the Junior Fellows be appointed to perform the particular duties?—I think so.

315. If the teaching Fellows are sufficient what is the purpose of appointing deputies?—The teaching staff would be diminished by the incapacity of any of its members; but the deputies need not necessarily be drawn from outside the teaching staff.

316. There are twenty-six Fellows, and the Provost has told us that for fifty years there have been only two incapacitated?—There is a crisis approaching which makes it probable that the ages of some of the Junior Fellows and of the members of the Board will be more advanced than formerly.

317. Deputies would be a temporary expedient, not a general provision regulating the College?—A provision to be resorted to at any time, but only in case of necessity.

318. The Professors are not on the foundation, they are not a part of the corporate body?—I believe not.

319. Lord Rayleigh.—Do you propose that the number of permanent Fellows should be reduced, or that any addition should be made to them?—I should leave the number of permanent Fellowships as at present, but create some new temporary Fellowships, and ultimately make all Fellowships temporary in the first instance, widening at the same time the basis of examination.

320. Then you propose that there should be a gradual merging of the Professorships in Fellowships?—Yes, so far as regards Professorships which require the teacher's chief energies. We state—

"We believe that where a subject is important enough to form a part of the general education, and to require the teacher to devote his chief energies to the work of the place, he ought to possess an equal footing in the place with the Fellows. This end could in the future be attained by widening the basis of Fellowship so as to allow of Fellows being elected for distinction in those subjects which at present form the departments of Professors."

321. Judge Flanagan.—For what period are the Professors elected?—Some for life, some for five, some for seven years.

322. How many are elected for life?—Five or six. Two of those present are elected for life. Professors are not elected for life until they have proved their capacity for teaching.

Professor Dowden.—We appear as representatives of the Professors at large, but it is impossible to avoid calling attention to the distinction, within the body of professors between those who devote themselves wholly to University work and those who have extra-University professions. The claim of those who devote themselves wholly to the work of the University appears to me to be much stronger than that of the others.

323. Lord Rayleigh.—I suppose that the inference to be drawn from your statement is that the Advowson Fund might be properly applied to carry out the objects which you have in view. Will you explain in what way that would be done best?—No great institution can be considered in a healthy condition so long as the position of a large portion of the working staff remains a matter of just discontent. If the position of the Fellows is unsatisfactory, that of the Professors—a body almost as numerous and equally engaged in carrying on the education of the place—is far more unsatisfactory. There is no promotion whatever, and only in some instances has a pledge of any pension been given. As set forth in our statement we should be given, after a certain number of years' service, an assured position; we should be elected for life. In my case and that of Dr. Atkinson that has been already done. In my own case after being once re-elected, I was appointed for life. What we desire is that such an arrangement should be extended as widely as possible. Secondly, we should be given a direct interest in the success of our work. The object would be attained in a general way in proportion as we were made an integral part of the University. I do not propose that the Professors should be paid by fees for attendance on their lectures. I am not in favour of that. Thirdly, we should have an expectation of promotion. Last, there should be a provision for retirement when incapacitated through age or infirmity, and such provision should not be limited to the Professors in whose cases it already exists, but should be extended as widely as possible. I may touch on one more point. I approach it with some reluctance. An allusion is made in our statement to the smallness of the salaries of some Professors. For myself I feel that I have been somewhat liberally dealt with, but I may perhaps take my own case as

341. Lord Belmore.—Whom do you represent?—The Fellows who are junior to me.

342. When did you get your Fellowship?—In 1867.

343. How many Fellows are junior to you?—Six. I represent five of them. I do not include Mr. Fitzgerald, who got his Fellowship this year. From 1867 to 1873 there were six Fellows elected, including myself. For them I speak.

344. What do you complain of?—The stagnation in promotion, as it affects the juniors among the Junior

Tyrrell's is an exceptional case, as he is Professor of Latin. Mr. M'Clay's about £300, Mr. Palmer's, I have already stated, £233.

360. Do you reckon in those cases their rooms and commons?—I do not. I speak of hard cash exclusive of chambers and commons.

361. Is there any other grievance connected with recent legislation which you think demands redress?—I think I stated incidentally that one complaint I have is that the University is not secularised. There are offices open to clerical Fellows which are not open to lay Fellows.

362. Mr. Galbraith.—You mean the Readerships in the Chapel?—Yes, and others too. The Readerships were created since the passing of the Irish Church Act. That was a step rather in the contrary direction to what we might have expected.

363. Judge Flanagan.—You said that there ought to be a fixed basis for the income?—For instance, the Professor of Greek gets £200 a year as a fixed basis, and the Professor of Latin £200 a year, and their proportion of the tutorial fees. But the Tutors who take pupils have no fixed basis.

364. In the event of the recurrence of an exceptional year, such as that of the Crimean War, or a succession of such exceptional years, you anticipate that the tutorial fees would go down?—They would go down. In such years there is a great tendency on the part of young men to go into the army.

365. Then you would have to reduce the fixed basis to a lower figure?—No, I would preserve the same fixed basis always; in such years the fluctuating part would fall.

366. Are the revenues of the College absorbed in the payment of Tutors and Professors?—I presume they are, or nearly so. But the tutorial fund might be distributed on some fixed basis. Somehow or other, there ought to be a fixed basis to a man's income.

367. You stated as a grievance that there are many clerical offices which you cannot accept, and therefore, that the clerical Fellows are at a better position than the lay Fellows?—Yes.

368. Is not that their own fault?—There are no livings now, and they were the chief inducement to the lay Fellows to take orders.

369. Then you propose that the emoluments of those offices, which are open to clerical Fellows alone, should be taken from them and distributed among all?—No; but some of those offices ought to be thrown open, such as lectureships in Hebrew, and the inequality might be remedied further by the creation of offices which lay Fellows might hold.

370. Mr. Porter.—You have given us instances of the rate of promotion among the Fellows, before the stagnation commenced, the cases of Mr. Ferrar, Mr. Mahaffy, and Dr. Traill, whose average of promotion was five years?—Yes.

371. Since that promotion has been much slower?—Yes.

372. How do you account for that?—By the loss of livings and loss of bishoprics. Fellows used to get nearly as many bishoprics as livings. Between bishoprics and livings, we should have had two or three vacancies at least since the Church Act. In twenty-seven years, from 1843 to 1869, ten livings were taken by Fellows. That is an average of about one every three years. If that be so there would have been two or three vacancies by livings since the Irish Church Act.

373. Only some of the larger livings were attractive to Fellows?—That was not always so. Dr. Lee resigned his Fellowship for a small living, and so did his predecessor.

374. Have there been vacancies by death or succession among the more important livings since the Church Act?

Lord Belmore.—Drumragh was vacant last year.

Judge Longfield.—And Clonfeacle.

375. Mr. Porter.—Were there any special circumstances making the rate of promotion quicker before the period of stagnation began?—No; vacancies were rather more numerous than usual perhaps. I think six years is about the average time a man remained on the junior grade before the Act.

376. Judge Flanagan.—What is the difference between the incomes of the different grades?—Last year it was £160. It runs from £140 to £160.

The Rev. Joseph Carson, D.D., S.F.T.C.D., Bursar.

377. Lord Belmore.—Will you be so good as to state from what sources the revenue of the College is derived?—I cannot answer that question better than by presenting a balance sheet of the income and expenditure of the College for the last four years, 1873–76, which was prepared by myself annually in the discharge of my duty as Bursar, and laid before the Board on the 20th of November in each year. I have not received the authority of the Board to do so, but I do not think that the Board would have the least objection to your seeing the balance sheet.

[The balance sheet was handed to Lord Belmore.]

378. The income of the estates is £42,504 11s. 2d.?—Yes. This was the net amount of income received from the estates in the year 1876. The other sources of income of which the particulars are set down in the balance sheet bring the income up to £61,171 4s. 7d. The expenditure is given in the table and shows a balance of income over expenditure in each year of about £700.

379. We understood from the Vice-Provost that the income and expenditure were about equal without counting the Advowson Fund?—Yes. In the years 1875 and 1876, a sum of about £8,100 was expended on the new Anatomical Museum in the Park. Taking the one-half of this sum, and deducting it from the expenditure of each of the years 1875 and 1876, it would raise the margin of income over ordinary expenditure in those years to about £4,800 or £4,900, so that practically the Vice-Provost is right.

380. Was not a portion of the sum received for the Advowsons, the compensation for three livings purchased by the College?—Yes, and the money derived from these three Advowsons of Killeshandra, Killileagh and Clogherny, was applied in redeeming a portion of the tithe-rent charges on the College estates.

used as this money in the same manner as is done with respect to those College estates which the Board have no power to part with, and which are held in perpetuity for the general purposes of the College. He added, however, that the Board were at liberty to apply the *interest* of this money in the same way in which the rents derived from the estates are used; namely, for the purposes of general collegiate expenditure. But counsel was of opinion that the sum of £25,700 received for the three livings purchased by the College, stood on quite a different footing, and that the Board were not bound to preserve it intact, as a separate fund. What was actually done was this. The Board invested in Government Stock the sum of £24,397, received for the eighteen Crown Livings; and they then took the £25,700 which had been received as compensation for the three Advowsons above mentioned and £18,753 that had accrued for interest, making altogether £44,453. The £18,753 was the interest on the whole sum. The above sum of £44,453, was paid over to the Commissioners of Church Temporalities, and by this payment the tithe rent charge on the College estates was redeemed to the extent of about £2,000 a year.

Dr. Carson again referred to the balance sheet. Practically the amount of the net rents from the Old estate and the Baldwin estate, viz., £10,840 in all, is larger than it would have been by about £2,000, if the tithe-rentcharge had not been redeemed in the manner above explained; inasmuch as the tithe rent-charge is one of the items deducted from the gross rental, before the net amount is set down in the account.

291 As to the Divinity School: what we want

Jan. 8, 1872.

Rev. Joseph Carson, D.D., S.F.T.C.D.

O'Brien, as Archbishop King's Lecturer, with a salary of £700 a year. At that time the Board had no power to put a charge on the estates of the College. The only power they possessed was to charge any new salary on the fund arising from the general payments made by the students. The Board considered, and fairly so, that the eminence of the Professor whom they appointed would of itself attract a large number of students both from Ireland and England, and that the fees paid into the College funds, under the name of Decrements, would enable them to pay the salary of one of the principal teachers of the School; in other words, that the salary of Dr. O'Brien and his successors, would come out of the fees paid in by the students. No student ever paid special fees for Divinity lectures in the College. The payment of the salary of *Archbishop King's Lecturer* is made out of the *Cista Communis*. If the Divinity School were removed from the College, an important source of revenue would be lost to the College, by diminishing the inducement to students to come here. There had been as many as 165 students in the Senior Divinity class alone. The loss of the inducement to come to the Divinity School would therefore be a very serious injury to the College funds. I now come to the third item to which I referred above, of £300 for Theological Exhibitions. These exhibitions were created in 1858, and naturally furnished a strong inducement to young men of ability who intended to enter Holy Orders, to join the Divinity School. If the connexion between Trinity College and the Divinity School should be severed, the College would sustain a loss from the falling off of the students who have hitherto come here attracted by the exhibitions and prizes in the Divinity School, and who have paid their fees into the *Cista Communis*. In this, as well as in many other respects the College would suffer a very heavy loss.

384. £2,513 were paid in the shape of salaries?—Yes.

385. The other payments amounting to £165—what are they?—They come under the head of examination fees.

386. What is the exact amount of the College expenditure on the Divinity School for the last three years?—The entire amount of the College expenditure on the Divinity School, including salaries, examination fees, exhibitions, and prizes, on the average of the last three years, is £2,557 14s. There are three important points in which we differ from the Queen's Colleges—one as to Theological Degrees (to which I have already adverted), the second as to religious instruction for Students, and thirdly, attendance on Divine Service in the Chapel. Anyone who looks over the regulations of the Queen's Colleges will see that from the nature of the case it is impossible to have any Theological instruction in those Colleges, or authorized religious teaching, because one of the obligations imposed on their Professors is that they shall not touch on any religious subject tending to produce contention or excitement.

Dr. Carson read the Form of Declaration required to be made by a Professor of the Queen's Colleges upon entering into office, which contains the following passage:—

"I moreover promise to the said President and Council that I will not introduce or discuss in any place or capacity of Professor, any subject of controversy, political or

to receive the testimonium of the Divinity School. They may ordain whom they like, and it is of the utmost importance that they should be satisfied with the suitableness of the persons who may be appointed Professors in the School. I am in favour of a smaller number of members on the Board who may have the management of the Divinity School, than that suggested in the paper of Doctor Salmon. He wishes to make the Divinity Professors members of the Divinity Council. If that were adopted we might have a man voting for his own election to the office of Regius Professor of Divinity. I have had long experience as a member of Boards, and as far as that experience goes I am in favour of small Boards. I am strongly in favour of concentrating the responsibility in as small a number of men as possible.

867. The income of the College varies a good deal? The highest amount of net income received in the last five years was in 1874, when it appears to have been nearly £3,000 higher than it was in 1876. The interest on the Advowson fund is included in both years. The net income from the estates is subject to considerable fluctuations. The gross rental is for the most part fixed, but, in order to ascertain the net rental, account must be taken of deductions for poor rates, agency and other charges, and deductions under the head of improvements, in addition to those rents which may be in arrear. The College holds large tracts of land in Kerry, and especially in the neighbourhood of the town of Cahirciveen. When the former lease of these lands expired in the year 1840, the general condition of the tenants was most wretched, and a contrast very unfavourable to the College was not unfrequently drawn between these lands and the adjoining estate which belonged to the Marquis of Lansdowne. In order to remedy this state of things, the College has been obliged within the last ten or eleven years to expend a sum of over £12,000 upon the improvement of Cahirciveen and its neighbourhood, a considerable part of which expenditure is, as yet, unproductive. As an example of the nature of this outlay I may mention that, a few weeks ago there was an application from the Knight of Kerry that the College should contribute to the improvement of the pier at Renard Point, opposite to the Island of Valentia, for which the Grand Jury had voted a [illegible] grant of money. The Board agreed to grant a considerable sum for this purpose. Expenditure on improvements of this kind vary considerably from year to year. I need not say that the poor rates have immensely increased within the last few years. All these things have a tendency to cause fluctuations in the net income received from the estates. But there is another equally important source of fluctuation in the general collegiate income, viz., the payments from the Students' half-yearly fees, and the fees for degrees. These payments fluctuate to a great extent. The entrance fees also are liable to much fluctuation. All these considerations impose a great responsibility upon the Board in the financial management of the College, and thus it becomes very necessary to have always a considerable margin of income over expenditure in order to avoid the risk of a financial deficit. Another important cause of disturbance, as regards the balance of income and expenditure, may arise from delay in payment of the rents. There are three tenants of the College whose rents amount in all to £11,000 a year, and a considerable difficulty might arise if these payments were not made at the proper time. One of these tenants pays the College £5,000 a year. If there was any delay in the half-yearly payment of his rent it might make a difference of between £2,000 and £3,000 in the net receipts for the year.

868. Are the rents in the nature of headrents?—A great part of them is of this nature. About three-fourths of the College rents are paid by the immediate lessees of the College, who occupy the position of middlemen, and who have large beneficial interests in their perpetuity leases; and the remaining fourth is paid by tenants who are for the most part in actual occupation of the lands.

869. Judge FLANAGAN.—I believe you stated that the Regius Professor was originally appointed, not for the Divinity Students exclusively, but all the Students?—I referred to the Statute of George III.

870. Practically of late years are not his lectures confined to Divinity Students?—They are. Divinity Students are the only persons whose attendance is compulsory.

871. You also said that when Dr. O'Brien was appointed Archbishop King's lecturer his salary was increased?—Yes.

872. What was the old salary?—I believe it was £30 a year.

873. And it was raised to £700 a year?—Yes, in the year 1833.

874. Was there an increase in the number of students after that?—There was.

875. Could you show by any return the number of students who attended the Divinity School before the salary was raised?—Yes. It appears from a return sent in by the Board, dated November 17th, 1871, that the average number of Divinity Students during the five years 1828–32, was 115.

876. Do you consider that the effect was to attract a number of students whose fees were sufficient to make up the difference?—Owing to the division of the Divinity Students after the year 1833 into two classes, Senior and Junior, it is not easy to state precisely the pecuniary gain to the College arising from the change made in that year with respect to the office of Archbishop King's Lecturer. That some gain accrued to the College is certain, for I find in the return just referred to that the average number of Students, in the junior class alone, during the years 1846–50 (after the importance of the changes in the organization of the Divinity School had become generally known) amounted to 162. But I do not think that the fees arising from the increased number of Students was sufficient to make up the increase of salary. I am dealing simply with matters of fact, as they appear on the face of the returns. The Board decided to pay the increased salary of Archbishop King's Lecturer in Divinity, out of the decrements paid by the students, and I consider that they were authorized to do so because the students whose fees were applied in payment of that salary derived the benefit of the instruction of the Lecturer.

877. Judge LONGFIELD.—Might there not be this reason that the Board considered that they had a right to do what they liked with the decrements, but had no such right over the College lands?—That is quite possible.

878. Do you know what was the general condition of the Junior Fellows at the beginning of this century. Were they able to live on their incomes?—I have no means of knowing. Possibly that information might be got out of the books in the Bursar's Office. There is a clause in the Statutes containing an express prohibition against lending money or advancing money to any person.

879. Mr. GALBRAITH.—At the time that Judge Longfield alludes to some of the Fellows were very poor?—Everything depended on the number of their pupils. At present that cannot be, for there is a certain share of the Tutorial Fund which each Tutor must get. But there were instances of Fellows being very poor. The only difference now, which the number of pupils makes in the income of a Junior Fellow is this, that out of the entire annual amount of the Tutorial Fees paid by each student—£8 8s.—all of which originally went to the tutor—the tutor now gets £1 1s., and £7 7s. is paid into the Tutorial Fund. Some tutors who take more than ordinary care of their pupils, always have their chambers full, because parents are always glad to place their sons under the care of such Tutors, but they are frequently prevented from carrying their wishes into effect by the operation of a rule of the Tutorial system

Jan. 8, 1877.

Rev. Joseph Carson, D.D., S.F.T.C.D.

Nov. 6, 1877.

Rev. Joseph Carson, D.D., S.F.T.C.D.

called the Limit. What happens is this—a father who has a son to enter, and has a high opinion of one or more of the Fellows, takes his son to one of those Fellows, who replies, "I am full;" then he goes to another, who says, "I am full also;" then he goes to a third, who tells him that he is full also. The father is then frequently obliged to put his son under the care of a gentleman he knows nothing of. I think this rule of the Limit works very prejudicially for the interests of the public, and also of the College.

400. Mr. Mulholland.—The number of Divinity Students decreased after the Church Act?—Yes. The average number of Divinity Students, in both Senior and Junior Classes, in the seven years before 1869, was 163. In the seven subsequent years the average number was [illegible].

400a. Was that accompanied by a diminution in the total number of students in the College?—It was, but only to a slight extent. The total number of students is given in the Dublin University Calendar. For the seven years ending in 1869, the average number of students was 1,2[illegible]4. For the seven years after that date, the average number was 1,177.

Wednesday, November 7, 1877.

Nov. 7, 1877.

Present:—Right Hon. the Earl of Belmore, K.C.M.G., in the Chair; Right Hon. Mountifort Longfield, LL.D.; Right Hon. S. W. Flanagan; A. M. Porter, Esq., Q.C.; Rev. J. A. Galbraith, F.T.C.D.; John Mulholland, Esq., M.P., D.L.

Right Hon. M. Longfield, LL.D.

401. Lord Belmore.—I believe, Judge Longfield, that you have full information as to the method in which compensation should be valued on a claim by a patron of a living for the loss of the Advowson, and of the principles upon which it was valued in the case of claims made by the College?—I have examined carefully the claims put in by the College and the decisions of the Commissioners on the claims, and the reference to the actuary. The facts stated for the actuary were the net income of the living, the age of the Incumbent, and the fact that the parson had no residence in the parish. The first case came on for arbitration before Dr. Ball and myself, and in the judgment which we gave we laid down the principles on which the arbitration should proceed, and we stated certain cases in which an increase ought to be made in the valuation. One of the cases was where the patron was resident in the parish, and, therefore, where it was important to him to have the nomination of the clergyman with whom he and his family were in future to have frequent intercourse. The second case was where the patron was about to appoint a member of his own family to the living. We thought that the compensation ought to be higher in that case.

annually to the College. The half of that sum, viz., £8 8s. is paid to the Tutorial Fund, out of which the Tutor of the Student receives for himself £1 1s., and the remainder, £7 7s., is divided as before among all the Tutors, so that, since 1853, each Tutor has an interest in his pupils to the extent of one-eighth of the Tutorial fees paid by them.

409. Can you give an instance or illustration as to how that system of paying £1 1s. to the Tutor of the Student acts?—In my own case, in the years from 1859 to 1876, I gained by the new plan over the old plan £884.

410. In how many years?—In seventeen years, from 1859 to 1876, I gained £884; calculating simple interest at 4 per cent. on that sum as it accrued, I gained altogether £1,108 by the change from the old to the new system. When the Tutorial system was first adopted in 1834, there was a smaller number of Tutors, only fifteen. Four Tutors were added by a Queen's letter in 1840. Up to 1840 the fund was divided among fifteen Tutors, of which five were in the Senior grade, five in the Middle, and five in the Junior grade. After 1840 the fund was divided among nineteen. There were five in the Senior grade, nine in the Middle grade, and five in the Junior grade.

411. Judge Longfield.—What was the falling off in the fund during the Crimean war?—In the years 1854, 1855, and 1856, the fund was as follows:—In 1854, £9,360; in 1855, £8,919; in 1856, £8,148, and then it rose in 1857 to £8,631.

412. Can you give the Commissioners information as to what the income in the several grades was in the earlier period before 1849, and in the still earlier period when there was a smaller number of Tutors?—I can give the average of the incomes of the Tutors in the three grades in the eleven years from 1832 to 1849. The average income of the Senior grade was £951, of the Middle grade £687, and of the Junior grade 331. These are the averages of the incomes of the three grades for those ten years. At that time when a Fellow was elected he became at once a Tutor, and he participated in the payments made by students entering after he became a Tutor. Thus, in the first year of his Tutorship he divided only in the payments made by students of one class or year, in the second year in the payments made by two classes, in the third year in those by three, and so on. That has passed away since 1853.

413. Mr. Galbraith.—The sums you have mentioned are taken from items in the Junior Bursar's books?—They are taken from the Junior Bursar's books. In 1849 the actual income of the Senior grade was £858, of the Middle grade £611, of the Junior grade £420. Then in 1850, when there was a change, the income of the Senior grade was £730, that of the Middle grade, £518, that of the Junior grade £365, so that there was there a diminution of nearly £100 in the income of a Tutor of the Middle grade in that year. But these sums do not represent the whole income of the Tutors; they are paid in addition their considerable salary as Fellows, and they are also paid salaries for Divinity, History, and Elocution Lectures, and fees for examining; also the salaries of such college offices as they may hold—namely, Junior Dean, Proctor, Censor, Reader in College Chapel, Preacher, &c.

414. Judge Flanagan.—Can you give the actual sum in any particular year—take for example, 1867—in that year what was the sum payable to a Tutor in the Middle grade?—I have it here [illegible]. In

418. To that, add £100, and that would make it £631?—Probably £100 would be too little.

419. Judge Flanagan.—Have the Fellows the choice of chambers?

Mr. Galbraith.—The Provost gives away the chambers.

420. Judge Flanagan.—And he entertains any claim?

Mr. Galbraith.—Yes; Fellows may compete for them.

Dr. Stubbs.—I would wish to correct my former answer, that £100 would be the average of the additional income over and above each Fellow's share of the Tutorial Fund. I find that in 1874 the average addition to the Tutorial income would come close to £300.

421. Lord Emly.—That would make the income of a Fellow in the Middle grade in 1867 about £731?—Possibly not so much, as the payments to the Junior Fellows from the funds of the College have increased somewhat since 1867.

422. And in the Junior grade about £250?—I would say, looking at this book, that the average payments to members of the Junior grade in 1874 was £157 in addition to their tutorial income.

423. Mr. Forster.—And does that continue so still?—I should say so.

424. Judge Longfield.—Has the income of the Fellows increased within ten years?—It has certainly increased. I can tell it in my own instance.

425. Lord Emly.—Take your income in the years 1856, 1866, and 1876?—I received in 1856 from the College, £130 16s. 6d.; in 1866, £116 11s. 8d.; in 1876, £232 16s. 6d., independently of what I received from pupils. Taking the income of the Middle grade at £631 in 1867, I think it is not unfairly to add £114 in order to calculate the total income in 1867.

426. What do you attribute that to?—First, more was paid for examinations. There were also a few small offices created in the interval, and the salaries of offices have been slightly increased. For instance, I hold the office of Reader in the Chapel, the salary of which is £30 a year.

427. Mr. Mulholland.—What was the amount of the income of the highest grade in 1876?—I could tell you exactly what mine was. I was in the highest grade, and I can tell what my income was last year. In 1876 I received more than others, because I happened to have more pupils than other Tutors. I received last year, £735 16s. 8d. from the Tutorial Fund, and in addition to that I received from the Bursar, £323 16s. I received more than others from the Tutorial Fund because I had more pupils.

428. Does that include the whole?—It includes the whole.

429. Does that include chambers?—I have not taken chambers into account. In order to arrive at the number of pupils which each Tutor may enter in any year the average number of entrances for the preceding three years is taken, and divided by the number of Tutors who receive pupils, and then the quotient is increased in the proportion of 3 : 2. The average number of paying pupils which each Tutor has under his care is about eighty.

430. Lord Emly.—Could you give an estimate of what the value of rooms and commons is to a Fellow who wishes to reside?—Commons are worth 16s. a week, or 2s. 3d. a day. The rooms for an unmarried man residing in them ought to be worth £20

Jan. 1, 1877.

Rev. John W. Stubbs, D.D., F.T.C.D.

year I was paid for 274 half-yearly payments of my pupils, which would amount to 137 pupils, so that I had 100 over the average; but that might have arisen from replacements.

435. Lord Emly.—From replacements?—Men that have gone off the books come back again to their Tutors. Students also enter frequently in June and October, and join the existing Junior Freshman class, and so become Senior Freshmen in the next year. Such Students pay up the fees already paid by their class and this adds to the income of the Tutor under whom they enter.

436. Mr. Galbraith.—You have experience on the question of the College Livings, on which we are anxious to have your evidence, particularly as to the mode in which their value was estimated?—I may say that I took a great deal of pains in estimating the value of them, twenty five years ago. I compared my estimates with the accounts of my friends who took the livings and they were generally correct. To estimate the tax paid to the Commissioners you must take the value of the rentcharge and the value of the lands, add them together—find the charge on the glebe-house, and allow 5 per cent. on the part of this recoverable from the tenants on the parish, and 10 per cent. on the portion which is waste and not so recoverable. I assumed the poor rate at one shilling in the pound upon the rentcharge, and sixpence in the pound upon the rent of glebe-lands. You deduct these along with curates' salary and other charges upon the benefice from the gross amount in order to obtain the net taxable value (n), then the tax was $\frac{£n \times (n+5)}{5000}$.

The net value of the living is then found by deducting the Ecclesiastical Tax from n. Take Clogherny.—the gross value of Clogherny was £1,407. The charge on the Glebe was £1,615—there was one curate to be kept, one church to be served. The tax to the Ecclesiastical Commissioners, £313 6s. The net value is £1,133 and a house. That is after payment of all charges, poor rate, and the tax on the living. £1,133 and a house was the net value.

437. Did you take into account the agent's fees?—No; as a matter of fact I did not take into account the agent's fees. The agent's fees would be five per cent. That would be £50 a year.

438. Lord Emly.—£1,133 and a house—does that include the whole of the Glebe land?—I charged as if it was let up to the hall-door. Clonfeacle became vacant in 1849, the value of that benefice was taken in 1843, I revised it, and the valuation was then accurate. The gross value was £1,850. There was a charge of £2,800 on the Glebe-house to be paid. There were two curates, and two-thirds of the salary of a third to be paid by the rector, the remaining one-third was paid by a chaplaincy. There were three churches to be served. £788 was the net value of the living. The benefice of Clonfeacle on the last occasion was vacant just after the famine. The poor rate was high, the landlords throughout Ireland could not get their rents, and far better land than the Glebe lands was in other parts of the country, at that time difficult to be let. A good deal of the rent of the land was paid in labour, not in money. That was considered an unsatisfactory arrangement, so that although the net value was stated at £788 it might not be anything like that. The Clergyman who accepted should pay £2,800 charge on the Glebe-house, and it required at least another £1,000 to furnish the house, stock the land, and pay institution fees. £3,800 was a serious sum for a young man to be obliged to provide when entering a benefice.

house, and was taken …
and the net value was …

442. The clergyman …
Yes, and he did re…
one.

443. Drumragh.—T…
The charge was £900, …
the tax was £732.

444. After deducti…
There was one curate …
be served.

445. That is in the …
into account the char…
because without the ch…
get for £50 a year, w…
in country parishes, …
chaplaincy. Practical…
from it. Besides, I …
parish of Clonfeacle.

446. Tullyagnish.—
the value of this livi…
Achison. He gave me …
me what he received …
actual experience.

447. In what ye…
gross value of Tu…
charge on the Glebe …
be kept. The net valu…
The tax was £132 10…

448. Derryvullen.—
of Derryvullen myself …
every point in order …
in the value I put on …

449. Mr. Galbraith …
This was the value w…
vacant, and Mr. Lod…
was £1,094, the charge …
third another charge …
There were two curat…
value was £762, and …

450. None of these …
No; but they include …

451. Mr. McLenna…
Derryvullen is under …
returned at less than …
here as £832?—The …
The gross value of …
£1,100.

452. Lord Emly.—…
which the valuation …
know that the Colleg…
wrong.

453. Mr. Galbraith …
value of Ardstraw. …
in 1847 what was the …
A little over £890. …
the income of the …
Salmon was a Tutor …
his case; after having …
a Tutorial income of …
a Tutor, he had only …
and when he was fifte…
the same source was …

454. Judge Longfield …
—Dr. Salmon got his …
of five years he was …
come was £700. At …
income was £532. …
In fifteen years, that …
only £491 from the T…

455. Was that …
number of replacements …
the number of pupil…

[illegible]

Thursday, November 8, 1877.

Nov. 8, 1877.

Present:—Right Hon. the Earl of Belmore, K.C.M.G., in the Chair; Right Hon. Mountifort Longfield, LL.D.; Right Hon. S. W. Flanagan; A. M. Porter, Esq., Q.C.; Rev. J. A. Galbraith, F.T.C.D.; John Mulholland, Esq., M.P., D.L.

Rev. Samuel Haughton, M.D., F.T.C.D.

is thought by some to be hostile to religion. I have had much experience of the benefit obtained by Divinity Students from attending my lectures. It gives them a clear comprehension of what Geology is, and how a complete knowledge of that science enables an educated man to point out that there is no hostility between it and religion. That is a strong reason why future clergymen should be educated within the walls of the College. Another reason is, that I have a very strong objection to separate Theological Colleges. In the Roman Catholic and Greek Churches there are separate Theological Colleges. They always lead in my opinion to extreme views. The future clergyman should be characterized by moderation, and that is produced by contact with equally educated men who are not going into the Church. In the present condition of the Irish Church I should dread that a Theological seminary started outside the walls of Trinity College would probably fall into the extremes of low church dogmas; clergymen imperfectly instructed as it would have to fight against giants, themselves unprovided with the true weapons for a contest with the opponents of all religion. I consider that a low church clergyman would be especially unfit and unable to deal with such opponents. The tendency of Theological Colleges is always to an extreme, either to low church exaggerations of particular dogmas, or to high church imitations of the ceremonies of another Church, which ought to be out of place in the Church of Ireland. What I dread is, that exclusive education which has a tendency to extremes, and which will develop an absence of the spirit of moderation. Above all, the absence of the training which mixing and contact with educated men will give. The result of separation would also be to prevent Students from England, who have hitherto come in considerable numbers, from coming in future. English Students do not come to the Divinity School alone. It is the University which attracts them. A Divinity School in connexion with the Church of Ireland would not have the same attraction. What brings Englishmen here is the celebrity of the education in our College.

465. Do you think that the numbers from England would be materially reduced merely by the Divinity School being removed from the College?—I do not think that the Divinity School is the best managed school in our University, but it is stated to be conducted on a very good system. We are more distinguished for other branches of science. Students are attracted by the Medical School, and the celebrity of the Professors who lecture in it.

466. Judge Flanagan.—What you appear to apprehend from a separation is, the Divinity Students not having a secular education?—They certainly would not.

467. Is there any reason why the heads of the School should not make it a condition that the Students should have had a secular education?—That would be to make an impossible condition. Suppose the heads of Maynooth College ordered that the Students should have a degree from Trinity College, they could not carry it out.

468. What difficulty would there be—could not the Divinity School make it a condition that the Students should be graduates of Trinity College or the Queen's University or Oxford or Cambridge?—A degree with residence might remove the objection.

469. Is not residence of Students in Trinity College the exception?—Not in the case of Divinity Students. Medical Students also must reside. What is in my opinion wanted is the training of clergymen of the Church for the contest which I have mentioned. You must have the clergymen scientific men or the Church will be at great disadvantage, and I think men would be better trained in a Divinity School connected with the College than in a separate Theological seminary. I think there can be little doubt that the tendency of a Theological seminary would be downwards.

470. Mr. Mulholland.—With regard to the management of the school have you formed any opinion? By whom should it be managed?—I have a strong feeling in favour of what Dr. Salmon proposes—a joint Board. From my own knowledge the University Council works uncommonly well.

471. Judge Flanagan.—You think the University Council works very well?—It works very well. There are minor defects in it which we hope to get rid of—but it has done a great deal of valuable work.

472. Suppose that by the gradual working of Fawcett's Act, the Fellows should all be of a religion different from the Church of Ireland or of no religion?—That is looking forward to a very remote time. That state of things could be dealt with when it arises.

473. By an Act of Parliament or how would you deal with it?—I think Dr. Salmon's plan is that certain classes should be represented, and that there ought to be members named by the Board. I would trust the Board of Trinity College. Whatever might be their religious opinions they will always be able and respectable men, and I would trust them to act loyally towards the Church of Ireland, and to nominate good men for the school.

wish that the govern-
the General Synod?
y own idea and wish
Bishops. But what-
ment, it is must have
Synod.

ately to the General
ected partly by the
ral synod!—I think
date transfer to the
able. I am sure that

the permanent body for the administration of the school, I should object to it. I admit that within certain limits it would be safe, but I should decidedly object that it should be continued unless the regular [illegible] should be [illegible]. It is clear with regard to the administration of the school that it would be for the present perfectly satisfactory. With regard to the appointment of Professors and lecturers in case of vacancies I think they should be all made under the authority of the General Synod. The object of appointing an [illegible] body would be to meet practical difficulties not with a view to make any alteration in the system of the school; but for the oversight of the discharge of the duties already existing in the case of Professors and assistant lecturers.

518. Mr. [illegible].—Your impression is that the course in the Divinity School was arranged by the Professors?—Mainly by the Professors, subject to the approval of the Board.

519. And that approval is given as a matter of course?—Yes, practically.

Rev. R. [illegible]

FRIDAY, NOVEMBER 9, 1877.

Nov. 9 1877.

Present:—Right Hon. the EARL of BELMORE, K.C.M.G., in the Chair; Right Hon. MOUNTIFORT LONGFIELD, LL.D.; Right Hon. S. W. FLANAGAN; A. M. PORTER, Esq., Q.C.; Rev. J. A. GALBRAITH, F.T.C.D.; JOHN MULHOLLAND, Esq., M.P., D.L.

ANTHONY TRAILL, Esq., LL.D., M.D., F.T.C.D., and D. WILLIAMSON, Esq., F.T.C.D., examined.

A. Traill, Esq., LL.D., and D. Williamson, Esq., F.T.C.D.

520. Lord BELMORE.—You wish to give evidence as to the necessity of a scheme of retirement for Fellows in Trinity College in connexion with the Junior Fellows' document?—Dr. Traill.—I divided the subjects of the observations I am about to make into four.—First, the necessity of a scheme of retirement; secondly, the special scheme of the Board; thirdly, the Advowson Fund; fourthly, the Divinity School. First, then, as to the necessity of a scheme of retirement——

521. Will you explain the statement in page 3 of that document, viz.: that during the next thirty years the average duration of a Junior Fellowship will be thirty-nine years, and that in eight cases that period will range from forty-three to forty-five years?—I take the Fellows' ages in 1877, and then write down for every year the values of their lives in the form of a decimal. I then add together as many of these decimal fractions as will give me the integer seven, equal to the number of Senior Fellows. This gives the number of years hence at which it may be expected that any Fellow will be included amongst the seven Senior Fellows. Thus in three years from the present time the chance of survivorship of the eight at the top (excluding the Provost), is ·66, ·75, ·85, ·99, ·93, ·90, ·91, ·91, the sum of which is equal to seven, from which it is to be inferred that in three years there will be seven survivors of these eight persons. The youngest of these being now aged fifty-nine will, if alive, then be sixty-two, and as he obtained his Fellowship at the age of twenty-four, the duration of his Junior Fellowship before co-option will then have been thirty-eight years.

Again, in fifteen years from the present the chance of survivorship of the sixteen at the top of the list of Fellows is ·31, ·08, ·28, ·11, ·30, ·46, ·48, ·48 ·48, ·48, ·56, 54, ·54, ·61, ·54, ·52, the sum of which is 7·16, from which it is to be inferred that in fifteen years there will be at least seven survivors of these sixteen persons. The most junior of these being now aged fifty-seven will then, if alive, be seventy-two, and as he obtained his Fellowship at the age of twenty-nine, the duration of his Junior Fellowship before co-option will then have been forty-three years. The youngest of these sixteen persons being now aged fifty-three cannot on the same calculation expect to become a Senior Fellow before thirteen years, when he will, if alive, be sixty-six; but as he obtained his Fellowship at the age of twenty-two, he will also have served as a Junior Fellow for forty-four years. When this calculation is extended over thirty years, so as to include the last of the Junior Fellows (excepting the one elected in 1877) and tabulated for each individual Fellow, the figures which represent the number of years at contest at which each Fellow would arrive at the Board, counting from the year in which he obtained his Fellowship, are as follows:—38, 38, 40, 42, 42, 43, 44, 44, 44, 45, 44, 43, 43, 41, 39, 36, 35, 35, 35, 33, 35, 31, 34, 34, 34; the average of which is 39, and the eight extreme cases are marked thus ⌒. This proves the statement in the document, and it completes the previous table, showing the average duration of a Junior Fellowship for the last 240 years.

The table, when completed, would stand thus:—

[illegible]	[illegible]	[illegible]
From 1637 to 1686,	From 1657 to 1730,	5 years.
From 1696 to 1746,	From 1710 to 1783,	16 years.
From 1740 to 1780,	From 1783 to 1802,	22 years.
From 1780 to 1841,	From 1810 to 1854,	23 years.
From 1841 to 1873,	From 1858 to 1877,	23 years.

The above figures not only show an extraordinary period of stagnation approaching in the immediate future, but they also show that even at the end of thirty years things have no prospect of returning to what has been their normal state; for the average duration of a Junior Fellowship at the end of that period will still be thirty-four years.

522. What is the shortest period in which a man was co-opted between the years 1760 and 1841?—I am not sure as to that. The present Provost was co-opted in 19 years, Dr. Moore in 16 years, Dr. Hart in 23 years, Dr. Toleken in 23 years.

523. Judge LONGFIELD.—Even before the repeal of the Celibacy Statute, were there not instances of Fellows whose promotion to the Board was long delayed?

Mr. Williamson.—Yes—for instance Dr. Hare was elected in 1800, and co-opted in 1837.

524. If Dr. Romney Robinson had not resigned his Fellowship, when would he have been co-opted?

He would have been co-opted in 1843. He would have been 30 years a Junior Fellow.

Dr. Traill.—Still in the whole period, from 1760 to 1841, the average is only 23; and it is also to be remarked that these figures only convey a small idea of the real amount of stagnation which exists, and is about to increase in the body of Fellows, because they only show the number of years of service as a Junior Fellow before reaching the Board, but they do not show the number of years each Fellow will remain in each grade. This is a much more serious consideration, because as a Fellow in the senior grade of tutors has a competence on which he can live comfortably at any rate, it does not matter so much to him personally to be delayed in

[illegible] sinecures which can be held by persons in other respects quite incapacitated from governing the College. As examples I may mention the offices of Vice-Provost, Catechist, Senior Dean, and Librarian, the last of which should be considered one of the most important posts in the University, instead of being merely an appendage to the income of a senior Fellow. On an examination of this year's calendar it will be seen that two offices are held by each of four members of the Board.

530. Is the examination for a Fellowship such that the man who gets the most marks must be elected?—The best man is always elected.

531. It does not depend on the number of marks?—Technically he is elected by the votes of the members of the Board, but practically the man having the highest marks is always elected.

Mr. Williamson.—The Fellowship candidates are diminishing gradually. Only one man that I know of has commenced to read for Fellowship during the last two years. For three years previous to this year there has been no vacancy. Many, who formerly would have been Fellowship candidates, are now going to Cambridge.

532. Mr. Mulholland.—Have you considered what the effect of an annual election independently of a vacancy would be?—Dr. Traill.—Only to increase the number of malcontents at the bottom of the list of Fellows.

533. Have you estimated the effect of a retirement scheme, in creating vacancies for Fellowship?—We went carefully into that calculation, and we found that if we assume the age at which men obtain Fellowship to be twenty-six, and provide for five retiring places for men about seventy years of age, then, according to the tables of mortality, there should be one vacancy per year, on the average.

534. Have you got the number of vacancies between 1740 and 1790?—There were fifty-eight vacancies.

Mr. Williamson.—There was then a much smaller number of Fellows. Fifteen was the number of Junior Fellows, the number of the Senior Fellows being the same as now.

535. Lord Belmore.—Was it the custom of Senior Fellows to take College livings?

Mr. Williamson.—Several of them have taken livings.

536. In some of the livings the income is in a great measure derived from the glebe lands—for example, Clogherney?—Very much so.

537. Mr. Mulholland (to Mr. Williamson).—How many years were you in the junior grade before you got into the middle grade?

Mr. Williamson.—I was particularly unfortunate. I remained for six years a non-tutor, and it was seven years more before I was promoted into the middle grade.

538. Had not the Fellows an equivalent for the stagnation in the repeal of the celibacy statute, by which they got leave to marry?—Dr. Traill.—The real benefit from that was obtained by men high up in the body.

539. Judge Longfield.—Were there any other causes for the stagnation—do you not think that the tutorial system had the tendency to prevent men tak[illegible]

[illegible] paid by the Senior Bursar to the Junior Fellows, [illegible] a year?—[illegible] than £[illegible] a year.

540. Judge [illegible].—Do I understand you to say that [illegible] of the principal reasons for [illegible] the livings was the [illegible]—I think it was a very strong reason. [illegible]

541. Judge Longfield.—Prior to [illegible] of Dr. [illegible], when the celibacy [illegible] passed, [illegible] what proportion of the Fellows took livings?—I cannot say.

Mr. Williamson.—A very large proportion I am sure.

[illegible]

547. Mr. Mulholland.—In what year was the change made in the [illegible] of the Tutors?—In [illegible] or [illegible].

548. Lord Belmore.—You wish to give evidence on the special scheme of retirement proposed by the Board and by the Junior Fellows. What do you consider to be the essential differences between these two schemes?—Dr. Traill.—The scheme proposed by the Junior Fellows points to a provision being made for [illegible] five retiring places, [illegible]. The scheme also points to a fixed age, seventy, as the proper time for retirement. The necessity for each of these provisions being taken together will be obvious, when it is remembered that within a list of [illegible] Fellows at present, there exist one group of five within a year of each other in age, and another group of six within [illegible] of each other in age, the average age of the latter group being within three years [illegible] of the former. The scheme put forward by the Board points to no fixed age for retirement, and prevents the possibility of a provision for an average number of retiring places, which by its machinery would prevent the bringing of these particular periods of stagnation which, [illegible], must come upon the College in fourteen years from the present date.

549. Will you point out the particular part of the scheme put forward by the Board which prevents the possibility of making a provision such as you describe?—[illegible] the creation of a [illegible] for the purposes of the scheme, and it further provides that in years when there might be no retired Fellows or a number less than the income derived from such capital sum would admit of, the balance of such income shall not accumulate for the purposes of the scheme, but shall be expended with the ordinary revenue of the College. The result of this provision, [illegible], would there be five retiring places (except in the extremely unlikely contingency of most of the [illegible] persons being Senior Fellows), [illegible] like a provision for an average of five retiring places. It might also easily happen, that by [illegible]

[illegible], 1878. J. [illegible], Esq., [illegible], and [illegible] Williamson, Esq., [illegible].

ure that the College might with quite as much reason lay claim to this compensation received by the Church as that the Church should lay claim to the Advowson Fund paid over to the College. (4) The balance remaining, after all the above explanations and deductions, was handed to the College. The fact that in calculating the value of the Advowson, as much use has been made of the figures representing the values of the incomes of those College livings, has not unnaturally caused many to fall into the error of supposing that the Advowson Fund was a portion of the capitalised value of the College livings, and that therefore the Church had at least a moral if not a legal claim upon it. Besides considerations that, I think, make it plain that the Clerical Fellows as such have no individual claim against the Advowson Fund. Their claim, if worth anything, would be based upon an Advowson Fund calculated according to the principles laid down in the Duke of Devonshire's case by the arbitrators, Judge Longfield and the present Lord Chancellor, where the valuation was that of a purely lay property, disregarding any clerical right of succession in the owner of the Advowson, but it should be based upon what would have been the Advowson Fund, if it had been calculated according to the principles laid down in the case of the Rev. Mr. Moore, of [illegible], (in which the arbitrators were the present Lord Chief Justice of the Queen's Bench and myself, with the Rev. Mr. [illegible] as umpire). In this case the owner of the Advowson was in orders, with a right of succession to the benefice, and the value of the Advowson was enormously increased by the arbitrators by a very substantial amount. The clerical members of the Corporation of Trinity College, Dublin, occupy a precisely analogous position to that of the Rev. Mr. Moore, and had the arbitrators in his case they would have gone back to the Church Temporalities Commissioners, and might have got a larger compensation, so as to have had the value of the Advowson Fund increased by the amount equal to the value of those [illegible] interests. Had this been done they might have shown individual claims against the increased Advowson Fund, but it seems to me to be perfectly clear that they can have no claim whatever as clergymen against the Advowson Fund as at present constituted. Having disposed of the various outside claims against the Advowson Fund, and having shown that it was paid to the College as compensation for that loss of patronage which entered a means of promotion amongst those Fellows of Trinity College who did not accept the College livings, as well as advantage to those who did, it seems to me to be incontrovertibly established that the obvious and natural allocation of the Advowson Fund is that for a scheme of retirement.

557. You say that the College got the same compensation as any other lay proprietor of an advowson—do you consider that any moral claim exists on behalf of the Church against the advowson fund on this account?—I consider that in general the Church has a strong moral claim upon those who have received compensation for privileges as members of that church, but I think it must be easily seen that the analogy fails if the argument be pressed against the Corporation of Trinity College. In the first place, it is no longer necessary that the Fellows shall be clergymen, and therefore, whatever remains of the trust should be held impartially for all denominations as far as they can win their way into the corporation by open competition. But further, any ordinary owner of an advowson could, before disestablishment, have sold his advowson and put the money into his pocket, and, therefore, he could have given it back to the Church as a free gift. As he could have done this before disestablishment, he is also free to do so after disestablishment, and hence the force of the moral argument in his case, that he should assist the Church in her hour of need rather than make a private profit. But the Corporation of Trinity College was not at liberty before disestablishment to sell the advowsons of the Crown livings, and even if it were persuaded that with the consent of all their members they might have mortgaged those advowsons which they possessed, under the letters patent of 3 Geo. III., it is quite clear that the money so obtained should have been applied to secure the flow of promotion amongst the Fellows, because the preamble of those letters patent states that the object for which these advowsons were purchased was to "ensure a more frequent succession of Fellowships in the said College."

558. You wish to give evidence as to the question of the future connexion of the Divinity School with Trinity College in the future, and of its future government?—Do you think the Divinity School should remain connected with Trinity College or that it should be separated from it?—I am strongly of opinion that the connexion should continue. I think it essential for the proper training of Divinity Students, that they should be educated with all other students in their studies, and mix freely with them in every-day life. It must also be remembered that our Divinity Students are not preparing solely for the ministry of the Church of Ireland, but that many of them are for the Church of England, and some of them for other Protestant denominations. No good reason could be assigned for separating the Theological Faculty from the University of Dublin, and as degrees in Divinity can now be taken by laymen, it is only the proper function of the University to supply teaching in the necessary subjects of examination.

559. Do you think there should be any modification in the government of the Divinity School?—Yes; as the Board of Trinity College may at some future period not consist of clergymen, provision should be made, at least, that only such members of it as were clergymen should have governing powers in respect of the Divinity School. Further, as the recognition of our Divinity Testimonium by the Bishops of the Church of Ireland is only discretionary, it is very important that they should as far as possible be brought into intimate connexion with the government of the Divinity School, so that they might be induced to make it a general rule that before ordination they should require candidates to produce the Divinity Testimonium.

560. What governing body would you suggest for the future?—I think the number should not be much larger than at present, and, in my opinion, the best selection that could be made would be; three persons to be named by those members of the Board who were also members of the Church of Ireland, the two Divinity Professors, and one person to be chosen by the assistants of the Professors, and three persons to be chosen by the bench of Bishops—nine in all.

561. What powers would you give to this governing body?—They should have the power of electing the Professors and other teachers of the School, or of removing them from time to time. They should have the control and direction of all studies in the Divinity School, and should have the control of all money for payment to them, subject only to a veto by the Board of Trinity College in the case of any proposal to disturb the primary allocation in the Divinity School of funds belonging to Trinity College.

562. From what funds would you pay the salaries and supply the wants of the School?—As long as the Professors are elected from amongst the Fellows of Trinity College, their salaries should be paid as at present, but as the supply from that source will probably become limited, sufficient funds should be supplied from other sources, possibly from the confiscated Church Funds, to enable the governing body to fill as far as possible vacancies in their chairs, and to give suitable salaries to the successors of the present Professors. The funds of Trinity College should still bear the expense of all local requirements of the School, and should also pay a capitation fee for each Divinity Student upon the books of the College.

563. The time may come when there is no clerical Fellow to take the Professorship of Divinity?—Yes;

[illegible]

Dec. 7, 1877.

A. Traill, Esq., LL.D., M.D., and R. Williamson, Esq., F.T.C.D.

and then, in my opinion, the £1,200 a year should go into the College funds. The capitation fee would be a reasonable sum to be paid by the College.

565. Do you think that the Church would be satisfied with having only three representatives on the Board?—The three representatives of the teachers would be as much representatives of the Church as of the College. I do not consider that the Divinity School of Trinity College is the property of the Church of Ireland. Many pupils of the school go to the English Church. Some of my pupils have become Presbyterian ministers. The number of men for the English Church is very large. I put the school on a wider basis than the Church of Ireland.

566. How many students of the Divinity School belong to other churches?—I should say between the Church of England and the Presbyterian Church the proportion would be about one-third.

567. Do you consider that there is any obligation on Trinity College to keep up the Divinity School?—I do.

568. Judge Flanagan.—Do I understand you to say that a layman can now get a theological degree?—Yes.

569. Therefore you consider that the school should be open for the benefit of laymen generally?—That change was only made about a year ago.

570. If the Divinity School was entirely separated, do you consider that the pupils in the Divinity School would be hurt by the separation?—Yes.

571. In what respect?—A Divinity School belonging to the Church would never have the same prestige as a Divinity School attached to the University. I think the natural tendency of it would be to educate the Divinity Students in theology alone, and not in arts. I consider that the education of a clergyman in arts is as important as his education in theology.

572. What difficulty would there be in the Governors of the Divinity School requiring that the students should have an education elsewhere in arts?—I think the tendency of all theological colleges is to look to instruction in theology alone. A number of men were ordained at the time of the disestablishment of the Church who had not a degree in arts, and they don't compare favourably with those who have degrees.

573. Do not the Bishops require candidates for ordination to be examined?—It is the Chaplain's duty to examine candidates; but I do not think that chaplains examine in anything but theology.

574. Mr. Galbraith.—In some cases of exigency, have not the bishops made it a condition for ordaining them that they should afterwards go through the arts course?—Yes. I have heard of a great number of clergymen on whom that condition was imposed.

575. Mr. Porter.—Is it not the fact that, under the present system, a man may take a degree in theology without arts?—He can take out a testimonium, but not a degree.

576. Lord Belmore.—He must be a B.A. before taking a degree in Divinity?—Yes, and so it is also in the Engineering School.

Jan. 9, 1878.

Wednesday, January 9, 1878.

Present:—Right Hon. the Earl of Belmore, K.C.M.G., in the Chair; Right Hon. Mountifort Longfield, LL.D.; Right Hon. S. W. Flanagan; A. M. Porter, Esq., Q.C.; Rev. J. A. Galbraith, F.T.C.D.; John Mulholland, Esq., M.P., D.L.

Rev. J. A. Galbraith, F.T.C.D.

The Rev. J. A. Galbraith, F.T.C.D., one of the Commissioners.

577. Lord Belmore.—I believe, Mr. Galbraith, that you wish to put in a document?

Mr. Galbraith.—I wish to put this document in evidence; it is a copy of a statement signed by nineteen of the Junior Fellows and forwarded by them to the Prime Minister, and I believe that it was mainly this which induced the Government to issue this Commission. I desire to put it in for the purpose of showing what were the grievances from which the Junior Fellows considered themselves to be suffering, when they applied to the Government for an inquiry by a Royal Commission.

APPENDIX.

APPENDIX II.

of Trinity College, Dublin, as to the present condition of
sity of providing an adequate system of retirement for Fellows
the discharge of their duties.

and they beg to lay before them the following proposal:—

In the year 1873, the Irish Church Temporalities Commissioners handed over to the College as compensation for the loss of its advowsons, together with accrued interest, the sum of £138,839 3s. 1d. This, with interest since earned, must amount to a sum of at least £150,000. Considering the origin of this Fund, namely, as compensation for the loss the College suffered in being deprived of its rights of nomination to twenty-one Benefices, the Junior Fellows maintain that its legitimate application would be to provide retiring places for Fellows incapacitated by age or infirmity for the discharge of their duties, and therefore propose that it should be set aside for that purpose.

From the experience derived from the past history of the College, it can be shown that, if provision be made for four retiring places, the evils apprehended will be in a great measure, if not altogether, obviated. It can also be shown that the Advowson Fund will be more than sufficient for this purpose.

While the Junior Fellows maintain that the establishment of such places should be the first charge on the Advowson Fund, they are of opinion that under the present circumstances of the College an adequate scheme of retirement should be provided for Professors, who are not Fellows, whenever they may become disabled by age or infirmity for the discharge of their duty, and accordingly, that any residue of the Advowson Fund, aided, if necessary, by the general funds of the College, should be applied to that purpose.

The Junior Fellows, having failed to obtain the consent of the Board to the establishment of an adequate Scheme of Retirement, and being fully convinced that the future welfare of the College must depend on the three conditions which have been already specified, namely,

A vigorous Governing Body,
An active and efficient Staff of Teachers,
A sufficient number of Fellowship Vacancies,

urgently request that Her Majesty's Government will advise Her Majesty to issue a Royal Commission to inquire into the facts they have above alleged, and which they are prepared, if called on, to substantiate.

The Junior Fellows have been induced to approach Her Majesty's Government, not merely from foreseeing the evils which are certain to arise before long from the present course of legislation if no remedy be now applied, but also because, even at present, grave dissatisfaction is felt, both within and without the College, respecting the three points already adverted to—Firstly, as to the Governing Body, from the fact that there are at present two Senior Fellows who are wholly incapacitated for the discharge of any duty incidental to their position; Secondly, from the unprecedentedly advanced age of a large number of the Junior Fellows still engaged in the work of instruction; Thirdly, from the fact that there has been no Fellowship Examination for three consecutive years, and that there is at present no certainty of one being held in 1877.

Signed by the Committee appointed to act on behalf of the Junior Fellows,

Joseph A. Galbraith.	George F. Shaw.
Samuel Haughton.	Benjamin Williamson.
John K. Ingram.	Anthony Traill.

Appendix III.

Statement of Provost and Senior Fellows of Trinity College.

APPENDIX III.

STATEMENT of the Provost and Senior Fellows.

The Provost and Senior Fellows of Trinity College beg leave to make the following statement in reference to the subjects of inquiry specified in the Royal Commission:

I. With regard to the [illegible] for only [illegible] consequences arising from the lack of patronage, they submit an extract from a proposal for a new statute, which was laid before the Visitors in last December by them, with the approval of all the Junior Fellows, viz.:—

"Whereas it is expedient that provision should be made for the retirement of any of the Fellows of the College of the Holy and Undivided Trinity of Queen Elizabeth, near Dublin, who may become permanently incapacitated for the due performance of their duties, by reason of old age, sickness, or any [illegible]; and whereas the incomes of each of the said Fellows consist partly of a fixed salary, and partly of other payments distributed according to the standing amongst the Fellows, and partly also of the share of any Professorship, Lectureship, or office to which such Fellow may have been appointed; and whereas the funds of the said College have been recently increased by the [illegible] of certain sums of money as a compensation for the loss of certain Advowsons to the [illegible] of such rights of [illegible] event of any Non-Tutor Fellowship becoming vacant, to omit to fill up or elect to the same until by such means the Non-Tutor Fellowships shall be abolished: And whereas it is expedient that a fixed rule should be laid down for such omission to elect Fellows, and that provision should be made, as far as possible, for the election of a Fellow in the said College every year, it is proposed that until the total number of Junior Fellows shall be twenty-eight, one Fellow shall be elected every year, and that not more than one Fellow shall be elected in any one year unless the number of Junior Fellows shall be less than twenty-three on the first day of Lent in any year, on the happening of which event two Fellows shall be elected in such year; provided always, that in no case shall more than two Fellows be elected in any one year, and that the number of Tutor Fellows now existing shall not be increased."

II. The Provost and Senior Fellows are not aware of any [illegible] Advowsons [illegible] the Fellows in Priest's Orders have [illegible] the presentation to benefices. This claim has in fact been already put forward by some of the Fellows as a legal claim, but the legal advisers of the College state that no such claim can be established in law.

[illegible]

[illegible]

IV. [illegible]

[illegible]	[illegible]	[illegible]	[illegible]		1873	4150	5	0
[illegible]	[illegible]	[illegible]	[illegible]		1874	150	0	0
[illegible]	[illegible]	[illegible]	[illegible]		1875	148	1	0
[illegible]	[illegible]	[illegible]	[illegible]		1876	111	4	0
[illegible]	[illegible]	[illegible]	[illegible]					

V. [illegible]

[illegible]

"May 8, 187[illegible]

[illegible]

"May 27, 187[illegible]

"The following resolutions of the Divinity School Committee were communicated to the Board:—

"1. That the Divinity School Committee do very gratefully accept the resolutions of the Provost and Senior Fellows on the subject of the Divinity School, and request them to put the matter in the hands of their Law Advisers for such ratification as may be requisite to insure the legal permanency of the arrangement.

"2nd. That the Divinity School Committee respectfully suggest to the Board the advisability of effecting the security of the pecuniary part of the arrangement, by capitalizing the income requisite for maintaining the Divinity School, and handing over this capital to the Representative Body in trust for that purpose.

"(Signed). "L. H. [illegible],
"Hon. Sec. of the Divinity School Committee.

"The Board agreed to the first of the above resolutions, but they were evenly divided on the second resolution, four voting for it, and four against."

Another plan for the government of the Divinity School has been proposed by the Rev. Dr. Salmon, Regius Professor of Divinity, in a letter to the Registrar, which is forwarded herewith.

These two plans have been submitted to the Legal Adviser of the Board, who has given it as his opinion in each case, that the plan proposed could be carried out only by Act of Parliament.

The above statement represents the opinions of the Board, collectively, on the several subjects referred to in the Royal Commission: individual Members of the Board are understood to entertain special views in reference to certain points connected with these matters, which may have to be brought before the Commissioners in separate communications.

By Order of the Board,

Thomas Stack, Registrar.

Trinity College, April 21, 1877.

APPENDIX IV.

Statement proposing a scheme of Retirement.

Fellowship, up to the period of cooption, was five years, and that eighteen Fellows were promoted to Bishoprics. From 1690 to 1740, the average Junior Fellowship lasted for ten years, and six Fellows became Bishops. From 1740 to 1790, the average length of a Junior Fellowship was fifteen years, six Fellows becoming Bishops; and from 1790 to 1841, the average duration of a Junior Fellowship was twenty-three years, and the number of Bishoprics to which Fellows were appointed was seven.

These results may be tabulated as follows:—

From 1660 to 1690	Average duration of Junior Fellowship.	5 years;	Number promoted to Bishoprics,	18
" 1690 " 1740	" "	10 "	" "	6
" 1740 " 1790	" "	15 "	" "	6
" 1790 " 1841	" "	23 "	" "	7

This table excludes all the present Senior Fellows, the last of whom obtained Fellowship in 1841, and was not coopted until the year 1876, after thirty-five years' service.

But a different state of affairs has since arisen, owing to three circumstances:—

(1) The Repeal of the Celibacy Statute in 1840.

(2) The creation of ten additional Fellowships by the Legislature of that year, which were filled up between the years 1840 and 1850, in addition to those which fell vacant during that period in the ordinary course of events.

(3) The Disestablishment of the Church in 1869.

If a calculation be made, in accordance with the ordinary laws of mortality, extending over the next thirty years, so as to include all the existing Junior Fellows, for the purpose of arriving at a result analogous to that tabulated above as the record of the past, it will be found that if the present system continues as it is, and if no provision for retirement be made, the average duration of a Junior Fellowship before cooption will be thirty-nine years, and in eight cases that period will range from 43 to 45 years.

It might be supposed at first sight, on a consideration of the three circumstances above mentioned, that the last, viz., the Disestablishment of the Church, could not have much effect as compared with the other two, inasmuch as since the Repeal of the Celibacy Statute, and in consequence of the diminution of the incomes of the Livings by the Church Temporalities Act, College Livings have not been so freely accepted by the Fellows as in former days. It will be found, however, that with respect to the creation of vacancies in Fellowship, the Disestablishment of the Church must produce a very serious effect. Since 1841 thirteen vacancies among the Fellows have been produced by ecclesiastical preferment, exclusive of Bishoprics—ten owing to College Livings, and three to Professorships of Divinity; and during the same period there have been but thirty-five Fellows elected, including those added on by the Letters Patent of 1840. If we compare with these numbers those relating to the periods between 1740 and 1800, and between 1800 and 1841, we shall find that in the former period twenty-eight College Livings were accepted by Fellows, the whole number of elections to Fellowship being fifty, and that in the latter period twenty-four Livings were accepted by Fellows, the whole number of elections to Fellowship being forty-nine. It thus appears that the proportion of the vacancies caused by Church preferment to the total number of vacancies did not much alter during the century previous to the Disestablishment of the Church.

All the avenues of exit and retirement from Collegiate work which have hitherto depended on College Livings or promotion to Bishoprics have been effectually and for ever closed by the Act of 1869, and, as a result of this and of the other two circumstances already mentioned, it can be shown that if the body of Fellows be maintained at its present number, and without any provision for retirement, no present or future Junior Fellow can expect to reach the Board until after his 60th year, and that half the Board at any time must be over 70 years of age. These evils will, in the immediate future, be seriously increased, owing to the accumulation of Fellowship elections within a short period under the Legislation of 1840. There are in the present year sixteen Fellows, Senior and Junior, over 64 years of age, from whose ages may be shewn, as a consequence of the laws of human mortality, that of these in fourteen years there will probably be eight survivors, the youngest of whom will be 70 years of age, and at least one of them will be still a Junior Fellow.

A tabular statement is subjoined, of the most favourable conditions as to age which can happen among the Members of the Board, at the corresponding dates:—

arising from the College Livings, but lost the right to appoint some of its Fellows to receive them. These incomes have been confiscated, like any other Church property, the incumbents receiving compensation for their life interests, as in every other case; and the capital sum paid to the College represents the compensation to the Corporation for the loss of its rights. The Fellows having been the persons who had the right to [illegible] to all effects, to the pecuniary benefits arising from the exercise of the patronage by the Board, it seems evident that they are justified in claiming that the Advowson Fund shall be primarily devoted to redressing the evils arising from the stagnation in their body produced by this action of the Legislature.

Having now pointed out the evils which are at present felt, and those which are to be apprehended in the future; having shown the absolute necessity of a proper Scheme of Retirement, not only for Fellows of advanced age and long service, but also for Fellows throughout the Body who may be overtaken by infirmity or incapacity; and having further shown that the Fellows have an incontrovertible claim upon the Advowson Fund for the purposes of such a scheme, the Junior Fellows proceed to lay before the Commissioners the main features of a plan for carrying the foregoing principles into effect.

They are as follows:—

(1). Retiring pensions to be provided for Fellows ascertained to be incapacitated by age or infirmity for the effective discharge of their duties; the Visitors being empowered and required to inquire into the existence of such incapacity.

(2). Power of voluntary retirement of Fellows at or after the age of 70, on one of the pensions provided.

(3). Retiring salary for Fellows, after retirement, to be the income belonging to their position as Senior Fellows, exclusive of special offices.

(4). In the case of the retirement of a Junior Fellow, such retiring salary, adapted to the case, to be allowed as the Board and Visitors may approve.

(5). The application, to these objects, of the annual interest of the Advowson Fund, so far as it may be required for the purpose.

(6). The residue to be devoted to general collegiate purposes, amongst which the provision of suitable [illegible] for Professors, not being Fellows, should hold an important place.

(7). The retirement at present provided for Senior Fellows by the Letters Patent of 18 Vict., to be modified so as to be available only in cases of temporary incapacity; and leave of absence, in no case to extend beyond two years.

(8). Any Senior Fellow availing himself of such temporary leave of absence to be required to pay a suitable income to the Junior Fellow who is called on to discharge his duties at the Board.

The Junior Fellows do not propose a system of compulsory retirement, though they do not see any objection in principle to such a system, provided that existing interests were carefully compensated. But many thoughtful minds believe that the system of voluntary retirement above described will be found to be ineffective, unless it be further provided—(1), that no Senior Fellow should be eligible to hold the annual offices of Bursar, Senior Lecturer, or Registrar, after seventy years of age, or any of the other annual offices after seventy-five; and (2), that no Senior Fellow should hold more than one of the offices in any year. To secure the latter object, it would be necessary that all restrictions, whereby certain of these offices are not tenable by Junior Fellows, should be removed. It might be considered equitable that existing Senior Fellows, in case of retirement at, or after seventy, should obtain additional compensation for the loss of the minor offices.

If an adequate scheme should be now put in operation, the result will necessarily be a recurrence of existing difficulties, and fresh demands for a really efficient remedy. No plan will afford a satisfactory solution of the questions at issue which does not secure the three great objects of which we have spoken above, and in which the College and the Public are so deeply interested—a vigorous governing body, an efficient teaching staff, and a sufficient number of Fellowship vacancies.

(Signed),

Michael Roberts.	T. K. Abbott.
Samuel Haughton.	John R. Leslie.
John W. Stubbs.	Thomas T. Gray.
R. Townsend.	J. P. Mahaffy.
John K. Ingram.	Anthony Traill.
H. R. Poole.	Francis A. Tarleton.
George F. Shaw.	R. Y. Tyrrell.
J. W. Barlow.	William S. Burnside.
B. M. [illegible].	W. S. M'Cay.
Benjamin Williamson.	Arthur W. Panton.

Appendix IV. Statement concerning a Scheme of Retirement.

APPENDIX V.

Statement submitted to the Dublin University Royal Commission of the claims of certain of the Fellows of Trinity College, Dublin, in Holy Orders, for compensation for the loss of their right of succession to the livings formerly in the gift of Trinity College.

Appendix V. Statement of the claims of certain of the Fellows of Trinity College being in Holy Orders, for compensation.

At the passing of the Irish Church Act, in 1869, Trinity College, Dublin, was the owner of twenty-one Advowsons—eighteen granted by Letters Patent of James I., dated August 29, 1610, and three subsequently purchased by the College, in 1737, 1766, and 1828.

After the passing of the Irish Church Act, the College claimed and was paid Compensation for the loss of these Advowsons, under the 29th section of that Act.

The following are the names of the Benefices in respect of which Trinity College received compensation, and also the amount of the Annuities awarded to

The invariable practice of the Governing Body of the College, when any of these Benefices became vacant, was to offer such Benefice to each of the Clerical Fellows in rotation, in order of seniority, the Fellow accepting it being bound to resign his Fellowship within a year from the date of his appointment.

The annual income of many of these Benefices far exceeds the income derivable from a Junior Fellowship. Moreover, as the duties of a Parish are of a less exacting nature than the duties of a Fellow and Tutor of Trinity College, and therefore compatible with a state of health and constitution more or less unfitted for the efficient discharge of the various duties

APPENDIX V. — Statement of the claim of certain of the Fellows of Trinity College, Dublin, in Holy Orders, for compensation.

The custom of offering a Living, when vacant, to the Clerical Fellows in rotation, in order of seniority, has never in any instance been violated; and no person not a Fellow has ever been presented by the Board to a Living in the gift of the College until such Living had, in the first instance, been refused by all the Clerical Fellows.

This custom of offering the Benefices, when vacant, to the Clerical Fellows in rotation, according to seniority, is recognised in the Statutes of the College. In the Letters Patent, or Statute of Celibacy, 52 Geo. III., 1811, and in the Statute of 3 Vict., 1840, repealing the Celibacy Statute, the following clause occurs (MacDonnell's Statutes, vol. I., p. 245; and again, p. 299): "And Our will and pleasure further is, that, during such year, such Fellow so marrying, and giving such notice as aforesaid, shall be entitled to such choice or option of Ecclesiastical Benefices in the gift of the Provost, Fellows, and Scholars of the said College as he would have been during such year entitled to have had, if he had remained unmarried."

Again, the Letters Patent dated 23rd March, 1763, 3 Geo. III., authorising the College to purchase Advowsons, contain the following recital:—"And whereas our said Lieutenant-General and General Governor of our said Kingdom of Ireland having represented to Us that the purchasing of such Advowsons will cause a more frequent succession of Fellowships in the said College, and by that means tend very much to the encouragement of learning in our said Kingdom of Ireland, We, &c."

This recital proves that these Advowsons were purchased for the express purpose of being given to the Fellows; and also shows conclusively that this was the use which had always up to that time (1763) been made of the eighteen Livings then in the gift of the College. Hence, it seems impossible to avoid the conclusion that the Benefices were vested in the College for the primary purpose of causing a more frequent succession of Fellowships—and this purpose would be wholly defeated if there were no obligation to offer the vacant Livings to the Fellows, and it will also follow that the Fellows had the right to demand such offer, and as a matter of fact their right was always admitted, and never called in question. Indeed, the Board considered themselves so bound by this custom, that if an ex-Fellow wished to exchange Livings with another Incumbent, he was obliged, in the first instance, to obtain a consent from all the Fellows in Holy Orders that they would not accept his Living when he had vacated it for the purpose of the exchange; or if (as occurred in 1823, and again in 1833), while the Celibacy Statute was in force, a Fellow wished to marry before he had secured a Living, he procured the signatures of all the Fellows in Holy Orders to an agreement that they would refuse the first vacant Living, and allow him to accept it. Many similar cases might be quoted all going to prove that the Fellows in Holy Orders never allowed their right of choice or option of Ecclesiastical Benefices to be interfered with, and the Board have always recognised and acknowledged this right.

Under these circumstances, when the Irish Church Act came into operation, several of the Fellows in Holy Orders applied to the Commissioners of Church Temporalities in Ireland for Compensation, under the 48th section of the Act, for the loss of their right of succession to these Benefices. It will be seen from the Report of the Judgment of the Commissioners in the case, that the Commissioners disallowed the claims of the Fellows, upon the grounds that the Fellows were not "Ecclesiastical persons within the meaning of the Act," and that the right of succession provided for by the 48th section was a right incident to that Ecclesiastical status. At the same time, they were clearly of opinion that the Fellows had proved a right of succession, "of such ancient standing and such uniform observance, that we may take it to have the force of law" (Judgment, p. 3). Again (p. 6), "We are disposed to think that this right, though somewhat difficult of estimation, is a right of succession within the true meaning of that term." And at pages 8 and 16, the Master of the Rolls and Mr. Justice Lawson pointed out that the claim for Compensation of the individual members of the Corporation, in respect of that right of succession, should be asserted against the sum paid to the Corporation in respect of these Advowsons. "The Act of Parliament," said the Master of the Rolls, "by its 16th section, gives to the Corporation itself the fullest measure of Compensation for the entire Advowson, which, of course, covers the very next Presentation, to the right of succession to which Compensation is claimed by individual Members of the Corporation." And again, "It would appear more just and equitable that where the entire Advowson vested in the Corporation is compensated for by payment in full to the Corporation, a right to a next Presentation, vested in a Member of that Corporation, should be adjusted by the Corporation, out of the Funds it has got as Compensation, rather than that the same thing should be doubly paid for." "The individual Members of the Corporation," said Mr. Justice Lawson, "who have subordinate rights against the Corporation, must assert these against the sum paid to the Corporation in respect of these Advowsons. I am very far from saying that the Fellows have not such a right. I only decide that they have it not against the Commissioners." These judgments, pronounced upon Appeal, and after long deliberation, by Judges of high authority, contain clear expressions of opinion as to the existence of a legal right of succession in the Clerical Fellows, and as to the funds out of which they ought to receive Compensation for the loss of this right of succession.

We submit that our position in respect of these Livings is precisely similar to that of the Chancellor and Prebendaries of Christ Church, Dublin, in respect to the Benefices named in the 45th section of the Irish Church Act, to whom the Irish Church Temporalities Commissioners, as directed by that section, awarded Compensation.

In support of this view, we beg to refer the Royal Commissioners to the decision of the Arbitrators in the case of the Advowson of Drumgoon, in the county of Cavan. The Arbitrators in the case were the present Lord Chief Justice of the Queen's Bench, on the part of the Irish Church Temporalities Commissioners; Dr. Anthony Traill, F.T.C.D., on the part of the Claimant; and the Rev. Joseph A. Galbraith, F.T.C.D., as Umpire. It will be seen, by the result of this Arbitration, that a considerable sum was granted to the Claimant, for the loss of his right of presenting himself, in addition to the sum already awarded to him by the Church Temporalities Commissioners, for his loss, as Lay Patron, of the Advowson merely.

We desire, therefore, to lay before the Commissioners our claim to Compensation for the loss we have sustained in consequence of being deprived by the Irish Church Act of our right of succession to the Livings which, previous to the passing of that Act, were vested in the Corporation of Trinity College, Dublin; and we, at the same time, beg to submit that the sum of money received by the Corporation of Trinity College, Dublin, as Compensation for the loss of its Advowsons, should be held to represent the Livings in respect of which it was given, and that we have the same rights against this fund as we should have had against the Livings if still subsisting.

(Signed),

JOHN W. STUBBS, D.D.
BENJAMIN DICKSON, D.D.
JAMES W. BARLOW, M.A.
RICHARD M. CONNER, M.A.
THOMAS K. ABBOTT, M.A.
THOMAS T. GRAY, M.A.
JOHN P. MAHAFFY, M.A.

APPENDIX VI.

STATEMENT of the CLAIMS of the CHURCH of IRELAND with reference to the DIVINITY SCHOOL, submitted to the DUBLIN UNIVERSITY [illegible] COMMISSIONERS.

The Committee empowered by the Synod of the Church of Ireland to represent them before the University Commission, beg to submit the following statement with respect to the Divinity School of Trinity College:—

The Commissioners will be aware that Trinity College has, since its foundation, been the school in which the Irish Clergy have been trained. The supply of Clergy to the Irish Church is stated in the [illegible] to have been the principal object for which Trinity College was founded. The Fellows were not only, with one or three exceptions, obliged on pain of deprivation, to take Holy Orders, but on their election each took an oath that he would make Theology the main object of his studies. Accordingly, the body of Fellows has always included in its members many learned divines, from whom theological students have received professional as well as secular instruction; and for many years past the Irish Bishops have made it an ordinary condition of Ordination that the candidate should produce the certificate of the Trinity College Divinity School.

Ever since the passing of the Dublin University Act of 1873 the Synod has felt the greatest anxiety as to the effect of that Act on the Divinity School. Not that there has been interference with the present condition of the School, which the Act was so framed as not to interfere, the Divinity professorships being expressly exempted from its operation. But at the time the Bill was framed, it was foreseen that it would indirectly affect the Divinity School in such a way that further legislation of some kind would in future have become absolutely necessary. The Divinity School, like the rest of the College, has been under the government of the Provost and the senior members of the Fellows. By the Statutes of the College these have been almost all Clergymen, and they have always possessed the full confidence of the Church. [illegible] the present governing body of Trinity College. But the Fellows in future may not only be all Laymen, but need not even be members of the Church. The Divinity School of Trinity College will be practically lost to the Church of Ireland whenever it happens that the body which appoints the lecturers, which controls their teaching, and which prescribes the course of study, consists of persons either not belonging to the Church, or who, though nominally adhering to it, do not enjoy the confidence of its members in matters connected with Theology.

Besides the injurious effect of the Act of 1873 on the future government of the Divinity School, it threatens in another way to destroy the efficiency of the School. As the law stands at present the Regius Professor of Divinity must be chosen from among the Fellows or Ex-Fellows. There was no inconvenience in this arrangement as long as the Fellows were almost all Clergymen, and from their [illegible] the Clergymen in the Church most likely to devote themselves to theological teaching. But as there is no obligation on future Fellows to study Theology, it is possible that the body to which the office is now limited might not furnish a single person competent to fill it, and it is certain that in any case the choice of the electors would be most injuriously restricted. Even at the present moment there are so many of the Fellows who have not taken Holy Orders that if a vacancy occurred immediately, the choice would be among a considerably smaller number of persons than on the occasion of former vacancies.

It has been felt that even the immediate loss of the Divinity School to the Church of Ireland would be a less evil than this prospective loss; for if the Divinity School had been immediately taken away, no doubt compensation would have been provided, such as was given in the case of Maynooth and of the Presbyterian Theological Colleges. But no such compensation is likely to be given if the loss is postponed till these precedents have had time to be forgotten; besides that the eventual loss would be likely to happen as the result of a number of successive changes, no one of which might seem to present a sufficient claim for compensation. The Synod has, therefore, been exerting itself ever since the passing of the Dublin University Act of 1873 in order to obtain such a settlement of this question that the Church of Ireland may not be placed in a worse position with respect to the education of its Clergy than the other religious denominations affected by the Act of 1869. When that Act was before Parliament it was recognised that the withdrawal of public aid from an institution for clerical education demanded more cautious legislation and more liberal provision for existing interests than even the disendowment of a Church, and accordingly, Parliament dealt in the most liberal manner with the College of Maynooth and the Presbyterian Theological Colleges affected by that Act. The result has been that these institutions have now permanent endowments producing incomes nearly, if not quite, equal to that which they enjoyed before the Act of 1869.

If the means at present available for the education of candidates for Orders are not permanently secured to the Church, two sources present themselves from which similar compensation may be made, and on either of which the Synod considers that the Church has just claims, viz., the fund administered by the Irish Church Commissioners and the funds of Trinity College. As in the case of Maynooth and of the Presbyterian Colleges, compensation had been made out of the fund administered by the Church Commissioners, it was out of the same fund that the Church of Ireland, in the first instance, attempted to obtain compensation. Accordingly, the Synod both memorialised the Government that the precedent established in the case of the other religious bodies should be followed in the case of the Church of Ireland, and also petitioned Parliament to the same effect. The Secretary to the Divinity School Committee received an answer to their memorial from the Private Secretary of the Prime Minister, declining, on the part of the Government, to entertain the question until the whole subject of the distribution of the Church surplus came before them for consideration. The Committee of the Synod greatly regretted this reply, not only because it left the question unsettled for an indefinite time, but also because it was a refusal to concede to the Church of Ireland what was granted to the other religious bodies, provision for the education of whose Clergy was not postponed till the ascertainment of a surplus, but was regarded as a claim to be satisfied before any surplus could be said to have arisen. As there are some parts of the Church's loss in connexion with the Divinity School which, as it will presently appear, cannot fairly be made good from any other source, the Church can only hope that its case may be fully considered by Parliament when they come to deal with the whole question.

The claim of the Church on Trinity College is that on which the Commissioners are directly called to pronounce. It is needless to say much to establish the claims of the Church of Ireland on that Institution. It seems not unreasonable that whatever claims the Church fairly has should be satisfied out of the funds here before devoted to its service, before these funds are applied to any new purpose. It is not necessary to speak of funds which the Board hold only as trustees, having been given by the donors specially for the uses of the Divinity School; for it may be assumed that

Appendix VI. — Statement of the Claims of the Church of Ireland with reference to the Divinity School.

[illegible] Body of the Church of Ireland towards the maintenance of the Divinity School, on the following conditions, viz., that the students of Trinity College shall continue to receive instruction in the school as hitherto, without charge.

"III. That the students in the Divinity School shall be allowed to continue (as at present) to have the use of the Lecture-rooms in Trinity College for Theological instruction; provided that the lecturers are subject to ordinary collegiate discipline, and that they accommodate their time of lecturing to the requirements of public instruction in Trinity College.

"IV. That the Board of Trinity College are willing to assign a similar privilege to any other religious body desirous that its candidates for orders should be instructed in Trinity College."

The Committee accordingly had a conference with the Board, in which they expressed their approval of these resolutions, except that in resolution No. 2, they suggested the advisability of limiting the annuity to the particular term of the arrangement by capitalizing the proposed annual payments and handing over such capital sum to the Representative Body to hold for the purposes of the Divinity School. The Board referred the scheme to their legal advisers, who reported that an Act of Parliament would be necessary in order to give effect to the plan. The Committee accordingly had the draft of such a Bill prepared, and sent it to the Board, asking for their co-operation in submitting it to the Government. The Committee were informed by the Registrar of the College in January last that the Board had not come to any decision on this request, and also that they had a different scheme under consideration.

Negotiations between the Board and the Committee were interrupted by the announcement on the part of the Board that they had applied to the Government for a Queen's Letter authorizing the alteration [illegible] of a scheme of endowment for Fellows and Professors. Although, as has been stated, a difference of opinion has existed as to whether or not this is the fund which is properly applicable to satisfying the claims of the Church of Ireland; yet, the Committee always held that it was that which was primarily applicable to this charge, and that in any case its existence facilitates the discharge of the equitable claims of the Church on the funds of the College, the Committee felt that they would neglect their duty if they allowed it without remonstrance to be applied to another purpose before the claims of the Church of Ireland had been fairly weighed. For the Church would thus be exposed to the risk that it might hereafter be said that it had been [illegible] compensation, [illegible] from which compensation might have been made. The Committee, therefore, addressed the Government, asking them not to advise Her Majesty to issue the proposed Queen's Letter, until the question of the Divinity School had been at the same time considered, and some arrangement made in satisfaction to the Church of Ireland. The Committee acknowledge that by advising the Queen to appoint the present Commission the Government has completely attained their wishes in this matter.

The Committee, therefore, beg the Commissioners to give their best consideration to the claims here laid before them on behalf of the Church of Ireland. They will be happy to give either by viva voce representation or by written statement, any further explanation the Commissioners may desire, either as to their general views or as to the details of any particular plan which may recommend itself to the Commissioners as likely to afford the best solution for a settlement of this question. The Committee have only to add, in conclusion, that the Church of Ireland has no desire for a separation of its Divinity School from Trinity College. It would rather be its wish that the School should remain in as close connection with the College as the alteration made in the character of the governing body of the College by the Act of 1873 will permit. The Church would have no objection to having its Divinity School connected with a University where, besides, [illegible] of all religions without distinction, and would be well content that its students and teachers should be subject to the general discipline of such an institution; but the Church could not recognise the Divinity School as [illegible] were conducted and its course of study regulated by persons of a different religion.

APPENDIX VII.

Appendix VII. — Statement by some of the Fellows of Trinity College, with respect to the proposed separation of the Divinity School from Trinity College.

STATEMENT submitted to the DUBLIN UNIVERSITY ROYAL COMMISSION by some of the *Fellows* of Trinity College, with respect to the proposed separation of the Divinity School from Trinity College.

The undersigned Fellows of Trinity College avail themselves of the permission of the Royal Commissioners, conveyed in the letter of their Secretary to the Registrar of Trinity College, to submit reasons which, in their opinion, render it unadvisable that the School of Divinity now established in Trinity College should be severed from its present connexion with the College.

By reference to the Charter of Queen Elizabeth, which was confirmed and extended by Charles I., it appears that Trinity College was not established or endowed specially or mainly for the education of the Clergy of Ireland. The Charter states that the object of the Foundation was, that the youth of Ireland should be piously and liberally educated; that they should be assisted in the pursuit of learning and in the cultivation of virtue and religion; and, in order to carry this object out to the fullest extent, the Students have been granted, by the Charter of Elizabeth, the right of obtaining Degrees, in proper time, in all Arts and Faculties, including Theology. The Act of Parliament of the present reign, which abolishes tests, declares that it is expedient that the benefits of Trinity College, and the University of Dublin, and of the Schools in said University, as places of religion and learning, should be freely accessible to the nation; and the Act declares that, so long as the University continues to teach and grant Degrees in Theology, the Professors and Lecturers in Divinity shall be excluded from the operation of the Act. As long as the present Charter remains in force, the University must continue to grant Degrees in Theology: and Trinity College has always given instruction, in conformity with the spirit of the Charter, in all Faculties in which it grants Degrees (except, perhaps, Music).

No Fellow of the College will in future be required, as a condition of holding his Fellowship, to take any religious test or to be ordained to Holy Orders. There is nothing, however, which discourages a Fellow in future from becoming a Clergyman if he thinks fit to select that profession; on the contrary, the existing Statute requires the Tutors (who must be Junior Fellows) daily to attend to the culture of their pupils in piety and literature, on pain of being deprived of those pupils. The Deans are appointed to see that piety to God, as well as moral conduct, be preserved among the Students. One of the Senior Fellows must be elected annually as Catechist, to see that the Students are instructed in Sacred Literature by his assistants; and the College Chapel must be kept open, and morning and evening prayers offered, every day in it. All these duties incident to a Fellowship would

[illegible] historical [illegible] on Professors who [illegible] present time in a way [illegible]. Even now [illegible] similarity [illegible] the teaching staff of the [illegible]. The Professors who are [illegible] energetic and [illegible] great Institution. The [illegible] for the first time, [illegible] interests of [illegible] indispensable. But still [illegible]

lecturers, and that in some few cases an increase of salary to Professors has been made by the Board; but the existing arrangements cannot be considered as final, when regard is had to the smallness of the salaries received by some of the Professors who devote themselves wholly to forwarding the study of their several branches of learning. Further, in the Decrees recently made, with reference to certain Professors, it is provided that in no case shall the amount of the pension exceed two thirds of the Professor's salary, an arrangement which might be just if the salaries of the Professors were large, but when the entire salary is small, its reduction in the case of one who has spent his life in the service of the College is a manifest hardship, which would be still greater in the case where the larger portion of the Professor's income

dinations would furnish a favourable introduction, and their salaries a reasonable help. The remaining half would, probably, become Candidates for life Fellowships. The Assistant Lecturers would be selected from both classes. Their number might be allowed to vary according to the wants of the College; but, under existing circumstances, seven would probably suffice.

Such temporary Fellowships, attainable at an early age, would seem to furnish the stimulus at present so much needed; while, at the same time, they would supply men of various acquirements to fill the offices of Lecturers, and so adapt the teaching of the College to the wants of the time. On the other hand, the diminution in the number of life Fellowships would lessen considerably the time in which the Junior Fellows would hereafter be engaged in Academic Teaching, and lower the age of their appointment to the Administrative Offices. But in order to derive the full advantage of these arrangements, the life-Fellowships should be attainable at an early age. This may be effected by appointing a limited, but adequate course for Examination, account being taken of the answering of the Candidates at the Degree Examination. By these means the Examination might be made to test the ability of the Candidates, rather than the extent of their knowledge; and by varying from time to time the subjects of Examination, highly qualified men in various branches of knowledge might be introduced into the permanent body. It would not be unreasonable to expect that a life Fellowship might be obtained before the Candidate had reached the standing of Master of Arts; and the many years of exhausting toil now spent in preparing for the Fellowship Examination would be saved, to the great advantage of the men themselves, as well as that of the Institution in which they were thenceforward to labour.

It is hardly necessary to observe, that the proposed diminution in the number of life Fellowships should be effected gradually—as by omitting to fill more than one vacancy in any year, whatever the number of actual vacancies.

I have only a few words to offer on the other question which is under the consideration of the Commissioners. I earnestly hope, for the sake of the College, no less than for that of the Church of Ireland, that the future relation of the Divinity School to the University may be settled upon the basis of the Resolutions of the Board of November 3, 1874, and January 15, 1876. I believe it to be of the utmost importance to both bodies, that the connexion of the Divinity School with the College should be as close as is compatible with a separate and independent government; and I believe that such connexion can be maintained only by means such as are there proposed. I would, however, suggest the adoption of the reasonable proposal contained in the second of the Resolutions of the Divinity School Committee, of May 31, 1876.

H. Lloyd,
Provost of Trinity College.

APPENDIX X.

STATEMENT of A. S. HART, Esq., LL.D., Vice-Provost.

In compliance with the suggestion of the Secretary of the University Commissioners, I venture to offer some observations on the subjects of their inquiry, namely, the rate of succession to Fellowships; the future prospects of the Divinity School; and the application of the Advowson Fund.

With regard to the first subject, it appears from inspection of the University Calendar, that the number of Fellows elected during the last 180 years was 211, and that this corresponds nearly with the average rate of succession, but that, unfortunately, this rate has been by no means uniform; for on taking consecutive periods of 13 years, I find that, from 1823 to 1835 the number was 13; from 1836 to 1848 it was 27; and in the last 13 years it was only 9. This irregularity in the rate of succession has given rise to several evils. First, the reasonable expectation of at least one vacancy in every year (an expectation which is not much too high, even after the abolition of Church Patronage) induces some of the best scholars in almost every class to waste their energies in preparation for a possible examination, which fails to occur within the expected time, and thereby to injure their chance of success in some other pursuit; secondly, the disappointment of a few of these distinguished scholars has the effect of deterring their successors from similar studies, and so when an unusually large number of vacancies occur, it is impossible to find a corresponding number of sufficiently prepared Candidates; and thirdly, when a large number of Fellows of nearly the same age are elected, as, for example, in the interval between 1836 and 1848, the natural result is the inconvenience now apprehended, that all these men will become superannuated at about the same time, and that there is an insufficient number of young and active men. While on the other hand it may probably be found, a few years hence, that the rate of succession to Senior Fellowships will be inconveniently rapid, inasmuch as the present practice of excluding Senior Fellows from the office of teachers makes it undesirable that promotion to this post should take place in less than 15 or 20 years.

Under these circumstances, I think that no good object would be gained by a permanent increase in the number of Fellows, or by increased rapidity in the average rate of promotion to a Senior Fellowship, but that the existing evils would be most effectually remedied by an arrangement which would equalize the rate of succession to Fellowships, one Fellow being (as nearly as possible) elected in every year, and by a further arrangement for providing retiring pensions for Fellows who from any cause may become incapacitated for the discharge of their duties. This latter provision has already been made for Life Professors by the Board and Visitors, under the authority conferred on them by Royal Letters, 18 Vict.; and application has recently been made to the Government for authority to make a similar provision for incapacitated Fellows, and also for an enactment which would render the rate of succession more uniform. If this proposal is adopted, I think that it will in great measure remove the evils at present complained of.

It has been suggested that a scheme for superannuation of Fellows at a definite age would be better than the proposed arrangement, but I cannot concur in this view. It is clearly more desirable to remove incompetent officers at any age, than to remove those who are perfectly competent merely because they have reached a certain age; and as the funds available for the purpose are limited, it would be useless to attempt both objects. It is also to be remembered that the chief duties of Senior Fellows are administrative, and can be satisfactorily performed by men of advanced age, if not otherwise disqualified.

Secondly, with regard to the Divinity School, I believe that it is generally admitted that it is for the interest both of the Church and of the University that there should be as much cooperation as possible between them in conducting this School. It is for many reasons desirable that in their secular studies the Clergy and Laity should be united as at present, and even in a great part of their professional studies the Candidates for Orders might profitably avail themselves of the Lectures of University Professors. The teaching of Greek and Hebrew, for example, does not involve the peculiar doctrines of any Church; and even in the subjects of Ecclesiastical History, Moral Philosophy, and Natural Religion, the University Professors might be found to give useful instruction. It will, however, be necessary that the dogmatic teaching in the Divinity School of the Church of Ireland should be under the control of the Ecclesiastical authorities of that Church, and they must, therefore, have the right of appointing several of the teachers who have hitherto been appointed by the Provost and Senior Fellows; and it would be only reasonable that a sum of money sufficient to pay these teachers should be transferred to the Divinity School from the College Funds, which would hereafter be relieved from this payment. This transfer of authority could be effected without any change in the existing arrangements of the School.

The Provost and Senior Fellows have already expressed their willingness to concur in some such arrangements, and also to enter into a similar arrangement with any other religious body which desires that their Ministers should receive their education in the University. The chief advantage which Trinity College would gain from such arrangements is, that the religious instruction of her Students who belong to any such Body would, of course, be superintended by the teachers in its Divinity School—an advantage which is at present possessed only by those Students who are members of the Church of Ireland.

Thirdly, as to the application of the sums of money received by Trinity College as compensation for the Advowsons and Rights of Presentation which were the property of the College. It appears that some of these Advowsons were purchased by the College, and that the others were granted by King James I., in precisely the same manner that other confiscated property was given by him to the College, at the same time, and under no other condition than the general one that all College property should be used for the benefit of the College. This object was generally attained in the present case by using the Rights of Presentation for the purpose of creating vacancies among the Fellows; and it seems reasonable that the money now received as a compensation for this right should be used for the same purpose—with this difference, however, that future retirements should only be encouraged when beneficial to the College, although under the former system these retirements necessarily depended on the will of individual Fellows.

ANDREW S. HART,
Vice-Provost of Trinity College.

15th June, 1877.

Availing myself of the permission of the University Commissioners, I desire to offer the following remarks on the subjects to which their inquiries have been directed:—

1. Causes well known have brought about a state of things in Trinity College—as regards the succession of vacancies—which requires the application of remedial measures. With this view an important suggestion has been made by the Provost and Senior Fellows, with the approval of the Junior Fellows. It has been embodied in the form of a proposed Queen's Letter, and is now before the Commissioners. It is, in my opinion, good so far as it goes; but I have always felt that it is an imperfect remedy, and requires considerable additions, if a result permanently satisfactory is aimed at.

It is expected that, under the provisions proposed, there would be, on the average, one vacancy for Fellowship to be filled each year. This anticipation might be realised; but it proposes, in my opinion—as good being had to the encouragement due to the talent and energy of the youth of the University—but a meagre result. The ordinary case would be this, after (say) five years of laborious study—subsequent to the degree of A.B.—a candidate would each year succeed to a Junior Fellowship. According to existing arrangements [which it is not proposed to alter] the pecuniary value of that Fellowship would, for several years, be but small. It would, no doubt [barring the occurrence of War or other interfering causes], gradually, though slowly, improve; but it would not, according to reasonable anticipations, until after an incumbency of some thirty years or more, be equal to the incomes of those who are moderately successful in the career of the learned professions. When this came to be fully appreciated, a Fellowship in Trinity College, with its preliminary labour and risks, and its subsequent slender competence, would cease to be considered a prize. It is needless to point out the probable result. The ablest and most energetic young men would carry their talents (as they have already begun to do) to the better market, offered elsewhere, and the University of Dublin would have to supply itself with its staff of Fellows and Professors from an inferior stock.

With the means at our disposal, there is no remedy for this evil but an expedient which has been used elsewhere with advantage, and which may be applied amongst us with the additional safeguards suggested by experience in other Universities. I mean the institution of Terminable Fellowships.

In the recent discussions relative to the Universities

I believe that the institution of such Fellowships, two or more to be competed for each year, would offer prizes which would be highly valued by the able young men of the University. These prizes ought to be awarded as the result of a Special Examination, so as to have the honourable distinction which belongs to the title of a Fellowship. Such a distinction would facilitate the advancement of the holder in the line of life which he might select as most suited to him. His choice, though to be left free, would generally take the direction of the learned professions; and it may be observed that a Fellowship would furnish a strong recommendation for appointments in a department which is now assuming in England and elsewhere the proportions of a great Profession—I mean that of Schoolmasters.

I am strongly of opinion that the institution of such Terminable Fellowships, with their immediate advantages and distinctions, and the facilities and prospects which they would offer for future advancement, would, perhaps, more than any other measure which could be adopted, tend to infuse fresh life and energy into our whole Collegiate system.

And here, I think, it is important to remark that our present Fellowship system has frequently led to the waste of talents which might be better employed in other ways. A young man of talent and energy has often applied himself, and with success, to obtain a Fellowship, because it is the crowning Honor of the Academic career. Having obtained it, he will not relinquish it, though he may have no true taste or vocation for academic life or pursuits. And in this way it has often happened that a man who might have been useful, or even brilliant, in some other career, has passed a comparatively useless and obscure life as the result of his Collegiate success.

The institution of Terminable Fellowships, which it would offer inducement and reward to the able young men of all classes in the University, would afford a means of obviating the evil to which I have referred, and would at the same time add to the ranks of the several professions, men of special academic culture and training, and in this way, as I believe, materially promote the public good. At the same time, the Permanent Fellowships would be filled by selected men [chosen by such an examination as is proposed by the Provost] who would have a special fitness and vocation for their work, and so the interests of the University would be better secured. I observe, also, that as is remarked by the Provost, a considerable addition to the teaching-power of the University would be derived from the Sessional Fellows. Our

number (say) to six. The Fellows thus liberated from the work of Tuition might do more work as Teachers than at present.

I add the following suggestion—though it bears but indirectly on the general subject—that the value of a Junior Fellowship would be greatly enhanced, if the present very inequitable mode of distributing income by means of what is known as "the Tutorial System" were abolished—and the income of the Fellow increased according to his length of service.

II. I would not add to the number of the Senior Fellows; there are at present enough for the administrative duties they have to discharge, and it does not appear to me that anything would be gained by converting the Senior Tutors into Senior Fellows.

III. The guaranteed life interests of the present Fellows preclude the application to them of any system of compulsory retirement; and the method of retirement recommended in the proposed Queen's Letter is probably as good as the case admits of; but for any Fellow hereafter elected, I think, with a view to keep up the due succession and regularity of vacancies in the body of Permanent Fellows, it would be well to prescribe a compulsory resignation on attaining the age of seventy years.

This might be effected by purchasing for each individual elected to a Permanent Fellowship a deferred Government Annuity, commencing at the age of 70. This would imply (supposing the amount of the Annuity to be £1,000 per annum, the average age of those elected to Permanent Fellowships to be 27, and one Annuity to be provided for each year) an annual expenditure of from £400 to £700. This would be a cheap price to pay for getting rid of the possible recurrence of stagnation-difficulties, for insuring a regular succession of vacancies among the Permanent Fellows, and for preventing the injurious results which are apprehended, from having a Board containing, perhaps, several members of very advanced age. If such a plan as this were regarded with favour, its operation might, perhaps, be accelerated by voluntary arrangements made with some of the existing Fellows.

APPENDIX XI. — Statement of the Rev. Thomas Stack, M.A., Registrar.

IV. As regards the Divinity School I am much indisposed to any legislation which might have the tendency of separating the education of the Divinity Students from that of the general body of the Students, or of withdrawing it from the wholesome influence of the general government of the College.

It is, moreover, to be considered that our Divinity School contains, from time to time, many Students who look forward to employment in the Church of England, the Colonial Episcopal Church, and some even in the Dissenting Protestant Churches. For such a School the government might rather be desired of a University than of any special ecclesiastical authority. It will, according to the chances of human life, be from twenty-five to thirty years before the Board of Trinity College will be without a majority of clergymen in its body; and if it be supposed that it may ultimately come to consist chiefly, or altogether, of laymen, there seems to be no reason why the government of the Divinity School might not be conducted on a plan analogous to that of the existing University Council—according to the proposal which has been made by the Regius Professor of Divinity. I conceive that such a plan of management would be most advantageous to the Divinity School, the University, and the Church of Ireland, and more free from risk than any other which has been proposed.

THOMAS STACK,
Senior Fellow of Trinity College, Dublin.

Trinity College,
December 22, 1877.

APPENDIX XII.

STATEMENT of the Venerable WILLIAM LEE, D.D. Archbishop King's Lecturer in Divinity.

APPENDIX XII. — Statement of the Venerable William Lee, D.D.

TO THE MEMBERS OF THE ROYAL COMMISSION, &c.

In the following remarks as to the subject-matter of the Royal Commission for inquiring into certain matters connected with Trinity College, Dublin, I desire, at the outset, to observe, that I abstain from offering any opinion on the proposals of either the Provost and Senior Fellows, or the Junior Fellows, respecting schemes of retirement. I confine myself to the question of the Divinity School, and the preservation of its present connection with Trinity College.

1. I wish to express my dissent from the proposal to transfer the management of the Divinity School from the hands of Trinity College to any external body. My dissent is founded on considerations connected partly with the interests of religion, partly with the interests of the University itself.

(a) It seems to me to be essential to the interests of religion that the clergy of every religious denomination should not be destitute of the culture which enters so largely into the civilization of the present age. The severance, however, of the Divinity School from Trinity College involves, as an almost inevitable consequence, the result that the future clergy of the Disestablished Church of Ireland are no longer—as a class—to receive a university education. It is very well to say that university students are to continue, when the Divinity School is separated, "to receive instruction in the school as hitherto without charge;" but a few moments' thought will confirm what experience has taught those who have studied the question—namely, that university students will not resort to an external school as to the character or efficiency of which there will be no guarantee whatever. An external institution of an inferior class will offer no inducement to that large proportion of our Divinity Students who are now ordained in England. Even now, our B.A. Degree, together with attendance for one year in some one of the many theological colleges existing in England, is recognised by the English Bishops as sufficient qualification for Holy Orders; but destroy the university character of our Divinity School, and the entire class of English students who matriculate here for the purpose of joining it, will at once disappear, and this to the great detriment of Trinity College.

(b) When one remembers the social grade to which future candidates for the ministry of the Irish Church will probably belong, it can scarcely be supposed that their pecuniary means will enable them, in any case, to seek a university education. All that can be hoped for is to attract to a theological school of high character, a class of men fitted by their early training, and the culture which a university education supplies, to uphold worthily the interests of religion.

(c) The only possibility of maintaining a theological school at all in connexion with the Irish Church, seems to me to rest on the preservation of the present Divinity School on its present basis. It is in the highest degree improbable that Parliament will now sanction a large endowment, from whatever source, of any institution, in the interests of a Church which it has just disestablished; and without a considerable endowment—affording its teachers an income comparable to the average income held out by other professions to capable men—a theological school, apart from Trinity College, cannot be maintained in Ireland. Students of Trinity College, we are told, are not to pay any fees at all; while for others—the

APPENDIX [illegible]. — Statement of the Venerable William Lee, D.D.

probable candidates for Holy Orders in the future—say, fees which are not fixed at this lower point, would be above their reach. For the present school, on the other hand, connected with Trinity College, a supply of competent teachers is at hand, and need not fail for the future, as I hope to show presently. The present salaries secure an adequate income for the two Chief Professors; and for the other Professors, as well as the Assistant Lecturers, the prestige of the University and the nature of the work, have always proved sufficient to attract an able body of teachers, although at a small remuneration. The transfer of the Divinity School with its present endowments to some external body will, no doubt, preserve the incomes of the two Chief Professors—unless, indeed, as is possible, their incomes be reduced by the [illegible] in the most important positions, in the judgment of their future paymasters; but, in such case, the degradation of the school would begin at the top. And if this be not done, then no margin of any significance remains for the payment of the other Lecturers and Professors.

II. It will be said, of course, that the continued connexion with Trinity College of a Divinity School, in the interest of any one religious denomination, is out of harmony with recent legislation. When it is borne in mind, however, that full opportunity is, by the consent of all, to be given to every other religious community, to endow a theological school in its own interests, and as the Chairs in the present Divinity School have been in past years endowed by private liberality; when the students, moreover, belonging to every denomination, are trained in due course to their degrees in theology, it seems an extreme application of logic to sever the time-honoured connexion with Dublin University of the school which produced Ussher, and King, and Magee, and Graves, and Elrington, and Archer Butler, and Todd, and O'Brien, in order to apply the maxim, "Væ victis," to the institution which educated these men.

III. Turning now to the University itself:—

The severance of theological study from a university is calculated seriously to lower its general character as a school of knowledge and of culture. To exclude from the curriculum the study of Theology is practically to exclude the study of Hebrew and the other Oriental languages, of Ecclesiastical History, of Greek and Latin, in their most important applications. The German Universities have never omitted the Faculty of Theology, [illegible] Theological Professorships [illegible] "the Queen of Sciences." The proposed transference, therefore, of the Divinity School, to external management, amounts to an actual degradation of an ancient University.

IV. The moral training of its students during the years of their life most susceptible of good or of evil impressions, is no small part of the work of a university. It is a fact familiar to all who have studied the question, and have observed its bearings, that there is an amount of respect and deference paid by students to those of their fellows and teachers who are clergymen, which they do not pay to those who are laymen, however respectable. If moral influence, which springs inseparable from the office of the minister of religion, be absent; if there be no influence to counteract the unrestrained license of modern speculation, a university necessarily becomes an instrument of evil, not of good, with consequences to the commonwealth which it is terrible to consider. It is, therefore, greatly to be desired that a clerical element should be maintained among the Fellows of Trinity College, both in the interest of the Divinity School, and in the interest of the University. To this end the retaining the Divinity School in its present status must largely contribute; but to this should, I consider, be added a change of our system, based upon a certain alteration of the Advowson Fund, which I consider imperatively demanded by the existing condition and prospects of Trinity College.

V. The dearth of Fellowship vacancies in late years, and the certainty that, if there be no radical change in our system, the present stagnation must continue, are causes which point to the gradual decay of learning and science in Ireland. With few exceptions, the flower of our youth—in fact, nearly all our distinguished graduates for some time past—have migrated to Oxford or Cambridge, attracted by the numerous prizes there held out to the various branches of scholarship, and discouraged by the closing of all avenues to distinction at home. I lay it down as a maxim that without two vacancies for Fellowship every year, one for a Classical Fellowship and one for a Science Fellowship (as Classical and Science Fellowships are understood in Dublin), the progress of our University will come to a stand. My suggestion, therefore, briefly stated, is as follows:—I would create twenty Decennial Fellowships; I would reduce the present number of Junior Fellows (permanent Fellows I should call them) to the original number of eighteen; I would abolish the existing studentships, which were, at best, a temporary remedy for the existing stagnation. Vacancies in the number of permanent Fellows I would fill up, without examination, from among the existing Decennial Fellows, according to the aptitude, in the judgment of the Board, exhibited in communicating knowledge; or according to the proficiency exhibited in some department of science—room, however, being left, in the case of exceptional eminence, for electing to the vacancy a Decennial Fellow whose Fellowship might have expired. The election, as I have implied, should be the Board's. Of the consequences of this I would not alarm. From the experience of many years I can bear witness to the wisdom and impartiality with which the Board have discharged their trusts and followed their views, in the government of Trinity College.

With some such modification of our existing system, I feel certain that (even when the Fellows are taken from the various religious denominations) there would be no lack of Fellows seeking Holy Orders in the Church of Ireland. Leaving out of sight the attraction of the study of theology, the Chief Professorships still hold out an incentive to natural ambition; and thus a supply of clergymen would be provided sufficient to uphold the high moral tone of the University, and to furnish the Divinity School with competent teachers.

VI. To complete the sketch which I have given, and to prove that it is not impracticable, I would give to each Decennial Fellow £[illegible] a year, with his rooms and commons, and this would require an expenditure of about £5,[illegible] a year. To meet this expenditure, however, the suppression of the studentships gives £1,[illegible] per annum, and the suppression of eight Junior Fellowships, i.e., of six Tutorial Fellows, giving, on a low calculation, £[illegible]; and of two non-Tutorial Fellows, giving, say £[illegible] a year, there would be £[illegible] per annum, thus leaving a charge of but £[illegible] on the interest of the Advowson Fund.

The plan, of which I have sketched the outlines, leaves a sufficient margin for any scheme of retirement which the present stagnation may render necessary, while it affords a means of reducing the number of Tutors, of which complaint is now made, and at the same time gives scope to Fellows relieved from the burden of routine work, for entering on the different paths of original research.

WILLIAM LEE,
Archbishop King's Lecturer in Divinity.

24, Merrion-square, South,
Nov. 3, 1877.

APPENDIX XIII.

LETTER of the REGIUS PROFESSOR of DIVINITY to the REGISTRAR of TRINITY COLLEGE upon the future prospects of the Divinity School.

Appendix XIII.

Letter of the Regius Professor of Divinity to the Registrar of Trinity College.

Trinity College, Dublin,
December 20th, 1876.

MY DEAR STACK,

You have asked me formally to lay before the Board the views concerning the future of our Divinity School which I had expressed in conversation with the Provost and Vice-Provost.

Its present condition is plainly anomalous. It is governed by a body which is now theoretically open to persons of all religions, and which at no distant time will actually be so. The Divinity School of Trinity College will practically be lost to the Church of Ireland, whenever the body which appoints the Lecturers, which controls their teaching, and which prescribes the course of study, consists of persons either not members of the Church, or in whom, though nominally members of it, the Bishops who have hitherto recognised the Certificates of the School can feel no confidence.

It is clearly just that the Church of Ireland should either, if it surrender the Divinity School of Trinity College, receive compensation, such as was granted to the Roman Catholics and to the Presbyterians for the loss of the public support given to Maynooth and to the Presbyterian Theological Colleges, or else, if the Church is not to receive compensation, that the government of the Divinity School of Trinity College shall be so modified that the Church shall continue to enjoy the benefit of it.

Hitherto only the first of these alternatives has been tried, but with no very encouraging success. The Church's claim to compensation has not been disputed; but, there being two sources from which compensation might be provided—either the fund administered by the Church Commissioners, or the resources of Trinity College—the guardians of each of these funds appear to hold that the claim ought to be satisfied by the other. It seems to me, then, that it is well worth considering whether, instead of persevering in trying to find a solution by this method, a better cannot be found by the other alternative.

I believe that one of the reasons of the failure of the attempts that have been made to arrange an immediate separation between the Divinity School and Trinity College is, that nobody really wishes for such separation. The members of the Church of Ireland are most desirous that the young men intended for Orders in their Church should not be trained apart from the laity, but that they should, as heretofore, share the studies and join in the society of those intended for secular professions. They would regard the establishment of a Protestant Maynooth as a great calamity; and they would accept most liberal terms of compensation for the loss of the Divinity School in Trinity College, if they were given the alternative of the continuance of that school as at present, with some security for its permanent maintenance. On the other hand, it can be as little the wish of any one interested in the College that it should give up the education of candidates for Orders in the Irish Church, who form so considerable part of the members of the College. I find that out of 243 Students who became qualified by standing to join the Divinity School this year, 71 actually did so; from which it may be estimated that, notwithstanding the serious diminution of the number of the Divinity Students following on the Act of 1869, they still form nearly 30 per cent. of the entire number. And it is not unlikely that this proportion will increase; for the School seems to be showing symptoms of recovery from the great shock it received.

On quite other grounds opinion has been almost universally adverse to the idea suggested by words of Mr. Fawcett's Bill—that the University should cease to give Divinity Degrees. It has been felt that Theology is an important department of study which it would be unworthy of the University to abandon. Those most anxious to maintain the non-sectarian character of the University have suggested that, though ceasing to provide teaching in Theology, it should continue to examine, and might confer its degrees on those who exhibit sufficient learning irrespective of their opinions. Others have suggested that teaching also might be provided by means of different Theological Faculties connected with different denominations.

It being, then, the desire of all persons interested in the question, that the Divinity Students of the Church of Ireland should continue to receive their education in Trinity College, the question remains, can any plan be devised for maintaining the connexion with the University of one or more Schools of Theological instruction, consistent with the subordination of all to a governing body open indiscriminately to persons of every religion? It appears to me that this question has been practically solved by the Queen's Letter, obtained in 1874, for the appointment of a University Council. By that legislation, the Board, while retaining its present authority, resigned all the powers which it would be unsuitable for a mixed body to exercise over a Theological School. The Theological Professorships having been exempted from the operation of that Queen's Letter, it seems to me that all that is now necessary is to obtain another Queen's Letter, appointing another Council, consisting exclusively of members of the Church, which shall have precisely the same powers in matters connected with the Divinity School which the present Council has in the other departments of education. If other Theological Faculties were instituted in the University, they would be governed in like manner.

The advantage of this plan is that it postpones indefinitely the question of compensation to the Church of Ireland, without risk to the Church of losing it altogether. If the proposed arrangement were once made, it would stand until the Crown or Parliament interfered with it. As long as it continued, the Professors would be maintained, and the course of study prescribed, by a body in which the Church could have confidence. If Parliament should hereafter decide that Theology should not be taught in Trinity College, it would at the same time determine whether compensation was due to the Church of Ireland, and out of what funds it should be provided. But the Church would be delivered from the existing danger of losing the Divinity School silently, as friendly members of the Board are replaced by unfriendly.

With regard to the constitution of the proposed Council the model of the existing Council might be followed, and there might be four different sections: (1). There might be members nominated by the Board. The harmony that has existed between the Board and the present Council mainly arises from the knowledge each body has of the feelings of the other, through the presence of influential members common to both. (2). Corresponding to the sections nominated by the Junior Fellows and by the Professors would be in this case members appointed by the teachers in the School. The two principal teachers, the Regius Professor and Archbishop King's Lecturer, are such natural advisers of the Council, that it may be a question whether they ought not to hold their position ex officio. (3). There might be members nominated by the Bishops. It is most important of all, that the management of the School should meet their approval, since it rests with them to determine whether they will require the Certificates of the Schools from Candidates for Orders. (4). There might be members nominated by the clerical and lay members of the Synod; or else by the members of the Senate who are also members of the Church. Except, perhaps, in the last case, there seems no advantage in the cumulative method of voting.

Appendix XIII.

Letter of the Regius Professor of Divinity to the Registrar of Trinity College.

With regard to financial matters, it may, perhaps, be enough to maintain the rule that no change should be made in the existing distribution except by the Board and Visitors. It might be provided that no plan affecting the Divinity School should be sent up to the Visitors except accompanied by a Report from the new Council. And of course this Council would have the power to recommend to the Board a new distribution if they should think it advisable.

The only other thing necessary for the welfare of the Divinity School on the new system is the removal of the restriction to Fellows of any Professorship, and of any similar restriction in other cases, if any such exists. This restriction was quite proper when every Fellow was bound to take Orders, and when the electors were able to choose among some of the most learned divines of Ireland; but the body of Fellows of the future might not include a single qualified person. I understand that some of the Junior Fellows think that the removal of the restriction would be unjust to them as long as any Junior Fellow can be found willing to accept the office; but this is a contention which it is impossible to maintain. It was never intended that the electors should have no range of choice, but be limited to one or two persons. The restriction of the office to Fellows, and the obligation of Fellows to take Orders, went together. But no Fellow elected since 1851 has taken Orders; none of these, therefore, can reasonably think it a grievance that he does not get rises by Divinity promotions. As their seniors rise to be on or near the Board, the number of Fellows qualified and willing to accept the Divinity Professorship is yearly diminishing; and unless a vacancy takes place tolerably soon, the choice of the Electors would be very injuriously hampered by existing rules.

I remain,

Faithfully yours,

George Salmon.

APPENDIX XIV.

Appendix XIV.

Queries by the Royal Commissioners, with the answers of the Provost and Senior Fellows.

Queries by the Royal Commissioners, with the Answers of the Provost and Senior Fellows.

Divinity Professors, Lecturers, and Teachers.

Query 1.—State all the private Endowments dedicated to the study of Divinity, or in any wise devoted to that purpose, with the names of the several Benefactors, and the trusts (if any) affecting such Endowments.

Query 2.—State the manner in which the property mentioned in the preceding question is invested, the amount of income arising therefrom, and how the same is disposed of.

Query 3.—State the dates at which the said several private Endowments were created.

Whether any and what additions have been made thereto by the College for the same purposes respectively.

And the dates of such additions being made.

Answer of the Provost and Senior Fellows.

1718.—£500 late Irish currency was given by the Most Reverend William King, Lord Archbishop of Dublin, towards founding a Divinity Lecture for the use of the Bachelors in the College.

1722.—A further sum of £500, being a bequest by said Archbishop King, was paid to the College for the further Endowment of the Divinity Lecturer. These Endowments were invested in the purchase of £958 17s. 6d. Bank of Ireland Stock, in the year 1833, and the income arising therefrom has varied from £35 to £43 9s. 11d. per annum, and has been applied in part payment of the salary of the Divinity Lecturer. The salary since 1833 has been £700 a year—the increase having in that year been granted by the Provost and Senior Fellows as a charge on the Endowments.

1833.—A sum of £1,000 was given by the Most Rev. Lord John George Beresford, Archbishop of Armagh, towards founding a Chair of Ecclesiastical History in the University. A further sum of £1,000 was given by the same Archbishop in 1851, for the same purpose. These two sums have been invested in the purchase of £833 6s. Bank of Ireland Stock. The income arising from this Endowment has varied during the last fifteen years, from £74 11s. 5d. to £113 16s. 6d. The Professor has, during that period, received a salary of £150 a-year.

Query 4.—Have any Public Grants from the Crown or from Parliament been made for the purposes of the Divinity School?

Answer.—No.

Query 5.—Furnish a list of all Professors and Lecturers appointed to give instruction in Divinity in the College; stating

The mode of their appointment.

The tenure of their offices.

The duties which they perform; and

The salaries or other emoluments which they receive.

Answer of the Provost and Senior Fellows.

(*a*.) Regius Professor of Divinity, appointed by the Provost and Senior Fellows from among the Fellows or Ex-Fellows of the College, who are Doctors in Divinity. The Professor holds the office for life, unless guilty of neglect of duty or other offence against the Statutes, or unless promoted to a Bishopric.

The prescribed duties are, to read a Prelection at the beginning of every Term, in which the order and matter of the studies of that Term are expounded. To give two Lectures in every week during the Term. To explain the Holy Scriptures in these Lectures. To expound also the controversies with all opponents as well of the Christian religion as of our Church. To hold Lectures also, and Examinations in Ecclesiastical History. To assign to the Students books, approved by the Provost and Senior Fellows, in which they are to be diligently examined. To prescribe Exercises in Theology. To furnish the Provost, at the end of each Term, with the names of Students remarkable for negligence or for diligence. To be Moderator in Disputations for Theological Degrees. To preach four Sermons each year in confirmation of the Christian religion. To read annually four public Prelections in Divinity, at such times and in such places as the Provost and Senior Fellows shall prescribe. To hold an annual Examination of the Students in Divinity, for two days, during four hours each day; in the morning of the first day in the Old Testament, and in the evening in the New Testament; in the morning of the second day in Ecclesiastical History, and in the evening of the second day in the Articles and Liturgy of the Church of England. The salary is £1,318 per annum.

(*b*.) Archbishop King's Lecturer, appointed by the Provost and Senior Fellows. He holds his office for life.

His duties are, to lecture Divinity Students during their first year, on two days in each week; during the Michaelmas and Hilary Terms on the Evidences of Natural and Revealed Religion …

on the Socinian controversy, and to preside at examinations of these Students at the end of each Term. The salary is £100 per annum.

(c.) Professor of Biblical Greek, appointed by the Provost and Senior Fellows. The tenure of the office is for five years.

The duties are, to lecture in two of the three Terms of each year in subjects to be appointed by the Board, and to assist at the Divinity Examinations held by the Professor of Divinity, and by Archbishop King's Lecturer. The salary is £100 per annum.

(d.) Professor of Ecclesiastical History, appointed by the Provost and Senior Fellows. The tenure of the office is for five years.

The duties are, to lecture twice a-week during two of the three Terms in each year for all Students requiring the testimonial of the Professor of Divinity, to hold an Examination in each year for Prizes in Ecclesiastical History, and to examine in Ecclesiastical History at the Divinity Professor's Prize Examination. The salary is £100 per annum.

(e.) Four Assistants to the Professor of Divinity appointed by the Provost and Senior Fellows.

The Assistants appointed before the year 1870 held the office usually during the continuance of their Junior Fellowship. The tenure of those subsequently appointed is fixed by the Provost and Senior Fellows at the time of their appointment.

The duties are, to lecture Students twice a-week during each Term in the second year of their Divinity Course, and to assist the Professor in the Divinity Examinations. The salary of each Assistant is £23 per annum.

(f.) Five Assistants to Archbishop King's Lecturer in Divinity, appointed by the Provost and Senior Fellows.

The duties are, to lecture Students twice a-week during each Term in the first year of their Divinity Course, and to assist Archbishop King's Lecturer in the Divinity Examinations. The tenure of office and the salary are the same as those of the Assistants to the Professor.

N.B.—The Senior of the nine Assistants receives £60 per annum.

Note.—The list given above does not include Catechetical Lecturers, or other persons appointed to give religious instruction to all classes of Students, as it is assumed that the questions are intended to refer solely to the Divinity School.

Query 6.—State the dates of the creation of the several Offices mentioned in the preceding questions.

Answer of the Provost and Senior Fellows.

(a.) The date of the creation of the Professorship of Divinity is not known, but it is recited in the Royal Letter, 26 Car II., "That there hath been for these many years, and still is, a Professor of Divinity in that our University and Colledge of the Holy and Undivided Trinity, near Dublin."

(b.) The date of the foundation of this Lecture by Archbishop King was 1718.

(c.) This Professorship was founded on May 15, 1838.

(d.) This Professorship was founded on March 23, 1852.

(e.) The first appointment of an Assistant Divinity Lecturer was on March 8, 1783.

(f.) The first Assistants were appointed on October 21, 1833.

Query 7.—State the nature and dates of change (if any) made in the salaries, emoluments, or duties of the several Offices before mentioned, during the last twenty-five years.

Answer of the Provost and Senior Fellows.

were received by him in the seven years preceding that time; and which were, from and after that date, transferred to the general funds of the College.

(b.) There has been no change since 1838.

(c.) None.

(d.) None.

(e) and (f.) In June, 1847, the salary of the Senior Assistant was raised from £38 13s. 9d. to £60 per annum; and the salaries of the Junior Assistants were raised from £27 1s. to £40 per annum each.

Appendix, XIV. Queries by the Royal Commissioners with the answers of the Provost and Senior Fellows.

DIVINITY SCHOLARSHIPS, EXHIBITIONS, PRIZES, &c.

Query 1.—State the number of Scholarships, Exhibitions, Prizes, or other rewards given to encourage or assist Students in Divinity.

Query 2.—State their value, and the conditions under which they are given or received, and the nature and value of such of these as proceed from Private Endowment.

Query 3.—State the Trusts (if any) affecting any Private Endowment given for the support or encouragement of Students in Divinity.

Answer of the Provost and Senior Fellows.

SCHOLARSHIPS.

In the year 1844 two Scholarships of £30 each, denominated "The Beddell Scholarships," were founded by the Committee of the Irish Society, for Students in the University who attend Lectures of the Professor of Irish and Divinity lectures, and pass each year an examination in Irish. The Scholars are elected and paid by Trustees named by the founders. The Examination for the Scholarships to be held annually, as soon after the Trinity Term Examination as possible. Open to Students of any standing in the University, and tenable for four years, if they shall keep their names so long on the College Books, and have not been admitted to Holy Orders. The Scholars are required to reside in or near Dublin, and attend the Lectures of the Professor of Irish (unless excused), and to attend Divinity Lectures; to pass an Annual Examination, at the commencement of Michaelmas Term, in the Irish Language; and to produce Certificates of having passed the Annual Examination.

EXHIBITIONS.

In the year 1797, an annuity of £50, late Irish currency, chargeable on the lands of Castlebanagh, County Kilkenny, was bequeathed by the Rev. William Downes, D.D., of Waterford, to the Provost, Fellows, and Scholars of Trinity College, for the foundation of five "Downes Exhibitions" of £9 4s. 8d. each, "to be given to Students in the Divinity line, at the discretion of the Provost and Senior Fellows; respect being had in such choice to narrow circumstances, and proficiency in learning; to continue till arriving at standing of A.M., death, resignation, or leaving College."

In the year 1858, six "Theological Exhibitions," three of the value of £60 and three of the value of £40 annually, were founded by the Provost and Senior Fellows, with the consent of the Visitors. The Examination for the Exhibitions is held every year, at the end of Hilary Term. Tenable for three years. Candidates must not be more than one year's standing as A.M., reckoned from the Michaelmas Examination of the Senior Freshman year; must have completed the Terms of the Divinity Curriculum; must present themselves at the Examination immediately subsequent to the term in which they have completed their Divinity Course. No person can be a Candidate a second time.

PRIZES, &c.

In the year 1798, £200 in Treasury Debentures was [illegible] [illegible]

APPENDIX XIV.

Queries by the Royal Commissioners, with the answers of the Provost and Senior Fellows.

these prizes were not awarded, and in the year 1873 the original Endowment, with interest for the time of the discontinuance of Prizes, amounting in all to £401 10s., was invested in the purchase of £136 Bank of Ireland Stock, and the income arising therefrom has varied from £10 7s. 3d. to £14 10s. 1d. per annum, which has been applied to the payment of £16 equal, in Prizes to the two best answerers at the Final Examination of the Junior Divinity Class.

In the year 1707, a sum of £1,000, late Irish currency, was bequeathed by Rev. William Downes, D.D., for providing Divinity Prizes for Bachelors of Arts of the University. This money was invested in 1869, in the purchase of £368 17s. 6d. Bank of Ireland Stock. The income arising therefrom has varied during the last seven years from £33 to £37 10s. per annum, and the following Prizes are given in accordance with the directions of the testator:—

"Dr. Downes' Divinity" Premiums of £10 2s. 2d. and £9 4s. 7d., for Written Composition.

Premiums of £11 1s. 6d. and £7 7s. 6d., for Extempore Speaking; and

Premiums of £5 7s. 8d. and £3 13s. 10d. for Reading the Liturgy.

These Premiums are awarded at Examinations held on three separate days, in the last week of Trinity Term. A Candidate must have attended with remarkable diligence as a Candidate Bachelor, or Bachelor of Arts, on Divinity Lectures, in two Terms.

"Archbishop King's Divinity Prizes."—£30 in Premiums, given at an Examination held by Archbishop King's Divinity Lecturer in Trinity Term. Such Students only can be Candidates for the prizes as are selected by the Examiners at the General Examination for the Junior Divinity Class.

"Biblical Greek."—Prizes of £10 and £5, awarded at an Examination to be held in Michaelmas Term, to Students of Senior Sophister or higher standing under that of A.M.

"Ecclesiastical History."—Prizes of £10 and £5, given at an Annual Examination to be held in Trinity Term by the Professor, open to such Students as shall have attended the Professor's Lectures during two Terms of the year in which they present themselves.

"Divinity Composition."—Premiums of £1 each are awarded in each of the three Terms of the Divinity Year to those Students in the Senior and Junior Divinity Classes, respectively, who are recommended by the Regius Professor and Archbishop King's Lecturer, for the best Written Compositions on subjects proposed during the Term.

In the year 1844, a Prize of £10 was founded by the Committee of the Irish Society, to be called the Bedell Prize, and to be given to the best answerer of the [illegible] Candidates for the Bedell Scholarship. This is paid by the Trustees of the Bedell Fund.

In the year 1853, a sum sufficient to produce an annual income of £7 12s. 6d. was contributed by friends of the Right Rev. Samuel Kyle, late Bishop of Cork, and was invested in Government Securities in the joint names of the Provost and Senior Fellows of Trinity College, the Professor of Irish, and the Dean and Archdeacon of Cork, all for the time being, the interest to be paid annually to Divinity Students at an Examination in the Irish Language, held during their Divinity Course, and to be denominated "The Kyle Prize." The income at present arising from this Endowment is £9 10s. 4d.

In the year 1868, a sum of £300 was given by the Right Hon. Richard B. Warren, Attorney-General for Ireland, and M.P. for the University, to be invested in Anglo-Egyptian Dutch bonds, for the purpose of founding an annual Prize of £10 in the Divinity School, to be called "The Church Formularies Prize." In 1873, at the desire of the donor, these bonds were returned to him, in exchange for £250 Debenture Stock of the Great Southern and Western Railway of Ireland, invested in the names of the Provost, Fellows, and Scholars of Trinity College.

The income arising from this Endowment is £10 a year; and it is applied to the payment of an annual Prize, according to the directions of the donor.

NOTE.—There are also Lectures, Prizes, and Endowments connected with the study of Hebrew, which since the year 1869 has formed a part of the Divinity Course; but as these were originally founded in connexion with Oriental Literature, and are at present made use of by Jews and Dissenters as well as by Members of the Church, they are not supposed to be included among the matters referred to by the Commissioners in their Queries.

There are also Private Endowments for the purpose of giving Prizes for Theological Essays to members of the University generally, but not limited to Students in Divinity.

APPENDIX XV.

Query I.—State the names of the Benefices in respect of which Trinity College received compensation under the Irish Church Act, 1869, and the following particulars concerning each of them, viz.:

The Diocese in which it is situate.

The Amount of Annuity awarded to the Incumbent by the Church Temporalities Commissioners; and

Of the Compensation awarded to the College in respect thereof.

Ann [illegible]

Names of Benefices for the loss of the Advowsons of which the College seeks compensation.	County in which situated.	Amount of Annuities payable by the Incumbent [illegible].	Compensation.		
		£ s. d.	£	s.	d.
Arboe,	Armagh,	606 [illegible] [illegible]	2,607	15	1
Ardtrea,		305 11 9	2,579	4	10
Clogherny,		1,[illegible] 14 7	11,791	[illegible]	5
Clonfeacle,		330 7 2	5,9[illegible]	7	[illegible]
Clonoe,			6,418	1	1
Desertcreight,		437 3 9	3,103	10	3
Aghalurcher,	Clogher,	750 11 10	6,141	15	5
Cleenish,		655 [illegible] [illegible]	[illegible]	[illegible]	[illegible]
Derryvullan,		480 [illegible] 11	6,194	[illegible]	11
Enniskillen,		843 [illegible] [illegible]	4,271	10	1
Ardstraw,	Derry,	1,433 [illegible] [illegible]	9,[illegible]	11	1
Cappagh,		1,034 14 [illegible]	7,[illegible]	15	[illegible]
Drumragh,		1,[illegible] [illegible] [illegible]	5,415	[illegible]	[illegible]
Killyleagh,	Down,	616 [illegible] [illegible]	4,[illegible]	[illegible]	[illegible]
Killeshandra,	Kilmore,	1,087 [illegible] [illegible]	[illegible]	7	7
Clondahorky,	Raphoe,	[illegible] [illegible] [illegible]	1,[illegible]	11	[illegible]
Clondevaddock,		412 [illegible] 7	2,[illegible]	10	[illegible]
Conwal,		[illegible] [illegible] [illegible]	[illegible]	10	1
Kilmacrenan,		[illegible] [illegible] [illegible]	5,1[illegible]	[illegible]	10
Raymoghy,		[illegible] [illegible] [illegible]	[illegible]	[illegible]	[illegible]
Tullyaughnish,		1,[illegible] [illegible] [illegible]	6,7[illegible]	[illegible]	1

NOTE.—The Provost and Senior Fellows have no official knowledge of the amount of Annuities awarded to the Incumbents. The figures given above are taken from a Return made by the Irish Church Temporalities Commissioners to the House of Commons, as the net annual value of the Livings of which the Incumbents had [illegible], [illegible] the value of [illegible]. The [illegible] of Clonoe does not appear in that Return, as it is [illegible] the Incumbent did not commute. The [illegible], however, [illegible], appears in a publication by the Chief Clerk of the Commissioners to have been £216 4s.

Query 2.—State briefly the names of the Title under which each Advowson was held, etc.:

Whether it was granted by the Crown, or Purchased by the College. In the latter case state Price paid for each.

Answer.—All the Advowsons, except the three hereafter named, were granted to the College by Letters Patent of 29th August, 1610, 8th James I. A copy of these Letters Patent is sent herewith.

Killyleagh.—Purchased on [illegible] July, 17[illegible], for £1,[illegible], of which [illegible] was a Bequest by the Rev. [illegible], D.D., Senior Fellow, in trust, to purchase an Advowson or Advowsons for the College.

Killeshandra.—Purchased 17th May, 17[illegible], for £3,[illegible].

Clogherny.—Purchased 17th June, 18[illegible], for £1[illegible].

NOTE.—Letters Patent of 3 Geo. III. were granted to the College, authorizing it to purchase such Advowsons. A copy of these Letters Patent is sent herewith.

Query 3.—Is there any Trust expressed in the grant of any of the said Advowsons?

State any such Trust therein contained.

Answer.—There is none, unless the [illegible] in Letters Patent of Geo. III. may be considered to imply a Trust in respect to the purchased Advowsons.

Query 4.—When a Benefice, in the Patronage of the College, became vacant, in whom did the power rest of presenting a clergyman thereto?

Answer.—The Provost and Senior Fellows, as the governing body of the College, presented in the name of the Corporation.

Query 5.—Was it the custom to offer the Benefice to each of the Clerical Fellows in succession, according to seniority?

Was this custom invariable, or were there any exceptions to it?

Answer.—It appears from the Register of the College that the custom of offering Benefices to the Fellows in Priests' Orders in succession (with the exceptions hereafter mentioned) has prevailed at least as far back as the year 17[illegible]. The entries in the Registers previously to that year are mainly of the fact of a presentation of a person to one of those Benefices.

On some occasions a Fellow who accepted a Living was allowed an option of taking a Living subsequently becoming vacant, if declined by all the Fellows then of senior standing to him; and in a few cases an exchange of a Living was allowed.

Query 6.—State the names of the Ex-Fellows who were in possession of College Livings on the 1st of January, 1869, with the dates of their respectively vacating Fellowships; and being appointed to the said Livings.

Answer.

Names.	Dates of vacating Fellowship.	Dates of Appointment to Livings.
Robert V. Dixon (Clogherny),	June [illegible], 18[illegible].	Feb. [illegible], 18[illegible].
Wm. A. Willock (Ardtrea),	[illegible]	[illegible]
James [illegible] ([illegible]),	[illegible]	[illegible]
[illegible] ([illegible]),	[illegible]	[illegible]
[illegible] ([illegible]),	[illegible]	[illegible]
John [illegible] ([illegible]),	June [illegible]	[illegible]
Henry [illegible] (Conwal),	[illegible]	[illegible]
John [illegible] (Tullyaughnish),	May [illegible]	Oct. [illegible]

Query 7.—Does the "University Calendar" give a correct list of the Fellows elected since 17[illegible]; and of the dates of their several elections, and of their deaths, or acceptance of College Livings?

Answer.—It is believed to do so.

Query 8.—Is there any case in the present century, in which an Ex-Fellow holding a College Living was permitted to exchange with the Incumbent of another

APPENDIX XIV.

Queries by the Royal Commissioners, with the answers of the Provost and Senior Fellows.

Livings, giving the names of the exchanging parties, and of the Benefices exchanged, together with the dates of such exchanges; and the names of the holders of the Livings on the 1st of January, 1878.

Names of Fellows who exchanged.	Names of Persons with whom exchange was made.	Names of Benefices.	Dates of Exchange.	Names of Holders of the Benefices on 1st January, 1878.
Thos. Romney Robinson, .	Hon. J. C. Moore, .	Enniskillen, Carrickmacross.	March, 1824, .	Samuel Greer. Thos. Romney Robinson.
John T. Rutledge, . .	Richard Verschoyle, .	Derryvullen, Armagh.	October, 1846, .	Richard Verschoyle. John T. Rutledge.

In May, 1818, the Rev. Arthur Henry Kenney, Ex-Fellow, resigned the Benefice of Kilmacrenan on promotion to the Deanery of Achonry; and the Rev. Anthony Hastings, who had not been a Fellow, was presented to Kilmacrenan by the College.

By order of the Board,

THOMAS STACK, *Registrar.*

Trinity College, April 13, 1877.

APPENDIX XV.

Query by the Royal Commissioners, with the answer of the Provost and Senior Fellows.

APPENDIX XV.

QUERY by the ROYAL COMMISSIONERS, with the ANSWER of the PROVOST and SENIOR FELLOWS.

DEGREES IN THE FACULTY OF THEOLOGY.

Query.—State the mode of conferring Degrees in the Faculty of Theology, the Lectures to be attended, and Examinations to be passed, the length of time which must be devoted to the study, the payments to be made, and all other conditions necessary to be performed in order to obtain each Degree in Theology.

Answer.—The rules at present in force are as follows:—A Bachelor in Divinity must be a Master of Arts or a Bachelor of Arts of three years' standing. He must likewise have undergone a special Examination in Divinity before the Regius Professor, according to Rules prescribed by the Provost and Senior Fellows, with the consent of the Regius Professor.

A Doctor in Divinity must be a Bachelor in Divinity of five years' standing. He must likewise present to the Regius Professor a printed thesis, in which he has treated of and explained some portion of Doctrine from the Holy Scriptures, or of the History of the Church, or of Dogmatic Theology. This thesis is to be approved of by the Professor.

Those who were students before the 26th Nov., 1875, may, up to the year 1878, obtain these Degrees under the Regulations formerly in force, which are as follows:—A Bachelor of Divinity must be M.A. of seven years' standing. Before the private grace of the House can be obtained for this Degree, the Candidate must perform the necessary exercises before the Regius Professor of Divinity, or his Deputy. These are, one Concio *ad Clerum* in Latin, and one Sermon in English *ad Populum*.

A Doctor in Divinity must be B.D. of five years' standing, and in Priest's Orders. The exercises performed before the Regius Professor of Divinity are, a Sermon *ad Populum* in English, and a Latin Sermon *ad Clerum*. When the Degrees of B.D. and D.D. are taken together, the exercises for both must be performed.

There are no Lectures to be attended.

The fees payable on taking these Degrees are as follows:—

S. Theologiæ Baccalaureus,	.	£13	15	0
S. Theologiæ Doctor,	. . .	26	0	0

By order of the Board,

THOMAS STACK, *Registrar.*

Trinity College, April 23, 1877.

APPENDIX XVI.

Additional Queries by the Royal Commissioners, with the Answers of the Registrar of Trinity College.

APPENDIX XVI.

ADDITIONAL QUERIES put by the ROYAL COMMISSIONERS with the ANSWERS of the REGISTRAR of TRINITY COLLEGE.

Query 1. What was the original salary of the Professor of Divinity, and what additions have from time to time been made thereto?

Query 2. By what authority was the advowson of the living of Killybegs purchased by the College?

Answer 1. The changes in the salary of the Professor of Divinity are as follows:—(1). King's Letter, Geo. II., salary named to £50. (2). 1 Geo. III., salary raised to £500. (3). 36 Geo. III., salary raised to £700. (4). 54 Geo. III., salary raised to £1,300 Irish = £1,200 British.

The present salary is £1,218. The £18 was added as compensation for Degree Fees by Decree dated 18th December, 1853 (pursuant to authority granted by Statute, 13 Victoria).

Answer 2. The record [illegible] in best answered by the following extract from the Registry:—1757, July 5. "This day Dr. Madden and Dr. Knight's [illegible] the conveyance to the College of the advowson of the Parish of Killybegs, pursuant to His Majesty's License."

The conveyance of the advowson is dated the 6th of July, 1757, and recites a License from the Crown to purchase it, dated 12th April, 1751, 24th George II.

The advowson was purchased as directed under the will of Dr. Gilbert, who bequeathed part of the purchase-money to the College for this purpose.

T. STACK, *Registrar.*

June 2, 1877.

Queries by the Royal Commissioners, with the Answers of the Provost and Senior Fellows.

Query 1.—A list of the references, in the Charters and Statutes, to the teaching of religion or to the Divinity School, or to any matters in anywise affecting the same.

Answer of the Provost and Senior Fellows.

1. The first reference to this matter occurs near the beginning of the Charter of Elizabeth, in the words, "Ut eo melius ad bonas artes percipiendas, colendamque virtutem et religionem adjuventur" [p. 2, ed. 1844]. These words are recited and confirmed in the Charter of Charles I. [pp. 1 and 3, ed. 1873]; and the same Charter, p. 4, repeats a certain provision of the Charter of Elizabeth—"Utpote seminarium tam istius Collegii, quam totius regni etiam et *Ecclesiae*."

2. In 13 Car. I., Cap. IX., De Cultu Divino [ed. of 1873 (containing additions and emendments extracted from 18 Vict.), p. 23], there are several allusions to religious worship; also to the office of Catechist, and to his assistants. The attention of the Commissioners to the whole Chapter is specially requested.

3. In the Litterae Patentes of 1 Geo. III., Cap. I. is concerned with the office of Professor of Divinity and his duties.

4. In the same Chapter, p. 68, the following words occur: "Cum vero permultum referat, ut juventus Academiae, illi praecipue qui sacris ordinibus destinantur, in sacris literis et religionis Christianae doctrina diligentius erudiantur, ea quam praecipue ob causam fundatum fuit hoc Collegium."

5. In the Letters Patent 51 Geo. III., at p. 85, are regulations concerning the Professorship of Divinity, with regard to salary and duties.

6. In the Letters Patent 18 Vict., occurs a regulation relative to the attendance on the Lectures of the Professorship of Divinity (quoted in p. 68, ed. 1873).

7. In 13 Car. I. Cap. XIII. [p. 33, ed. 1873], De Officio Decanorum—occur the following words: "Quo melius vera et pietas erga Deum, et morum probitas honestasque conservetur, statuimus et ordinamus, ut duo e Sociis quotannis in Decanos eligantur."

8. The Divinity School is not referred to by name in the Statutes, but it appears by 1 Geo. III., Cap. I., that Bachelors of Arts [as there described] were required to attend the Lectures of the Professor; and, until recently, Scholars, although not intending to enter Holy Orders, were obliged, under penalties, to attend the Lectures of the Professor of Divinity.

9. In Litterae Patentes, Car. I. Cap. X. [p. 29, ed. 1873], De Tutorum ac Pupillorum Officio, occurs a passage as follows: "Quod si Tutor quempiam suis pupillis ad pietatem et bonas artes quotidie erudiendis," &c.

10. In estimating the extent to which the teaching of religion was connected with Collegiate arrangements, attention may be drawn to the fact that the obligation by which the Provost must be "in sacris ordinibus constitutus," and by which the Fellows were bound, with few exceptions, to enter into Holy Orders, though removed within the last few years, had existed previously since the 13 Car. I. (vide ed. 1844, pp. 31 and 43).

Query 2.—A list of the Professorships and Lectureships held in connexion with the Divinity School, or for the purpose of giving Lectures or Instruction in the Scriptures or Theology, and of the sums paid to such Professors and Lecturers, distinguishing in each case the amounts paid out of the General College Funds, and derived from private endowments.

Query 3.—Scholarships and Prizes of every kind,

Answer of the Provost and Senior Fellows.

In the Return of the Provost and Senior Fellows, dated April 12, 1877, in pp. 1–7, will be found the Answers to these Queries, so far as they are directly connected with the Divinity School.

As it is understood that information in reference to instruction in Hebrew, and to the instruction given under the superintendence of the Catechist is desired—it is given in the following statement. These matters had been referred to in the Return of April 12, in pp. 6 and 7.

Catechetical Instruction.

The Catechist is one of the Senior Fellows, appointed annually by the Provost and Senior Fellows. The office was established by Statutes of Charles I., in the year 1637. His duties are to take care that the Students who are members of the Church of Ireland are instructed "in sacris literis," by means of questions and answers, on days and hours to be prescribed. The Salary is £200 a year. Assistants to the Catechist are appointed by him from among the Junior Fellows, or Masters of Arts. They hold office for the term in which they are appointed. Their number is usually about eight. First appointed in A.D. 1837.

Their duty is to catechise the Students during the first two years of their Course, in portions of the Bible, and in the Creed. They receive a stipend of four guineas each for the Term—and are employed to examine at the Catechetical Term Examinations, held in each Term, for which there are special fees.

Instruction in Hebrew.

The Professor of Hebrew is one of the Fellows elected by the Governors of Erasmus Smith's Schools, on the recommendation of the Provost and Senior Fellows. The office is tenable for life. It was endowed by Erasmus Smith about 1710.

The duties are to lecture all Students during the second and third years of their Hebrew Course, both those belonging to the Divinity School and others. The salary is £[illegible] per annum.

The Lecturer in Hebrew is one of the Fellows elected by the Provost and Senior Fellows. The office is usually held during the continuance of Junior Fellowship.

The duty is to take part in lecturing Students during the three years of their Hebrew Course. The salary is £80 per annum.

Two Assistant Hebrew Lecturers are elected by the Provost and Senior Fellows from among the Junior Fellows. The office is tenable during the continuance of the Junior Fellowship.

The duties are the same as those of the Lecturer. The salary is £50 per annum.

There is also, occasionally, an additional Hebrew Lecturer, with a stipend of £10 10s. for each Term.

Expenses connected with Catechetical Instruction.

	£	s.	d.
1. In Salaries,	806	[illegible]	[illegible]
2. In Premiums,	188	0	[illegible]
3. In Examination Fees and Payments for Lectures,	464	17	[illegible]

For Hebrew:

	£	s.	d.
1. Salaries,	[illegible]	[illegible]	[illegible]
2. Premiums,	[illegible]	[illegible]	[illegible]
3. Examination Fees,	[illegible]	[illegible]	[illegible]

Appendix XVIII.

Inquiries by the Royal Commissioners, and Answers of the Provost and Senior Fellows.

The following prizes, in reference to which inquiry is made, are paid out of the funds of the College, viz.:—

	£	s.	d.
Archbishop King's Divinity Prizes,	[illegible]	[illegible]	[illegible]
Biblical Greek Prizes,	[illegible]	[illegible]	[illegible]
And	[illegible]	[illegible]	[illegible]
Ecclesiastical History Prizes,	[illegible]	[illegible]	[illegible]
And	[illegible]	[illegible]	[illegible]
Divinity Composition Prizes of £[illegible] each (varying in each amount),			
Six Theological Exhibitions, [illegible] (per annum),	[illegible]	0	0

An inquiry is made respecting the [illegible] belonging to nine years [illegible] in p. [illegible] of Return dated April 24, 1877. The reply is—these amounts are made up of the sums annually paid, during the nine years stated, to Examiners at Divinity and [illegible] Examinations, and of the salary paid to an Assistant Lecturer in Hebrew.

The following Tabular Statements, I., II., III., IV., supply answers to the inquiries of the Commissioners as to the number of [illegible] Students, of Divinity [illegible] issued, and of the whole number of Students on the books in certain years. To these have been added—in order to make the information on this subject complete—Tables V. and VI., though not required by the Commissioners.

In Tables IV. and VI. the number of Students is given as it appears in the Books after the first [illegible] in December in each year, according to the [illegible] of [illegible] usually adopted in the College.

It is to be observed that, in the statements on Divinity Lectures, none are included except those who attended both the Professor and the Assistant Lecturer. Those who attended the Professor only, as a part of their duty as Scholars, are not reckoned.

[This remark does not apply to the years 1828–1833, during which period the form in which the Returns are kept makes it difficult to [illegible] as to the attendance, as above stated.]

I.—Return of Attendance on Divinity Lectures for each of the years from 1828 to 1833.

1828–29,	[illegible]
1829–30,	[illegible]
1830–31,	[illegible]
1831–32,	[illegible]
1832–33, (Session incomplete, Lectures interrupted by Cholera),	[illegible]

Note.—Attendance in the Junior Year commenced in 1833.

New System.

—	Junior Class.	Senior Class.	Total.
1833–34	73	161	[illegible]
1834–35	119	78	[illegible]
1835–36	[illegible]	[illegible]	[illegible]
1836–37	[illegible]	[illegible]	[illegible]
1837–38	[illegible]	[illegible]	[illegible]
1838–39	[illegible]	[illegible]	[illegible]

II.—Return of Attendance on Divinity Lectures in each year from 1856 to 1876.

—	Junior Class.	Senior Class.	Total.
[illegible]	[illegible]	[illegible]	[illegible]
[illegible]	[illegible]	[illegible]	[illegible]
[illegible]	[illegible]	[illegible]	[illegible]
[illegible]	[illegible]	[illegible]	[illegible]
[illegible]	[illegible]	[illegible]	[illegible]
[illegible]	[illegible]	74	[illegible]
[illegible]	[illegible]	[illegible]	[illegible]
[illegible]	[illegible]	[illegible]	[illegible]
[illegible]	[illegible]	[illegible]	[illegible]
[illegible]	[illegible]	[illegible]	[illegible]
[illegible]	[illegible]	[illegible]	[illegible]
[illegible]	[illegible]	[illegible]	[illegible]
[illegible]	71	[illegible]	[illegible]

Return of Attendance on Divinity Lectures—continued.

—	Junior Class.	Senior Class.	Total.
[illegible]	34	97	131
[illegible]	[illegible]	[illegible]	[illegible]
[illegible]	[illegible]	[illegible]	[illegible]
[illegible]	[illegible]	[illegible]	[illegible]
[illegible]	[illegible]	[illegible]	[illegible]
[illegible]	[illegible]	[illegible]	[illegible]
[illegible]	[illegible]	[illegible]	[illegible]
[illegible]	[illegible]	[illegible]	[illegible]

III.—Return of Number of Divinity Testimoniums issued in each Year from 1856 to 1876 (under each Year).

[illegible]	[illegible]	1867–68	[illegible]
[illegible]	[illegible]	1868–69	[illegible]
[illegible]	[illegible]	1869–1870	[illegible]
[illegible]	[illegible]	1870–71	[illegible]
[illegible]	[illegible]	1871–72	[illegible]
[illegible]	[illegible]	1872–73	[illegible]
[illegible]	[illegible]	1873–74	[illegible]
[illegible]	[illegible]	1874–75	[illegible]
[illegible]	[illegible]	1875–76	[illegible]
[illegible]	[illegible]	1876–77	[illegible]
[illegible]	[illegible]		

IV.—Return of the Number of Students on the College Books in each Year from 1828 to 1838.

[illegible]	[illegible]	1834	[illegible]
[illegible]	[illegible]	[illegible]	[illegible]
[illegible]	[illegible]	[illegible]	[illegible]
[illegible]	[illegible]	1837	[illegible]
[illegible]	[illegible]	[illegible]	[illegible]
[illegible]	[illegible]		

V.—Return of Attendance on Divinity Lectures in each Year from 1839 to 1856.

—	Junior Class.	Senior Class.	Total.
[illegible]	[illegible]	[illegible]	[illegible]
[illegible]	[illegible]	[illegible]	[illegible]
[illegible]	[illegible]	[illegible]	[illegible]
[illegible]	[illegible]	[illegible]	[illegible]
[illegible]	[illegible]	[illegible]	[illegible]
[illegible]	[illegible]	[illegible]	[illegible]
[illegible]	[illegible]	[illegible]	[illegible]
[illegible]	[illegible]	[illegible]	[illegible]
[illegible]	[illegible]	[illegible]	[illegible]
[illegible]	[illegible]	[illegible]	[illegible]
[illegible]	[illegible]	[illegible]	[illegible]
[illegible]	[illegible]	[illegible]	[illegible]
[illegible]	[illegible]	[illegible]	[illegible]
[illegible]	[illegible]	[illegible]	[illegible]
[illegible]	[illegible]	[illegible]	[illegible]
[illegible]	[illegible]	[illegible]	[illegible]
[illegible]	[illegible]	105	[illegible]

VI.—Return of the Number of Students on the College Books in each Year from 1839 to 1876.

1839	[illegible]	[illegible]	[illegible]
1840	[illegible]	[illegible]	[illegible]
[illegible]	[illegible]	[illegible]	[illegible]
[illegible]	[illegible]	[illegible]	[illegible]
[illegible]	[illegible]	[illegible]	[illegible]
[illegible]	[illegible]	[illegible]	[illegible]
[illegible]	[illegible]	[illegible]	[illegible]
[illegible]	[illegible]	[illegible]	[illegible]
[illegible]	[illegible]	[illegible]	[illegible]
[illegible]	[illegible]	[illegible]	[illegible]
[illegible]	[illegible]	[illegible]	[illegible]
[illegible]	[illegible]	[illegible]	[illegible]
[illegible]	[illegible]	[illegible]	[illegible]
[illegible]	[illegible]	[illegible]	[illegible]
[illegible]	[illegible]	[illegible]	[illegible]
[illegible]	[illegible]	[illegible]	[illegible]
[illegible]	[illegible]	[illegible]	[illegible]
[illegible]	[illegible]	[illegible]	[illegible]
[illegible]	[illegible]	1875	[illegible]
[illegible]	[illegible]	1876	[illegible]

By order of the Board,

Thomas Stack, Registrar.

Trinity College,
November 17, 1877.

XVII.—STATEMENT showing the NUMBER of STUDENTS who obtained the DEGREE of BACHELOR of ARTS from the Year 1856–57 to the Year 1876–77, both inclusive; and the NUMBER of DIVINITY TESTIMONIUMS granted during the same period.

Appendix XVII. Students who obtained the degree of Bachelor of Arts from the Year 1856–57 to the year 1876–77.

—	A. B. Degrees.	Divinity Testimoniums.	—	A. B. Degrees.	Divinity Testimoniums.
1856–57	161	60	1867–68	[illegible]	[illegible]
1857–58	[illegible]	64	1868–69	[illegible]	[illegible]
1858–59	[illegible]	67	1869–1870	[illegible]	[illegible]
1859–1860	144	[illegible]	1870–71	[illegible]	[illegible]
1860–61	[illegible]	[illegible]	1871–72	[illegible]	[illegible]
1861–62	[illegible]	[illegible]	1872–73	[illegible]	[illegible]
1862–63	[illegible]	[illegible]	1873–74	[illegible]	[illegible]
1863–64	[illegible]	[illegible]	1874–75	[illegible]	[illegible]
1864–65	[illegible]	[illegible]	1875–76	[illegible]	[illegible]
1865–66	[illegible]	[illegible]	1876–77	[illegible]	[illegible]
1866–67	[illegible]	[illegible]			

By order of the Board,

THOMAS STACK, *Registrar*.

March 23, 1878.

APPENDIX XVIII.

Appendix XVIII. Patent Roll of James the First.

PATENT ROLL of the eighth year of James the First—(Fifth Part, No. 2.)—GRANT to TRINITY COLLEGE, DUBLIN, of LANDS and ADVOWSONS in ULSTER.

Concerning a Grant of a Farm to the College, &c. of Queen Elizabeth, near Dublin, within the Kingdom of Ireland.

The King to all to whom, &c., Greeting:—

Know ye, that we, of our special grace, certain knowledge, and mere motion, have given, granted, and [illegible]

[illegible]

land; Drummore, being
Falaugh, being two balli-
ing one quarter of land;
of land, Moresagh,
being one quarter
two ballibors of land;
of land; Magelivagh,
Carigdrumagh, being one
land; Ballimakilly, being
being six ballibors
one quarter of land;

Caprogh, and Arleragh, in the Barony
and whatsoever of them are in the Co
aforesaid, with all their rights, members
nances. And also all and singular adv
tions, nominations, presentations, free
and rights of patronage of all and sing
tories and Vicarages of the several C
Parishes of Daghymoghy, Clondevadog
Aghanna, Kilmacrenan, Conwall, and
and whatsoever of them, with all their
bers, and appurtenances, are in the Cou
aforesaid. And also all and singular

College of the Holy and Undivided Trinity of Queen Elizabeth, near Dublin, and of their successors for ever.

To be held of us, our heirs, and successors, as of our Castle of Dublin, in our said Kingdom of Ireland, in free and common soccage, by fealty alone, and not in capite, neither in soccage in capite, nor by military service; rendering annually to us, our heirs, and successors, of and for the aforesaid territory, country, or precinct of land called Tonregy, and other premises above, by these presents before granted in Tonregy aforesaid, in said County Ardmagh, containing, as is said before, four thousand and one hundred acres of land, more or less, ten pounds, eighteen shillings, and eight pence, current money of England. And of and for the aforesaid territory or precinct of land called Coolmore, and other premises above by the presents granted before, in Coolmore aforesaid, in said County Ardmagh, containing, as is aforesaid, six hundred acres of land, more or less, thirty two shillings. And of and for the aforesaid territory or precinct of land called Slutmulrony, and other premises above by the presents before granted in Slutmulrony aforesaid, in the County Fermanagh aforesaid, containing, as is aforesaid, nine hundred acres of land, more or less, forty and eight shillings. And of and for the premises above by the presents before granted, in the County Donegall aforesaid, containing, as is aforesaid, four thousand acres of land, more or less, ten pounds, thirteen shillings, and four pence, current money of England. And of and for the aforesaid late abbey, monastery, or religious house, and other premises, above by these presents before granted in the site or precinct of the aforesaid late abbey, monastery, or house in the said County Donegall, six pounds, sixteen shillings, and sixpence, current money of England, at the receipt of the Exchequer of us, our heirs, and successors, of our said Kingdom of Ireland, or at the hands of our Vice-Treasurer, or Receiver-General of us, our heirs, and successors, of our said Kingdom of Ireland for the time being, at the Feasts of Saint Michael the Archangel and of Easter, by equal portions annually to be paid. And further, of our more ample special grace, certain knowledge, and mere motion, we have granted, and given leave, and by these presents, for us, our heirs and successors, do grant and give leave to the aforesaid Provost, Fellows, and Scholars of the College of the Holy and Undivided Trinity of Queen Elizabeth, near Dublin, and their successors, that they themselves, and any one of them from time to time, at his and their will and pleasure, during the space of seven years next following after the Feast of Easter last past before the date of these presents, may and can ship, convey, export, and transport beyond our said Kingdom of Ireland, or any part or parcel thereof, as far as into our Kingdom of England, and all our other dominions whatsoever, or into any other kingdom, country, territory, or dominion in parts beyond the sea, being in friendship of us, our heirs and successors, and not elsewhere, all and every grain, hides, tallow, wool, flax, linen yarn, cloth of every kind, and all other commodities and merchandizes whatsoever, from time to time, in or within the several Counties of Ardmagh, Tyrone, Colrane, Donegall, County of the City of Derry, Fermanagh and Cavan, or any one of them, in our Province of Ulster, increasing, happening, renewing, or arising from, or in the future to be increased, reduced to, renewed, or brought forth; and those commodities and merchandizes, so exported or transported thence, at their own will, to sell and to expose for sale, or to exchange for their greater convenience and usefulness, without account or payment of any custom, great or small, or of any subsidy, imposition, or sum of money, or of any other charge, or anything else therefor, to us, our heirs or successors, within our kingdoms, or any one of them, to be repaid, discharged, or done; willing moreover, and by these presents firmly enjoining, commanding, and directing as well all and singular treasurers, sub-treasurers, customers, collectors of customs, and examiners of taxes, as all other officers and servants of us, our heirs and successors whatsoever, of our said Kingdoms of England and Ireland, and of any one of them, that they themselves, and any one of them, from time to time, may permit the aforesaid Provost, Fellows, and Scholars of the College of the Holy and Undivided Trinity of Queen Elizabeth, near Dublin, and their successors, and any one of them, quietly and peaceably, in the form aforesaid, to ship, carry, export, sell and expose for sale, or exchange all and singular commodities, and merchandizes of this sort, without payment of any custom, great or small, or of any subsidy, imposition, or sum of money whatsoever, therefor, to us, our heirs and successors, in that behalf to be rendered or discharged. And these our Letters Patent, or the enrolment of them, will be as well to our said Treasurers, Sub-treasurers, Collectors of Customs, Examiners of Taxes, and other officers and servants whatsoever, a sufficient warrant and acquittance in this behalf, any statute, act, ordinance, provision, proclamation, or restriction, or any other thing, cause or matter whatsoever, contrary to the aforesaid, notwithstanding.

And further, of our more ample, special grace, certain knowledge, and mere motion, we have granted and given leave, and by these presents for us, our heirs and successors, do grant and give leave to the aforesaid Provost, Fellows, and Scholars of the College of the Holy and Undivided Trinity of Queen Elizabeth, near Dublin, and to their successors, that they themselves, and any one of them, from time to time, within the space of five years next following after the Feast of Easter last past, before the date of these presents, at his and their will and pleasure, may and can ship, carry, and export, and convey, of and from our Kingdom and Dominions in any one of them into our Kingdom of Ireland, and there discharge, unload, all and all manner of victuals and utensils in their houses or buildings to be had and used, and all and all manner of materials and instruments for edifices and structures to be made in and upon any lands within the aforesaid Counties of Ardmagh, Tyrone, Colrane, Donegall, County of the City of Derry, Fermanagh, and Cavan, or any one of them, and for the necessary instruction and maintenance of agriculture, and sheep, or birds of every kind, for store, English stocking and storing, and for cultivating and manuring of any lands within the several counties aforesaid, or any one of them, without account or payment of any custom, subsidy, imposition, or sum of money therefor, to us, our heirs and successors, in our Kingdoms, to any one of them, to be rendered or made.

And further, We will, command, and direct, to all and singular Treasurers, Sub-treasurers, Customers, Collectors of Customs, and Examiners of Taxes, and to all our other officers and servants whatsoever, of our said Kingdoms of England and Ireland, and any one of them, that they themselves, and any one of them, from time to time, may permit the said Provost, Fellows, and Scholars of the College of the Holy and Undivided Trinity of Queen Elizabeth, near Dublin, and their successors, and any of them, quietly and peaceably to ship, carry, transport, export, discharge, and unload, all and singular such victuals, utensils, materials, and instruments for making the aforesaid edifices and structures, and to be applied and used for the aforesaid purposes and uses, without payment of any custom, subsidy, impost, or sum of money therefor, to us, our heirs or successors, in that behalf to be rendered or paid. And these our Letters Patent, or their Enrollment, shall be sufficient warrant and exoneration in that behalf, to the treasurers, sub-treasurers, customers, Collectors of Customs, and any other officers and servants whatsoever. Notwithstanding any statute, act, ordinance, provision, proclamation, or restriction, or any other thing, cause, or matter whatsoever, to the contrary thereof notwithstanding. So as that this our grant or license

Appendix XVIII.

Patent Roll of James the First.

APPENDIX XVIII. — Patent Roll of James the First.

shall in no wise extend to any commodities, to be transported or imported into our said Kingdom of Ireland, with the intention that such merchandise or goods should be sold or exchanged.

We also will, and by these presents firmly enjoining, direct and command, that the aforesaid Provost, Fellows, and Scholars of the College of the Holy and Undivided Trinity of Queen Elizabeth, near Dublin, and their successors, and each of them, from time to time, within the space of two years next following after the Feast of Easter last past, before the date of these presents, may and can lawfully and freely enter into all and singular woods, underwoods, and woody lands in the several Counties of Ardmagh, Donegal, Fermanagh, Cavan, and Tyrone (except the Country of Coleraine, and the Countries of Glenconkeine, and Killetragh, extending from the Country of Coleraine to Ballyshanny, to be reserved and granted to the Mayor and Commonalty of our City of London), and there by the Assignment of our Commissioner (viz. in that behalf to be authorised, to cut and carry off all such and so much trees or timber as shall be sufficient for the edifices or structures to be erected in and upon the premises, or any parcel thereof, without any account of sum of money, or anything else, for such trees or timber, to us, our heirs or successors, or to any other person or persons to be paid or made.

We do further will, and by these presents enjoining, do direct and command, and the aforesaid Provost, Fellows, and Scholars of the College of the Holy and Undivided Trinity of Queen Elizabeth, near Dublin, and their successors, for themselves and their successors, covenant and consent to and with us, our heirs and successors, by these presents, that if the Commissioners aforesaid in that behalf authorised, within the space of two years, after the Feast of Easter last past before the date of these presents, shall assign to any other person or persons, for erecting structures or edifices in any part of the several Counties aforesaid, any trees or timber, growing or being in and upon the premises above by these presents before granted, or any part thereof, that then it may and shall be allowable for such person or persons, lawfully, quietly, and freely, to go and enter upon the before granted premises, or any or every parcel thereof, and within the space of two years as aforesaid, to cut and carry off all such and so many trees or timber, as so aforesaid to be there assigned, and convert them to the use aforesaid, without any account or sale of money, or anything else to be paid or made therefor, to the aforesaid Provost, Fellows, and Scholars of the College of the Holy and Undivided Trinity of Queen Elizabeth, near Dublin, or to their successors, and without any interruption, impediment, or hindrance of the aforesaid Provost, Fellows, and Scholars of the College of the Holy and Undivided Trinity of Queen Elizabeth, near Dublin, or their assigns; anything in these presents to the contrary notwithstanding.

We do also will, and by these presents firmly enjoining, direct and command, and the aforesaid Provost, Fellows, and Scholars of the College of the Holy and Undivided Trinity of Queen Elizabeth, near Dublin, for themselves and their successors, agree and covenant to and with us, our heirs and successors, by these presents, that the aforesaid Provost, Fellows, and Scholars of the College of the Holy and Undivided Trinity of Queen Elizabeth, near Dublin, and their successors, shall, and each shall, cause their several tenants in fee farm, and their several tenants for a term of a life, or lives, or of years, and each of them, to build and erect their mansion houses adjacent to each other, and near the chief house or mansion of the said Provost, Fellows, and Scholars of the College of the Holy and Undivided Trinity of Queen Elizabeth, near Dublin, and of their successors, in and upon the premises to be built or erected, and not here and there, or apart, as well for the mutual defence and protection of the said Provost, Fellows, and Scholars of the College of the Holy and Undivided Trinity of Queen Elizabeth, near Dublin, and their successors, and of their tenants aforesaid, as for the creation of several villages in and upon the premises, to the service and public good of our said Kingdom of Ireland.

We do further will, and by these presents firmly enjoining, direct and command, and the aforesaid Provost, Fellows, and Scholars of the College of the Holy and Undivided Trinity of Queen Elizabeth, near Dublin, for themselves and their successors, agree and consent to and with us, our heirs and successors, by these presents, that the aforesaid Provost, Fellows, and Scholars of the College of the Holy and Undivided Trinity of Queen Elizabeth, near Dublin, and their successors, from time to time, shall prepare and have ready in their mansion houses, to be erected or built in and within the premises, a sufficient number of arms to arm or equip a competent number of men for the defence or protection of the said Provost, Fellows, and Scholars of the College of the Holy and Undivided Trinity of Queen Elizabeth, near Dublin, and of their servants and tenants, against rebels and other enemies of us, our heirs, or successors, in our said Kingdom of Ireland.

And further we do will, and by these presents for us, our heirs and successors, do grant, and firmly enjoining, command, that the said territory or precinct of land called Toaghy, and all other territories, lands, tenements, and hereditaments, and all other and singular the premises above by these presents before granted, shall be, and be accounted from henceforth, one entire manor in fact and name, and for ever shall be called and reputed the Manor of Kilmacrenan; and that the aforesaid Provost, Fellows, and Scholars of the College of the Holy and Undivided Trinity of Queen Elizabeth, near Dublin, and their successors, shall have and hold within the said Manor 600 acres of land distinct and separate for demesne lands of the said Manor.

And further we grant and give licence to the aforesaid Provost, Fellows, and Scholars of the College of the Holy and Undivided Trinity of Queen Elizabeth, near Dublin, and to their successors, that they and their successors aforesaid, and every one of them, may and shall be able freely, and without the hindrance of us, our heirs and successors, to give, grant, and in what way soever alienate, all other and singular the premises before granted and whatsoever parcel thereof, to any person or persons, their heirs or assigns, not being mere Irish. To be held of the aforesaid Provost, Fellows, and Scholars of the College of the Holy and Undivided Trinity of Queen Elizabeth, near Dublin, and their successors, as of their aforesaid Manor of Kilmacrenan aforesaid, in free and common soccage, and by suit of Court to be held twice per annum. Rendering such rents and other lawful services as to the aforesaid Provost, Fellows, and Scholars of the College of the Holy and Undivided Trinity of Queen Elizabeth, near Dublin, and their successors, it shall seem better to obtain. Notwithstanding the Statute commonly called "Quia Emptores terrarum," or any other Statute, Act, ordinance, or proviso, or any other thing, cause, or matter whatsoever to the contrary notwithstanding.

And further we will, and by these presents for us, our heirs and successors, grant and give licence to the aforesaid Provost, Fellows, and Scholars of the College of the Holy and Undivided Trinity of Queen Elizabeth, near Dublin, and to their successors, that they, and each of them, may have and hold, and may and shall be able to have and to hold, in and within the precincts or limits of the Manor aforesaid, a Court in the nature of a Court Baron, to enquire, hear, determine, and operate all and singular such things and matters, and in the same manner and form as and like as they ought or are accustomed to be enquired into, heard, determined, or executed in any Court Baron within our said Kingdom of England, or within our said Kingdom of Ireland. To be held before the Seneschal or Seneschals by the said Provost, Fellows, and Scholars of the College of the Holy and Undivided Trinity of Queen Elizabeth, near Dublin, and their successors from time to time to be nominated and appointed; and before the free suitors of the said Manor of Kilmacrenan respectively. And in the said Court to hold pleas of all and singular actions, trespasses, covenants, accounts, contracts, detinues, debts or demands, whatsoever, which in debts or damages do not exceed a sum of forty shillings sterling, happening or arising in or within the premises above by these presents before granted, and the limits and bounds of the same. And that they and each of them shall have and receive, and from time to time may and can have and receive, all and singular profits, amercements, fines, commodities, advantages, and emoluments whatsoever to such Courts belonging or appertaining, or in any way therefrom issuing or arising, without account or any thing else therefor to us, our heirs or successors, to be rendered, paid, or performed.

We also will, and of our more ample special grace, certain knowledge, and mere motion, by these presents for us, our heirs and successors, grant to the aforesaid Provost, Fellows, and Scholars of the College of the Holy and Undivided Trinity of Queen Elizabeth, near Dublin, and to their successors, that We, our heirs and successors from henceforth for ever, annually and from time to time, shall exonerate, acquit, and keep indemnified, as well the aforesaid Provost, Fellows, and Scholars of the College of the Holy and Undivided Trinity of Queen Elizabeth, near Dublin, and their successors and each of them, as the aforesaid rectories, messuages, lands, tenements, hereditaments, and all other and singular the premises above by these presents before granted, and every parcel thereof, with their entire appurtenances, against us, our heirs, and successors, of and from all and all manner of corrodies, rents, fees, annuities, pensions, portions, sums of money and charges whatsoever, from the premises before granted, or from any parcel thereof to us, our heirs or successors, issuing or to be paid, or thereupon towards us, our heirs or successors, charged or to be charged, except from the rents, services, tenures, and other charges above for the premises in these presents reserved.

Willing therefore, and, by these presents firmly enjoining, commanding as well to the Treasurer, Chancellor, and Barons of the Exchequer, of us, our heirs and successors, as to all and singular the receivers, auditors, and other officers and servants of us, our heirs and successors whatsoever, of our said Kingdom of Ireland for the time being, that they and each of them, on the sole showing of these our Letters Patent, or their Inrollment, without any other Writ or Warrant from us, our heirs or successors, in any way to be obtained or prosecuted from time to time, shall cause to be made to the aforesaid Provost, Fellows, and Scholars of the College of the Holy and Undivided Trinity of Queen Elizabeth, near Dublin, full, entire, and due allowance and manifest discharge of and from all and all manner of such corrodies, rents, fees, annuities, pensions, portions, sums of money and charges whatsoever, except of the aforesaid rents, services, tenures, and other charges above for the premises in these presents as aforesaid reserved, from the premises before granted, or any of them, to us, our heirs or successors, issuing or to be paid, or thereupon towards our heirs or successors charged or to be charged, and by the aforesaid Provost, Fellows, and Scholars of the College of the Holy and Undivided Trinity of Queen Elizabeth, near Dublin, and their successors, payable, to be done or performed. And these our Letters Patent, or the Inrollment of them, shall be as well to the said Treasurer, Chancellor, and Barons of the Exchequer aforesaid as to the aforesaid

Appendix XIV.

Patent to purchase four Advowsons.

APPENDIX XIV.

TRINITY COLLEGE, DUBLIN.—PATENT TO PURCHASE FOUR ADVOWSONS.

George the Third, by the Grace of God of Great Britain, France, and Ireland King, Defender of the Faith, and so forth, to all unto whom these presents shall come, greeting: Whereas the Provost, Fellows, and Scholars of the College of the Holy and Undivided Trinity of Queen Elizabeth near Dublin, by their memorial presented to our right trusty and right well beloved cousin and counsellor George Dunk Earl of Halifax, our Lieutenant General and General Governor of our said kingdom of Ireland, have humbly besought us to grant them our royal licence to purchase in mortmain four advowsons in our said kingdom of Ireland; and whereas our said Lieutenant General and General Governor of our said kingdom of Ireland having represented to us that the purchasing of such advowsons will cause a more frequent succession of Fellowships in the said College and be of a [illegible] use in the encouragement of learning in our said kingdom of Ireland, we have been graciously pleased to grant their request. Know ye therefore that We of our special grace, certain knowledge, and mere motion, by and with the consent of the Most Reverend Father in God our right trusty and right well beloved councillor George Bishop of Armagh, Primate of all Ireland, our right trusty and right well beloved cousin and councillor Henry Earl of Shannon, and our right trusty and well beloved councillor John Ponsonby, Esq., Speaker of our House of Commons in our said kingdom of Ireland, our Justices General and General Governors of our said kingdom of Ireland, and according to the tenor and effect of our letters under our Privy Signet and Sign Manual bearing date at our Court at St. James's the [illegible] day of [illegible], 1762, in the second year of our reign and now enrolled in the rolls of our High Court of Chancery in our said kingdom of Ireland, have given and granted, and by these presents do give and grant to the said Provost, Fellows, and Scholars of the College of the Holy and Undivided Trinity of Queen Elizabeth near Dublin our royal licence to purchase in mortmain to them and their successors the advowson and right of patronage, presentation, and nomination of and to four several churches in our said kingdom of Ireland. And further, of our special grace, certain knowledge, and mere motion, by and with the advice and consent aforesaid, and according to the tenor and effect of our said letters, We have given and granted, and by these presents do give and grant, to all and every person and persons who now are or shall be seized or possessed of any estate in the advowson, right of patronage, presentation, and nomination of and to the four several churches which shall be so purchased by the said Provost, Fellows, and Scholars of the College of the Holy and Undivided Trinity of Queen Elizabeth near Dublin our royal licence to alien, grant, and convey the advowson, right of patronage, presentation, and nomination of and to the four several churches to be purchased as aforesaid to the said Provost, Fellows, and Scholars of the College of the Holy and Undivided Trinity of Queen Elizabeth near Dublin and their successors, any law, statute, or usage in our said kingdom of Ireland to prevent purchases of lands, tenements, or hereditaments in mortmain notwithstanding. And further, of our more abundant special grace, certain knowledge, and mere motion, by and with the advice and consent aforesaid, We have given and granted, and by these presents do give and grant to the said Provost, Fellows, and Scholars, that they shall and may, from time to time after such purchase and alienation so made, from thenceforth have, hold, possess, and enjoy the advowsons, presentations, and nominations of and to the several churches which they shall so purchase to them and their successors in our said kingdom of Ireland, the statute of mortmain now in force in our said kingdom of Ireland to prevent and prohibit alienations in mortmain notwithstanding. Provided always that these our letters patent be inrolled in the Rolls of our High Court of Chancery in our said kingdom of Ireland within the space of six months next ensuing the date of these presents. In witness whereof we have caused these our letters to be made patent. Witness our aforesaid Justices General and General Governors of our said kingdom of Ireland at Dublin, the [illegible] day of March, in the third year of our reign.

DOWDALL.

(Seal.)

Enrd. Mich. Nowlan, D. Clk. of the Crown and Hanaper.

APPENDIX XX.

List of Benefices formerly in the Patronage of Trinity College.

APPENDIX XX.

Table 1.

A List of Benefices formerly in the Patronage of Trinity College, with their Successive Incumbents, so far as they have been ascertained.

I.—DIOCESE OF DERRY.

1. Ardstraw Rectory, 1610.

Name.	Date of Election to Fellowship.	Date of Co-optation.	Date of Acceptance of Benefice.	Observations.
John Richardson,	1603	—	1617	Bishop of Ardagh 1633–54.
Michael Wisdom,	—	—	1639	
Oliver Williamson,	1651	—	1660	Dean of Clonfert, 1671–78.
Thomas Wetherall, M.D.	—	—	1663	
Adam Usher,	—	—	1690	
John Hall,	1688	1693	1713	
Claud Gilbert,	1690	1698	1735	Reg. Prof. of Divinity.
Robert Shaw,	1712	1730	1743	
John Pellissier,	1737	[illegible]	1745	Reg. Prof. of Divinity, 1746–53, V.P.
Thomas Leland,	1746	1761	1781	
Joseph Wilson,	1753	1767	1786	
George Hall,	1777	1790	1800	Provost, 1806–11. Bishop of Dromore, 1811.
Gerald Fitzgerald,	1765	[illegible]	1806	
Richard H. Nash,	1798	1811	1828	
James MacIvor,	1814	—	1847	

Annuity awarded to Incumbent, . £1,835 4 6
Compensation for loss of Advowson, . 8,831 14 1

2. Cappagh Rectory, 1610.

Name.	Date of Election to Fellowship.	Date of Co-optation.	Date of Acceptance of Benefice.	Observations.
Hermann Walker,	—	—	1644	
George Walker,	—	—	1656	Chancellor of Armagh, 1663–77.
Patrick Hamilton,	1651	1666	1671	
William Griffith,	1697	—	1703	
Edward Synge,	1710	—	1719	Bishop of Clonfert, 1730, of Ferns and Elphin successively
William Bingham,	—	—	1730	Presented by the Crown.
Wood Gibson,	1738	1760	1750	
Robert Browne,	1767	—	1786	Dean of Cork, 1819.
Richard Stack,	1779	—	1807	
William Magee,	1788	1790	1812	Bishop of Raphoe, 1819. Archbishop of Dublin, 1822.
James W. Trench,	—	—	1819	Presented by the Crown.
Henry H. Harte,	1819	—	1831	
Joseph Dennis,	1814	—	1849	Dean of Clonfert, 1855.

Annuity awarded to Incumbent, . . £1,234 15 8
Compensation for loss of Advowson, . . 7,955 12 4

3. Drumragh Rectory, 1610.

Name.	Date of Election to Fellowship.	Date of Co-optation.	Date of Acceptance of Benefice.	Observations.
Richard Walker,	—	—	1620	
Thomas Crompton,	—	—	1625	
—— Brisben,	—	—	1645	
Robert Echlin,	—	—	1667	Dean of Tuam.
Thomas Squire,	1701	—	1713	
Edward Hudson,	1720	—	1729	
James Knight,	1738	—	1756	
Henry Mercier,	1740	1763	1767	
John Forster,	1734	1743	1768	
William Day,	1774	—	1780	
Richard Stack,	1779	—	1791	
Robert Burrowes,	1782	—	1807	Dean of Cork, 1819.
John B. Chapman,	1820	—	1841	
George Sidney Smith,	1831	—	1847	

Annuity awarded to Incumbent, . . £1,096 2 0
Compensation for loss of Advowson, . . 9,615 5 7

II.—DIOCESE OF RAPHOE.

2. Clondevaddock Rectory, 1610.

Name.	Date of Election to Fellowship.	Date of Co-optation.	Date of Acceptance of Benefice.	Observations.
Robert Alden,	—	—	1632	
Alexander Mackgwyre,	—	—	1661	
Richard Ratts,	—	—	1677	
Benjamin Span,	—	—	1687	Resigned in 1694.
John Richardson,	—	—	1694	
William Caldwell,	—	—	1693	
Thomas Watkins,	—	—	1708	
Charles Vane,	—	—	1744	
Tobias Caulfield,	—	—	1714	
Joseph King,*	1719	1729	1733	
John Craig,*	1723	1736	1749	
John Beatty,*	1740	1758	1759	
John Forsayeth,*	1752	—	1766	Archdeacon of Cork.
John Torrens,	—	—	1783	
David Duncan,	—	—	1785	
Thomas Greene,	—	—	1788	
Alexander Crawford,	—	—	1807	
Charles W. Wall,*	1794	—	1814	
Samuel B. O'Malley,	1830	—	1836	Bishop of Cloyne, 1863.
William A. Butler,	—	—	1838	
Richard Gibbings,	—	—	1863	**Prof. of Ecclesiastical History, 1863–1878.**
Charles F. Stewart,	—	—	1863	
Alexander Geo. Stuart,	—	—	1868	

Annuity awarded to Incumbent, £883 9 3
Compensation for loss of Advowson, 6,252 12 5

3. Clondahorky Rectory, 1610.

Name.	Date of Election to Fellowship.	Date of Co-optation.	Date of Acceptance of Benefice.	Observations.
Thomas Knox,	—	—	1625	Bishop of the Isles.
James Neill,	—	—	1637	
Patrick Sheridan,*	1660	1661	1664	Bishop of Cloyne, 1679;
William Lloyd,	1671-3	—	1677	Bishop of Killala, 1690,
Edward Rogers,*	1680	—	1683	Chancellor of Cloyne, 1683–1730.
Robert Lloyd,	—	—	1692	
John Johnston,	—	—	1702	
Jonathan Rogers,	1716	1724	1730	
Benjamin Bacon,	1734	—	1751	
John Jolly,	—	—	1763	
Thomas Bedford,	—	—	1749	
William Hutchinson,	1779	—	1790	
Henry Moseley,	1792	—	1797	
William Ruttle,	—	—	1843	
Daniel Mooney,	—	—	1852	

Annuity awarded to Incumbent, £811 10 7
Compensation for loss of Advowson, 3,318 16 9

4. Conwall or Letterkenny Rectory, 1610.

Name.	Date of Election to Fellowship.	Date of Co-optation.	Date of Acceptance of Benefice.	Observations.
Dougald Campbell,	—	—	1632	
Patrick Sheridan,*	1660	1661	1668	Bishop of Cloyne, 1679.
Roger Waring,	—	—	1679	
Edward Rogers,*	1680	—	1683	**Chancellor of Cloyne, 1683–1730.**
Benjamin Span,	—	—	1703	
William Span,	—	—	1740	
John Whittingham,	1736	1746	1765	
Joseph Stock,	1763	—	1779	Bishop of Killala, 1798, of Waterford, 1810.
John Ellison,*	1782	—	1793	
Joseph Stopford,	1790	1802	1819	
Charles Boyton,	1821	—	1839	
Henry Kingsmill,	1826	—	1850	

Annuity awarded to Incumbent, £887 19 5
Compensation for loss of Advowson, 6,388 10 1

John Vinck,	—	—	1632	
John Leslie,	—	—	1662	
Philip Townsend,	—	—	[illegible]	
Samuel Wye,	—	—	1706	
Matthew Leslie,	—	—	1711	
Caleb Cartwright,	1724	—	1718	
Hugh Hamilton,	1751	—	1764	Bishop of Clonfert, 1796; of Ossory, 1799.
William Babington,	—	—	1767	
Thomas Parsons,	1765	—	1797	
Arthur Henry Kenney,	1800	—	1810	Dean of Achonry, 1812.
Anthony Hastings,	—	—	1812	
Henry Martin,	—	—	[illegible]	

Annuity awarded to Incumbent, £[illegible] [illegible] [illegible]
Compensation for loss of Advowson, [illegible] 7 10

B. Rathbarry or Kilmurry Rectory, 1810.

William Tynte,	—	—	[illegible]	
Nathaniel Foy,	1671	1610	1678	Bishop of Waterford, 1691.
Henry Davis,	—	—	1691	Presented by the Crown.
John Hall,*	1695	1692	1712	
James Knox,*	1720	1728	1754	
John Sisson,*	1730	1736	1749	
John Morton,*	1745	1750	1779	
John Fothergill,*	1743	—	1762	Archdeacon of Cork.
William Jephson,	—	—	1788	
John Walker,	1768	1791	1791	
John Usher,	1790	—	1796	Archdeacon of Raphoe, 1816
John R. Chapman,	1830	—	1836	
William A. Hughes,	—	—	1842	
James Brown,	1848	—	1848	
Joseph H. Singer,	1810	1840	1850	Bishop of Meath, 1851:
Frederick Goold,	—	—	1850	Presented by the Crown. Archdeacon of Raphoe.
James W. Irwin,	—	—	1868	

Annuity awarded to Incumbent, . . £810 13 0
Compensation for loss of Advowson, . . 5,800 5 8

C. Tullyaughnish Rectory, 1810.

William Cunyngham,	—	—	1639	
Tobias Pullen,	1671	—	1677	Bishop of Cloyne, 1694, of Dromore, 1695.
—	—	—	1683	
Alexander Kinne,	—	—	1705	
John Forster,	1734	1743	1760	
Henry Maxwell,	1740	1752	1767	
Stanley Wilder,	1744	1753	1763	
Michael Kearney,	1757	1758	1778	Archdeacon of Raphoe, 1798.
Cornelius H. Usher,*	1794	—	1814	
Charles Boyton,	1831	—	1836	
William Atkins,	1843	—	1844	Dean of Ferns, 1862.
John B. Leslie,	1855	—	1863	Resigned shortly after his appointment.
John Gwynn,	1853	—	1863	

Annuity awarded to Incumbent, . . £1,146 8 9
Compensation for loss of Advowson, . . 6,754 5 1

Appendix XX.

List of Benefices in the Presentation of Trinity College.

III.—DIOCESE OF KILMORE.

10. Killesherdoney Rectory, 1763.

Name.	Date of Election to Fellowship.	Date of Co-option.	Date of Acceptance of Benefice.	Observations.
William Martin,	1740	1761	1764	
William Kidney,	1809	—	1837	
John C. Martin,	1821	—	1851	Archdeacon of Ardagh 1864, of Kilmore 1866. Died 1874.

Annuity awarded to Incumbent, . £1,087 8 2.
Compensation for loss of Advowson, . 9,764 7 7.

IV.—DIOCESE OF DOWN.

11. Killyleagh Rectory, 1760.

Name.	Date of Election to Fellowship.	Date of Co-option.	Date of Acceptance of Benefice.	Observations.
John Fletcher,*	1734	1743	1754	
William Day,*	1754	—	1759	
Richard Stack,*	1770	—	1763	
William Magee,*	1788	1790	1812	Bishop of Raphoe, 1819, Archbishop of Dublin, 1822.
Peter Carleton,	—	—	1813	Presented by the Crown.
Edward Hincks,	1813	—	1825	
Edward B. Moeran,	...	—	1867	

Annuity awarded to Incumbent, . . £814 12 8
Compensation for loss of Advowson, . . 4,287 9 5

V.—DIOCESE OF CLOGHER.

12. Aghalurcher Rectory, 1610.

Name.	Date of Election to Fellowship.	Date of Co-option.	Date of Acceptance of Benefice.	Observations.
Robert Whitlaw,	—	—	1615	
Richard Howlett,	—	—	1634	Sequestered in 1638.
Gervase Thorpe,	—	—	1638	
[James Johnston, (during Commonwealth)	—	—	—	Ejected 1661.
William Dunkin,	—	—	1661	Instituted on Presentation of Trinity College Dublin.
Adam Nixon,	—	—	1690	do. do.
Thomas Bladen,	1709	—	1717	do. do.
William Gore (Dean),	—	—	1722	
John Hamilton,	1712	—	1724	Instituted on Presentation of Trinity College Dublin.
William Thompson,	1718	1723	1729	do. do.
Richard Radcliffe,	1744	—	1754	do. do.
Robert Law,	1746	—	1765	do. do.
William Ogle,	—	—	1787	do. do.
Robert Russell,	1780	—	1794	Ob. 1837.
George Sidney Smith,	1831	—	1838	Rector of Drumragh, 1867.
Maurice F. Day,	—	—	1867	Dean of Limerick, 1872. Bishop of Cashel.
William S. Burnside,	—	—	1868	

Annuity awarded to Incumbent, . . £750 11 10
Compensation for loss of Advowson, . . 6,311 16 5

* The mark denotes that the Incumbent held another living simultaneously.

Appendix B.B.

List of Benefices formerly in the Patronage of Trinity College.

V.—DIOCESE OF CLOGHER—continued.

13. Cleenish Rectory, 1616.

Name.	Date of Election to Fellowship.	Date of Co-option.	Date of Acceptance of Benefice.	Observations.
James Slacke,	—	—	before 1622	and in 1631.
Edward Slack,	—	—	1633	
George Parker,	—	—	1638	Presented by the Crown.
(or Usurpation) John Tilson,	—	—	—	Deprived 1661.
(Restoration) Andrew Hamilton,	—	—	1662	
James Auchinleck,	—	—	1664	(Ob. 1668) Instituted on Presentation of T. C. D.
Robert Smith,	—	—	1688	
William Mullart,	1686	—	1702	
John Dennis,	1697	—	1713 ?	1721 ?
Thomas Forster,	1738	1746	1746	
William Barry,	—	—	1760	Bishop of Clonfert, 1766, of Killala, 1773, of Limerick, 1780.
Thomas Cuthbert,	—	—	1789	Presented by the Crown vice Clere made Bishop.
Lancelot Dowe,	—	—	1795	
John Kilpatrick,*	1768	—	1784	Rector of Clonmel, 1798.
Hon. Percy Jocelyn,	—	—	1798	Bishop of Ferns, 1809, of Clogher, 1820.
Hon. Richard Ponsonby,	—	—	1810	Bishop of Derry.
John Barry,	—	—	1813	
William Alex. Willock,	1840	—	1844	

Annuity awarded to Incumbent, £906 8 10

Compensation for loss of Advowson, 4,552 8 2

14. Derryvullan Rectory, 1610.

Name.	Date of Election to Fellowship.	Date of Co-option.	Date of Acceptance of Benefice.	Observations.
James Heygate,	—	—	1622	Bishop of Kilfenora, 1630.
William Dickerson,	—	—	1628	
Thomas Marshall,	—	—	1630	
Robert Ash,	—	—	—	Deprived 1661.
(Petty Commonwealth) John Leslie,	—	—	1623	Instituted on Presentation of Trinity College Dublin.
William Gradon,*	1692	—	1701	do. do. (Rector of Clogher, 1702)
John Kinnaury,	1712	—	1722	do. do.
Hon. Charles Caulfeild,	—	—	1724	(Son of William, Viscount Charlemont.)
Patrick Delany,	1709	1719	1729	Dean of Down, 1744.
John Kearney,	1719	—	1730	
Thomas McDonnell,	1727	—	1746	
William Mauleverer,	—	—	1763	
Richard Gedley,	—	—	1767	
John Stack,	1781	—	1791	
Hugh Hamilton,	—	—	—	
George Miller,	1789	—	1804	Master of Armagh School.
William Thomas Leith,	1842	—	1846	
John Young Rutledge,	1830	—	1865	Rector of Armagh, October, 1865.
Richard Vanstavern,	—	—	1868	

Annuity awarded to Incumbent, £889 5 11

Compensation for loss of Advowson, 8,194 3 11

* This mark denotes that the Incumbent held another living simultaneously.

Name.	Date of Election to Fellowship.	Date of Cooptation.	Date of Admission to Benefice.	Observations.

V.—DIOCESE OF CLOGHER—continued.

15. [illegible] (secular name) [illegible] (ecclesiastical name) [illegible], 1610.

Name.	Date of Election to Fellowship.	Date of Cooptation.	Date of Admission to Benefice.	Observations.
[illegible]	—	—	before 1622	and in 1631.
John Smith,	—	—	1622	Instituted on Presentation of Trinity College Dublin.
Robert [illegible] (or [illegible])	—	—	1661	do. do. The same appears to have taken the benefice.
William [illegible],	1660	—	1669	Instituted on Presentation of Trinity College Dublin.
Richard [illegible],	1676	—	1682	do. do.
Ezekiel Webb,	—	—	1694	[illegible]
[illegible] Smith,	1677	—	1683	[illegible]
William [illegible],	—	—	1703	
Andrew Mitchell,	—	—	1706	
Caleb Cartwright,	1724	—	1728	Rector of [illegible].
[illegible]	—	—	1743	
[illegible]	—	—	1750	
William [illegible],	1739	—	1748	
[illegible]	—	—	1779	
Thomas R. [illegible],	1814	—	1821	
[illegible]	—	—	1823	
William Connor Magee,	—	—	1850	Dean of Cork, 1864. **Bishop of Peterborough, 1868.**
[illegible]	—	—	1868	

Annuity awarded to Incumbent, £[illegible] 5 [illegible]
Compensation for loss of Advowson, [illegible],974 [illegible] [illegible]

VI.—DIOCESE OF ARDAGH.

16. [illegible] Rectory, 1610.

Name.	Date of Election to Fellowship.	Date of Cooptation.	Date of Admission to Benefice.	Observations.
George Lee,	—	—	1603	Dean of Cork, 160[illegible]
[illegible]	—	—	—	
[illegible]	1617	—	1619	April 3, resigned in June.
[illegible]	1617	—	1619	June, and 1625 by Crown. **Bishop of Kilmore 1642.**
[illegible]	—	—	1623	
[illegible]	—	—	1637	
William [illegible],	—	—	1637	Killed in the Rebellion of 1641.
[illegible]	—	—	1693	
[illegible]	—	—	1668	C.
[illegible]	—	—	in 1679	
William [illegible],	—	—	1684	C.
[illegible]	—	—	1722	C.
James [illegible],	—	—	1722	C.
[illegible] Richardson,	—	—	1733	C.
William [illegible],	—	—	1736	C.
Edward [illegible],	—	—	1738	C.
Thomas [illegible],	—	—	1771	C.
James Montgomery,	—	—	1787	C.
Nathaniel Smith,	—	—	1808	C.
Wm. [illegible],	—	—	1829	C. [illegible]
John [illegible],*	1798	—	1836	[illegible]
William [illegible],	—	—	1863	[illegible]

Annuity awarded to Incumbent, £[illegible] [illegible] [illegible]
Compensation for loss of Advowson, [illegible] [illegible] [illegible]

* [illegible]

† [illegible]

Appendix III. List of Benefices in the Patronage of Trinity College.

VI.—DIOCESE OF ARMAGH—continued.

17. Ardtrea Rectory, 1610.

Name.	Date of Election to Fellowship.	Date of Cooption.	Date of Acceptance of Benefice.	Observations.
Anthony Wainwright,	1605	—	1617	Sep. 16. Resigned October 23.
Robert Ussher,	1611	—	1632	Provost, 1629. Bishop of Kildare 1635.
John Richardson,	1616	—	1637	Bishop of Ardagh 1633.
Thomas Bradley,	1618	—	1637	Presented by Crown.
William Vincent,	...	...	1661	[illegible]
Thomas Wilkinson,	...	...	[illegible]	[illegible]
Edward Wetherington,	1676	—	1682	
Christopher Jenney,	—	—	1698	
Richard Reader,	1683	—	1697	Christopher Jenney was Rector in 1701.
George [illegible],	1707	1717	1728	Bishop of Cloyne, 1738.
John [illegible],	—	—	1734	
Robert [illegible],	1721	—	[illegible]	
Jonathan [illegible],	1726	1734	[illegible]	
Gabriel Stokes,	1736	—	1760	Chancellor of Waterford, 1783–1806.
Robert M'Ghee,	—	—	1803	
Thomas Elrington,	1761	1795	1806	[illegible] Bishop of Limerick, 1820, of Leighlin and Ferns, 1822.
Thomas Meredith,	1800	—	1819	
[illegible],	1812	—	1819	
William Phelan,	1817	—	1830	[illegible]
James Kennedy,	1817	—	1830	
William E. Meade,	—	—	1841	

Annuity awarded to Incumbent, . . £[illegible] 11 3
Compensation for loss of Advowson, . . [illegible] 8 10

18. Clogherny Rectory, 1658.

Name.	Date of Election to Fellowship.	Date of Cooption.	Date of Acceptance of Benefice.	Observations.
Robert V. Dixon,	1838	—	1853	

Annuity awarded to Incumbent, . . £1,363 14 7
Compensation for loss of Advowson, . . 11,701 3 8

19. Clonfeacle Rectory, 1610.

Name.	Date of Election to Fellowship.	Date of Cooption.	Date of Acceptance of Benefice.	Observations.
George Lee .	—	—	1625	
Thomas Crantz,	—	—	1619	
Joseph Travers,	1634	—	1634	
Patrick Sheridan,	1660	1665	—	Bishop of Cloyne, 1679.
Francis Marsh,	—	—	166–	Bishop of Limerick.
Henry Maxwell,	1663	—	1667	Presented by Crown.
James Downham,	—	—	1646	
William Palliser,	1668	—	1681	Bishop of Cloyne, 1693, Archbishop of Cashel, 1694
Bartholomew Vigors,	—	—	1681	Instituted on Presentation of T. C. D. Bishop Ferns.
Peter Drelincourt,	—	—	1690	Presented by Crown.
Robert Echlin,	—	—	1722	
John Walmsley,	1703	1713	1722	Instituted on Presentation of Trinity College Dublin.
Charles Stewart,	1720	1730	1738	do. do.
Henry Clarke,	1724	—	1746	do. Reg. Prof. of Div. 1743.
William Lodge,	—	—	1777	Coll.
William Andrews,	1747	1761	1777	Instituted on Presentation of Trinity College Dublin.
William Richardson,	1766	—	1783	do. do.
Francis Gervais,	—	—	1830	Collat. Evicted on writ of Quare Impedit.
William Davenport,	1794	1813	1822	Instituted on Presentation of Trinity College Dublin.
James Wilson,	1800	1820	1823	do. do.
Henry Griffin,	1811	—	1827	do. Bishop of Limerick 1853.
Joseph Stevenson,	—	—	1854	Presented by Crown.

Annuity awarded to Incumbent, . . £936 7 2
Compensation for loss of Advowson, . . 8,[illegible] 7 6

Appendix XX.

List of Rectories formerly in the Patronage of Trinity College.

Name.	Date of Election to Fellowship.	Date of Co-optation.	Date of Acceptance of Benefice.	Observations.

VI.—DIOCESE OF ARMAGH—*continued.*

30. [illegible] Rectory, 1610.

Name.	Date of Election to Fellowship.	Date of Co-optation.	Date of Acceptance of Benefice.	Observations.
—— [illegible],	1637	—	1639	April 3. Resigned in June.
Robert Maxwell,	1637	—	1639	June.
Henry Leslie,	—	—	1638	
William Darragh,	—	—	1623	Killed in Rebellion of 1641.
Thomas Wilkinson,	—	—	—	
Edward Walkington,	1676	—	1682	Bishop of Down, 1695.
Christopher Jenney,	—	—	1696	Presented by Crown.
George Berkeley,*	1707	1717	1724	Bishop of Cloyne, 1734.
William White,	—	—	1724	
Rev. Charles Chetwood,	—	—	[illegible]	
Thomas [illegible],	—	—	[illegible]	
John O'Connor,	—	—	[illegible]	
Richard B. Vincent,	—	—	[illegible]	
Francis Hall,	—	—	[illegible]	
John [illegible],	[illegible]	—	[illegible]	
James T. O'Brien,	1820	—	1836	Bishop of Ossory, 1842.
Thomas M'Neece,	1836	—	1843	Abp. King's Lecturer in Divinity.
William Lee,	1839	—	1843	Do. do. Archdeacon of Dublin 1864.
William De Burgh,	—	—	1864	
Thomas Jordan,	—	—	1867	

Annuity awarded to Incumbent, . . £[illegible] 13 3

Compensation for loss of Advowson, . . 3,807 18 1

[illegible] with consent of the Provost and Fellows of Trinity College Dublin. The union, however, does not seem to have been long maintained.

31. [illegible] Rectory, 1610.

Name.	Date of Election to Fellowship.	Date of Co-optation.	Date of Acceptance of Benefice.	Observations.
William [illegible],	—	—	1634	
Robert Fairfield,	—	—	1636	
John Kerdiff,	1621	1644	1667	[illegible] in Rebellion of 1641. Dean of [illegible], 1667.
—	—	—	—	
John Clarke,	—	—	[illegible]	[illegible] 1670.
Thomas Wardman,	—	—	1690	Instituted on Presentation of Trinity College Dublin.
John Moore,	—	—	1694	do. do.
Theodore Maurice,	—	—	1733	do. do.
Richard Dobbs,	1734	—	1737	do. do. Dean of Connor.
James Lowry,	—	—	1745	do. do.
John Bush,*	1781	—	1787	do. do.
Thomas H. Porter,	—	—	1863	do. do.

Annuity awarded to Incumbent, . . £[illegible] 8 9

Compensation for loss of Advowson, . . 5,139 16 3

July 5, 1636. The advowson of this Rectory was acquired in the [illegible] of the [illegible].

* This mark denotes that the Incumbent held another living concurrently.

Table II.

List of Fellows of Trinity College who have retired upon College Livings since 1750.

Appendix III.

List of Fellows of Trinity College, who have retired upon College Livings since 1750.

Name.	Elected Fellow.	Co-opted.	Accepted Benefice.	Name of Benefice.	Name.	Elected Fellow.	Co-opted.	Accepted Benefice.	Name of Benefice.
[illegible]	[illegible]	[illegible]	[illegible]	[illegible]	[illegible]	[illegible]	[illegible]	[illegible]	[illegible]
[illegible]	[illegible]	[illegible]	[illegible]	[illegible]	[illegible]	[illegible]	[illegible]	[illegible]	[illegible]
[illegible]	[illegible]	[illegible]	[illegible]	[illegible]	[illegible]	[illegible]	[illegible]	[illegible]	[illegible]
[illegible]	[illegible]	[illegible]	[illegible]	[illegible]	[illegible]	[illegible]	[illegible]	[illegible]	[illegible]
[illegible]	[illegible]	[illegible]	[illegible]	[illegible]	[illegible]	[illegible]	[illegible]	[illegible]	[illegible]
Thomas Leland,	[illegible]	[illegible]	[illegible]	[illegible]	[illegible]	[illegible]	[illegible]	[illegible]	[illegible]
William Martin,	[illegible]	[illegible]	[illegible]	[illegible]	[illegible]	[illegible]	[illegible]	[illegible]	[illegible]
John Stokes,	[illegible]	[illegible]	[illegible]	[illegible]	[illegible]	[illegible]	[illegible]	[illegible]	[illegible]
William Andrews,	[illegible]	[illegible]	[illegible]	[illegible]	[illegible]	[illegible]	[illegible]	[illegible]	[illegible]
Hugh Hamilton,	[illegible]	[illegible]	[illegible]	[illegible]	[illegible]	[illegible]	[illegible]	[illegible]	[illegible]
Thomas Wilson,	[illegible]	[illegible]	[illegible]	[illegible]	[illegible]	[illegible]	[illegible]	[illegible]	[illegible]
[illegible]	[illegible]	[illegible]	[illegible]	[illegible]	[illegible]	[illegible]	[illegible]	[illegible]	[illegible]
Michael Kearney,	[illegible]	[illegible]	[illegible]	[illegible]	[illegible]	[illegible]	[illegible]	[illegible]	[illegible]
[illegible]	[illegible]	[illegible]	[illegible]	[illegible]	[illegible]	[illegible]	[illegible]	[illegible]	[illegible]
[illegible]	[illegible]	[illegible]	[illegible]	[illegible]	[illegible]	[illegible]	[illegible]	[illegible]	[illegible]
[illegible]	[illegible]	[illegible]	[illegible]	[illegible]	[illegible]	[illegible]	[illegible]	[illegible]	[illegible]
Joseph Stopford,	[illegible]	[illegible]	[illegible]	[illegible]	[illegible]	[illegible]	[illegible]	[illegible]	[illegible]
[illegible]	[illegible]	[illegible]	[illegible]	[illegible]	[illegible]	[illegible]	[illegible]	[illegible]	[illegible]
[illegible]	[illegible]	[illegible]	[illegible]	[illegible]	[illegible]	[illegible]	[illegible]	[illegible]	[illegible]
[illegible]	[illegible]	[illegible]	[illegible]	[illegible]	[illegible]	[illegible]	[illegible]	[illegible]	[illegible]
[illegible]	[illegible]	[illegible]	[illegible]	[illegible]	[illegible]	[illegible]	[illegible]	[illegible]	[illegible]
[illegible]	[illegible]	[illegible]	[illegible]	[illegible]	[illegible]	[illegible]	[illegible]	[illegible]	[illegible]
[illegible]	[illegible]	[illegible]	[illegible]	[illegible]	[illegible]	[illegible]	[illegible]	[illegible]	[illegible]
[illegible]	[illegible]	[illegible]	[illegible]	[illegible]	[illegible]	[illegible]	[illegible]	[illegible]	[illegible]
				[illegible]	[illegible]	[illegible]	[illegible]	[illegible]	[illegible]
George Hall,	[illegible]	[illegible]	[illegible]	[illegible]	[illegible]	[illegible]	[illegible]	[illegible]	[illegible]
Richard Graves,	[illegible]	[illegible]	[illegible]	[illegible]	[illegible]	[illegible]	[illegible]	[illegible]	[illegible]
				[illegible]	[illegible]	[illegible]	[illegible]	[illegible]	[illegible]
[illegible]	[illegible]	[illegible]	[illegible]	[illegible]	[illegible]	[illegible]	[illegible]	[illegible]	[illegible]
[illegible]	[illegible]	[illegible]	[illegible]	[illegible]	[illegible]	[illegible]	[illegible]	[illegible]	[illegible]
Thomas Elrington,	[illegible]	[illegible]	[illegible]	[illegible]	[illegible]	[illegible]	[illegible]	[illegible]	[illegible]
[illegible]	[illegible]	[illegible]	[illegible]	[illegible]	[illegible]	[illegible]	[illegible]	[illegible]	[illegible]
[illegible]	[illegible]	[illegible]	[illegible]	[illegible]	[illegible]	[illegible]	[illegible]	[illegible]	[illegible]
[illegible]	[illegible]	[illegible]	[illegible]	[illegible]	[illegible]	[illegible]	[illegible]	[illegible]	[illegible]

Table III.

Table showing some particulars of the application of the Provost and Senior Fellows to the Church Temporalities Commissioners for Compensation for loss of Advowsons, and the Sums awarded by the Commissioners.

Application of the Provost and Senior Fellows to the Church Temporalities Commissioners for compensation for loss of Advowsons.

Name of Benefice.	Net Annual Income of Benefice.			Age of Incumbent.	Compensation awarded.		
	£	s.	d.		£	s.	d.
Clondevaddock,	1,060	6	9	56	9,239	7	8
Arboe,	916	14	8	88	2,867	13	1
Drumragh,	1,173	3	4	45	6,412	8	7
Raymoghy,	740	3	1	48	3,992	5	9
Clonca,	571	13	8	48	2,523	1	1
Aghalurcher,	750	12	10	58	3,141	16	6
Desertcreight,	657	1	3	63	3,108	10	8
Enniskillen,	688	3	9	60	3,274	16	1
[illegible]	613	0	0	50	3,251	9	8
[illegible]	907	18	3	56	5,920	5	3
Ardtrea,	1,450	3	11	53	8,003	11	9
Derryvullan,	1,084	6	11	68	4,149	8	11
Kilmacrenan,	391	5	2	31	2,152	7	10
Killeshandra,	1,067	7	5	71	3,758	7	7
Cappagh,	1,204	9	4	49	7,001	14	11
Clondahorky,	334	3	6	36	1,202	12	6
Clonfeacle,	811	10	2	58	3,215	10	0
[illegible]	770	15	0	57	3,835	14	8
Aughnish,	381	9	9	32	2,379	4	10
Tullyaughnish,	1,196	11	7	41	5,684	2	1
Clogherny,	1,574	7	6	37	11,701	9	8

Appendix XX.

Net Value of Benefices, &c.

TABLE IV.

TABLE showing approximately the NET VALUES of the following BENEFICES, and the several incomes of the Three Grades of JUNIOR FELLOWS at the dates at which they respectively became vacant.

	Vacant.	Net Value.	State of Tutorial Fund.		
			Senior Grade.	Middle Grade.	Junior Grade.
		£	£	£	£
Ardtrea, . .	1847	960	535	440	427
Clonfeacle, . .	1849	790	558	544	129
Clondehorky, . .	1852	1,153	645	501	323
[illegible], . .	1857	760	560	441	334
Dromragh, . .	1857	735	596	323	348
[illegible], . .	1849	633	633	444	429
Clonmany, . .	1851	671	627	478	319
Tullyaughnish, . .	1853	734	487	478	310

To these sums should be added £171, being the average amount paid by the Bursar to each of the Junior Fellows out of the funds of the College in 1851. See Report of Dublin University Commission, 1853, pp. 134–136.

APPENDIX XXI.

Appendix XXI.

Memorandum showing the amount of compensation paid to Trinity College, for the loss of its Advowsons, by the Church Temporalities Commissioners.

MEMORANDUM stating the AMOUNT of COMPENSATION PAID to TRINITY COLLEGE, for the loss of its ADVOWSONS, by the Church Temporalities Commissioners, under the provisions of the Irish Church Act, and the application thereof.

I.

The sum received as Compensation for the eighteen Advowsons granted to Trinity College by the Letters Patent of King James I., dated August 29, 1610, was £[illegible] [illegible]s. 6d.

(See Parliamentary Paper, dated July 31, 1874, House of Commons, No. [illegible], p. 14, in which the sum paid for each Advowson is stated.)

The Board of Trinity College, acting under the advice of Counsel, invested the above sum of £[illegible] [illegible]s. [illegible]d. in the purchase of £[illegible] [illegible]s. [illegible]d., New Three per Cent. Stock.

The annual income paid on this Stock is £[illegible] [illegible]s.

II.

The amount received from the Church Temporalities Commissioners as compensation for the three Advowsons of Killeshandra, Kildallagh, and Clonbarney, formerly purchased by the College, and paid for out of the Clear Overplus, viz., . . .	£33,[illegible] 18 6
Add Interest on the entire Advowson Compensation Money received from the Commissioners, from July 1, 1869, to date of payment (deducting Income Tax), ...	10,[illegible] 6 11
Add Interest on Deposit Receipts for Advowson Fund received from Bank of Ireland, December 1[illegible], 1872, to March [illegible], 1873, ...	716 19 10
Add Half-year's Income on £[illegible] [illegible]s., being part of the old Clear Advowson Fund invested in Government Stock, due 5th October, 1873, net, ...	1,[illegible] [illegible] [illegible]
Making together the sum of . . .	£44,[illegible] [illegible] [illegible]

(See Parliamentary Paper as above, p. 14.)

If this sum had been invested in Government Stock, as was done with the Compensation for the eighteen Advowsons stated above, the amount of New Three per cent. Stock purchased thereby would have been £[illegible] [illegible]s. [illegible]d., and the annual income thereon would have been .	£1,449 7 11
Add the above amount of income arising from the eighteen Advowsons, .	[illegible] 18 6

III.

The Board of Trinity College were advised by Counsel that as the Advowsons of the three last mentioned Benefices had been purchased with funds taken from the Clear Overplus, the Board were not bound to invest the Compensation money paid for these three Advowsons; but that they were at liberty to apply this Compensation money, as well as the interest derived from the whole Advowson Fund, to the general purposes of the College. They therefore decided to allocate these payments towards the purchase, from the Church Temporalities Commissioners, under the [illegible] section of the Irish Church Act, of the tithe rentcharge payable on the Estates of the College.

The total annual amount of rentcharge payable to the Commissioners was .	£2,[illegible] [illegible] [illegible]
Deduct average amount of Poor Rates, .	1[illegible] [illegible] [illegible]
Net annual amount of Rentcharge, .	£2,437 13 2
Twenty-two and a-half years' purchase on this sum, ...	£5[illegible],[illegible] [illegible] 10

As before stated, a part of this, the purchase-money, namely, £44,[illegible] [illegible]s. [illegible]d., was provided out of the Compensation paid for the three Advowsons, along with the amount of interest stated above, and the balance, £[illegible] [illegible]s. [illegible]d., was paid out of the general funds of the College. The College, by this payment, escaped immediate exemption from the rentcharge [illegible]; but as this annuity (or, to be quite exact, an annuity larger by £[illegible] [illegible]s. [illegible]d., into which the rentcharge annually would have been converted, under the second part of [illegible] section of the Irish Church Act, [illegible]) would have ceased to be paid in fifty-two years without any payment, in order to calculate the real beneficial [illegible] to the funds of the College arising from such immediate payment, there must be deducted from the aforesaid annual sum of £2,437 13s. 2d. such a sum as, if invested at say 3½ per cent., would reproduce the sum of £5[illegible],[illegible] [illegible]s. [illegible]d., paid for the rentcharge to the Temporalities Commissioners at the end of fifty-two years.

The calculation is as follows:—

Annual immediate rentcharge as above,	£2,437 13 2
Deduct annual sinking fund, which, at 3½ per cent., would repay the purchase-money in fifty-two years, .	[illegible] [illegible] [illegible]

The portion of this increase, arising from the sum of £16,855 14s. 8d. (being Compensation for the three Fellowships and Interest on the whole Advowson fund, as above stated, is £1,[illegible] 10s. 6d.

The actual annual increase, therefore, in the College funds, arising from the payment for Advowsons, may be stated thus:—

(a) Interest on the Government Stock, purchased with the payment for the eighteen Advowsons, ... £3,[illegible] 16 0

(b) Increment of Income arising from the application of the Advowson payment (including interest), to the Fellowships of Compensation, as [illegible] above, ... £1,[illegible] 10 6

Total, . . . £4,[illegible] 15 6

(Signed), Joseph Carson, Bursar.

Trinity College, February 5, 1878.

Appendix XXI. Memorandum relating to amount of compensation paid to Trinity College, for the loss of its advowsons, by the Church Temporalities Commissioners.

APPENDIX XXII.

Appendix XXII. Appeal of the Fellows, in Holy Orders, of Trinity College, Dublin.

Appeal of the Fellows, in Holy Orders, of Trinity College, Dublin, heard before Viscount [illegible], Mr. Justice Lawson, and the Master of the Rolls, on the 3rd of June, 1873. Judgment was reserved and delivered on the 20th December, 1873.

The Master of the Rolls, upon the sitting of the Court, proceeded to deliver judgment (a):—

In this case several of the Fellows of Trinity College in Holy Orders, namely, the Rev. Mr. Stubbs, the Rev. Mr. Gray, and the Rev. Mr. Mahaffy, have appealed from a decision of Mr. Justice Lawson, who disallowed their claims to compensation, which were made under the 15th Section of the Irish Church Act, 1869. The facts upon which those claims were made, and upon which this appeal rests, are not disputed. Under Ancient Charters, or Grants from the Crown, the Corporation of Trinity College was, at the passing of the Irish Church Act, in 1869, the owner of a considerable number of Advowsons; the next presentation to each of which, upon avoidance, would be tendered to the Fellows of the College in rotation, according to seniority, in conformity with a usage of such ancient standing and such uniform observance, that we may treat it as having the force of law. Several of those livings exceed in annual value the income derivable from any of the Fellowships which the Appellants enjoy; and, therefore, it may be taken that if the Irish Church Act had not passed, there was a possibility or a probability, of one of those livings being tendered to the Appellants, or some one of them, varying more or less, according to the age and health of the incumbent for the time being, and of the Appellant.

We are disposed to think that this right, though one somewhat difficult of estimation, is a right of pecuniary value within the true meaning of that term; and, therefore, the question is, whether the Irish Church Act has given the right of claiming compensation for the loss thereof. It is clear enough that a Fellow of Trinity College in Holy Orders is neither the holder of a benefice nor the holder of a cathedral preferment; giving those terms the fullest signification, and the interpretation of them in the Irish Church Act is of the widest character. But it is argued that they were ecclesiastical persons, and, therefore, that they come precisely within the letter of the 15th Section of the Statute, and that as such they are thereby given the right to claim compensation for the loss being occasioned by the rights of presentation being taken from the College.

This question then turns entirely upon the true construction of the Statute. Now one of the very first canons of construction in reference to the interpretation of a statute is, that general terms made use of in it are to be construed with regard to its context; and nothing can be so opposed to principle and authority as the assertion that, because a general term, according to ordinary meaning, includes or embraces a particular thing or class within it, it must have that meaning in every statute or written instrument in which it happens to be used. No doubt, as a general rule, the ordinary grammatical meaning is to be given; but the context of the statute or written instrument can always serve to show—nay, more, to determine, that the term is used in a more restricted or different sense than understood ordinarily or in popular signification. Thus, in a statute, words which, standing by themselves, are capable [illegible] of one wide and [illegible] comprehensive, are shown, by reference to other portions of the same statute, and sometimes actually by reference to statutes in pari materia, to have a meaning so restricted and different from that which a mere perusal of them in the place where they are found would indicate, that the [illegible] and [illegible] interpretation of terms which in ordinary language are perfectly clear [illegible] only [illegible], until the reasons for such interpretation are clearly laid before the [illegible]. Lord Justice Turner, the very highest authority, in Hawkins v. Gathercole, 6 De G., M. & G., p. 21, after observing that in construing Acts of Parliament the words which are used are not alone to be regarded, and that regard must be had to the intent and meaning of the Legislature, says that the true meaning of the law upon this subject is to be found in the following passage, which was quoted from Stradling v. Morgan, in Plowden, Vol. I., p. 205, "In which it is said that the Judges of the law in all times past have so far pursued the intent of the makers of statutes, that they have expounded Acts which were general in words to be but particular;" and after referring to several cases the report contains the following remarkable passage, at p. 205: "From which cases it appears that the sages of the law heretofore have construed statutes quite contrary to the letter in some appearance, and those statutes which comprehend all things in the letter they have expounded to extend but to some things, and those which generally prohibit all people from doing such an act they have interpreted to permit some people to do it, and those which include any person in the letter they have adjudged to reach some persons only; which expositions have always been founded upon the intent of the Legislature which they have collected, sometimes by considering the cause and necessity of making the Act, sometimes by comparing one part of the Act with another, and sometimes by foreign circumstances; so that they have ever been guided by the intent of the Legislature, which they have always taken, according to the necessity of the matter, and according to that which is consonant to reason and good discretion." Taking the law as so settled, let the statute now in question be examined in its entirety and in detail. It is perfectly manifest that every ecclesiastical person, in the wide sense of that term, was never intended to be included in the provisions of this Act of Parliament. If that were so, one would expect to find clauses for the compensation of such persons, but none such exist. The compensation clauses, apart from the 15th Section, are carefully worded so as to embrace only the special classes of "Ecclesiastical Persons" therein particularly described, which are: "Every holder of any Archbishopric, Bishopric, benefice, or cathedral preferment," in or connected with the Church which was about to be disestablished, and every curate, [illegible]

(a) Mr. Fitzgibbon, Q.C., and Mr. [illegible], appeared for the Appellants: The Solicitor-General and Mr. [illegible], Q.C., appeared for the Crown.

APPENDIX XXXI. — Appeal of the Fellows in Holy Orders, of Trinity College, Dublin.

by the 15th Section of the Act; and it seems a strange proposition, that the Statute in its 46th Section has thrown its apparent policy to the winds and considered within it every ordained clergyman. Now one of the consequences of holding this position would be, that an ordained clergyman who had purchased an advowson before the passing of the Act, would, because he had the right to present himself on the next vacancy to the benefice, be entitled to compensation for his right of succession; while the same person would, as a matter of course, under the 15th Section, get full compensation for the loss of his advowson, which would include in it the same next presentation, thus getting compensation twice over for the next presentation. In truth, the 46th Section, if one regards its provisions and the interpretation clauses of the Act, plainly seems to indicate that the right of succession must be one flowing from or connected with some office or ecclesiastical preferment in the Church about to be disestablished; and this will appear more clearly by examining the several sections of the statute in which the term "ecclesiastical person" occurs. The first section in which this term occurs is the 14th, where the use of the term is by the very context limited in its meaning and application. The words are: "Without the consent of the ecclesiastical person under whom such curate or other officer may be serving at the time of the application being made for commutation."

In the 20th Section is it used twice, and there it is equally plain that it is used in a restricted sense. In Section 23 it is again used in the same way as only including those ecclesiastical persons entitled to commute, and who have agreed to commute. Again, it is used in the 27th Section in the same restricted manner. The use of the term in the 30th Section is a strong instance of the same limited meaning assigned to it in the Act of Parliament.

Then comes the 46th Section, which is as follows:—"The Commissioners shall ascertain whether the Chancellor and Prebendaries of Christ Church, Dublin, or any other Ecclesiastical Persons, are or are not entitled to any right of succession in the benefices of Kilcullen, Kildare, Saint Mary, Saint Thomas, and Saint George, Dublin, or any other benefice or benefices, and if entitled, shall award to them, respectively, such sum in compensation for the same as shall seem to them just."

Now, entirely apart from the interpretation clause, I should, on the general rules of construction, be prepared to hold that, inasmuch as the right of compensation in the instances quoted in the Section is expressly given as connected with offices or preferments in the Church, the words "or any other" ought to receive interpretation according to the rule "ejusdem generis;" for that construction alone would make the meaning of the 46th Section to be in unison with all the other provisions of the Statute; why, if ALL ecclesiastical persons were to be compensated for supposed loss of succession should the language of the Statute be so peculiar? But when the interpretation clause is examined it will be found that "ecclesiastical person," having explained itself by the context all throughout the Statute for the first time in this 46th Section, requires a meaning to be given to it, partly restricted and partly extended, which is answered by the interpretation clause, showing that "ecclesiastical

measure of compensation for the entire advowson, which of course covers the very next presentation, to the right of succession to which compensation is claimed by individual members of the corporation. It seems to me that the Fellows of Trinity College, though in Holy Orders, are not entitled to claim compensation under the Act; in other words, that the claim for compensation by the individual members of the corporation cannot be made good against the property vested in the Church Commissioners, but is, if it at all exists, a matter of adjustment between them and the corporation itself. A good deal of reliance during the argument was placed on the words in the recital in the statute, viz.:—"all just and equitable claims." I do not think that this recital, having regard to the way in which it is used, helps the contention; but it would appear more just and equitable that where the entire advowson vested in the corporation is compensated for by payment in full to the corporation, a right to a next presentation, vested in a member of that corporation, should be adjusted by the corporation, out of the funds it has got as compensation, rather than that the same thing should be doubly paid for, an intention which it is most difficult to impute to the Legislature. It appears to me, that to hold that the words "ecclesiastical persons" in the 46th Section are to be restricted to persons holding a benefice or cathedral preferment, as defined by the Act, accords with the general intent and provisions of the Statute, and is, having regard to the interpretation clauses, and the rules of construction I have referred to, absolutely required.

Nothing is of such frequent occurrence in our reports as words used in a clause, apparently in a most general sense, being restricted in their meaning. These cases are almost countless. I have selected a few of them which stand in different points of view, but the principles of which converge to illustrate what I have said, and the principles upon which our decision in this case must be founded.

By the Statute of the 3rd and 4th Vict., c. 105, a judgment is made an equitable charge in favour of the creditor against all the property of the debtor mentioned in it; viz., lands, rectories, tithes, hereditaments, &c., of or to which the debtor was, at the entry of judgment, seised or possessed for any estate or interest whatever, either at law or in equity. *Larger words cannot be conceived*; and it was held even in this country, where the incumbent could actually charge his benefice, that ecclesiastical rectories were not within the term "rectories." Why? Because in an earlier section of the same Act of Parliament, dealing with a wholly different matter, the word "rectory," though used apparently in the most general manner, was shown by the context to be confined to lay rectories.

The then Lord Chancellor of Ireland had held for a considerable time the opposite view; holding that the general words of the 22nd Section should get their full force and meaning; but he was obliged (when the matter was reviewed in the Court of Appeal in Chancery here), yielding to the rules I have mentioned, to reverse all his previous decisions, and to hold that the general meaning of the word "rectory" was to be restricted, and that lay rectories only were within the 22nd Section. That case will be found reported as *Stacey* v. *Fleming*, 14 Irish Chancery Reports, p. 23.

Appendix XXII. — Appeal of the Fellows in Holy Orders of Trinity College, Dublin.

ed by any glossary, I should hold, that the right of succession spoken of must, having regard to the context, and the whole frame of the Act, mean a right incident to the ecclesiastical status of the person in the Church. In the case named, of the Chancellor and Prebendaries of Christ Church, it means a right of succession to which, by virtue of the Chancellorship or prebend, the holder was entitled. Applying the ejusdem generis principle, the word "other" must point to that construction. These ecclesiastical offices were abolished by the Act, and the scheme of the Act is to give compensation for the loss of the office itself, and of any right to succeed to another office incident to the office held. It never could be held to apply to any right of succession belonging to a person in holy orders, growing out of the exercise of a right of patronage by the owner of an advowson entitled to compensation under the 15th section of the Act. The owner of the advowson may be charged with a duty or trust to present a particular person on the next avoidance, and the person so presented must be a clerk in holy orders, but his right to be presented does not grow out of his ecclesiastical status, but out of a special relation between him and the patron of the living. Thus, if a clergyman is himself the owner of an advowson, he may present himself on the next avoidance; but that is not a right of succession under the 40th section, but a matter to be considered in calculating the value of the advowson under the 15th section. I have always so held, and have disallowed such claims when presented under section 46. The same principle must apply where, instead of the clergyman being himself the owner of the advowson, another is owner of it with a trust or duty to present him. The Act provides that the entire capital value of the advowson is to be paid as compensation, and it would be absurd to hold, first, that the entire sum representing the value of the advowson should be paid to the owner or trustee, and besides that persons having rights as against him should be compensated out of the funds of the Commissioners, instead of out of the capital sum representing the entire value of the advowson. Now, applying that to the present case, how does the matter stand? The Corporation of Trinity College, consisting of the Provost, Fellows, and Scholars, have a number of advowsons, a sum of over £150,000 has been ascertained to be the value of those advowsons, and has been paid over to the corporation, and now represents those rights. Then it appears that by a usage of the corporation certain members of it, the Fellows were entitled in a certain order to be offered the presentation to those livings—that gives them a right, but not a right growing out of their ecclesiastical status, but incident to their office of Fellow, the being in holy orders being a necessary qualification for the enjoyment of the right. The status of Trinity College, and of its Fellows, is not affected by the provisions of the Church Act; but the College, like any other patron, owned the advowsons, and has been compensated for the loss, and the individual members of the corporation, who have subordinate rights against the corporation, must assert them against the sum paid to the corporation, in respect of those advowsons. I am very far from saying that the Fellows have not such a right. I only decide that they have no such right against the Commissioners, for that would be to make them pay for the same thing twice.

But the interpretation clause removes all doubt upon the matter. If the word ecclesiastical person, in the 40th section, had included [illegible], it would have included [illegible] compensation under that section by members of Cathedral corporations, who were entitled to succeed to other Cathedral preferments, and, therefore, the interpretation clause says an ecclesiastical person includes a person holding a cathedral preferment in [illegible] Cathedral, which [illegible]. We, then, have decided that the Chaplains of Christ Church, though laymen, were ecclesiastical persons within the meaning of the Act. The interpretation clause says the word ecclesiastical person shall mean any Archbishop, Bishop, or person holding any benefice; this excluding from it persons in holy orders who do not fill any of these positions.

[illegible] in my decision, in the case that a Fellow of Trinity College in Holy Orders, as such, is not an ecclesiastical person within the 40th section of the Act.

Lord Justice [illegible] concurred in the judgment already delivered, and stated that although the appellants had not succeeded, yet, as the case was a fair one for argument, the Commissioners would allow them their costs.

APPENDIX XXIII.

Appendix XXIII. — Rev. Joseph A. Galbraith to the Earl of Belmore.

Reverend Joseph A. Galbraith, F.T.C.D., to the Earl of Belmore.

Trinity College,
14 March, 1878.

Dear Lord Belmore,—With reference to the recommendation of the Commissioners that an election to one Fellowship, and one only, should be held every year, I have made the following calculations, which show that the number of Fellows existing under such a system will never be so great at any period as to impose a serious strain on the funds of the College.

I assume as the law of mortality that which is expressed in [illegible] Table ([illegible]), on which, I believe, with one exception, all Government dealings involving life contingencies are now conducted.

I have ascertained from the Senior Lecturer's books the ages of the Provost and Fellows. Taking one with another I assume that their ages at the middle of the year 1878 may be stated as follows:—One at each of the following number of years, viz., 78, 75, 68, 67, 66, 63, 61, 53, 51, 52, 41, 49, 47, 45, 37, 36, 35, 33, 33. Four at 60. Six at 57. Three at 38. Two at 54. In all thirty-four persons.

If we suppose a population to consist of one thousand males for each individual in this body, and of the same age, it follows from the assumed law of mortality, that it will, if not recruited, die off in successive periods, according to the following Table.

Appendix XXIII. — Rev. Joseph A. Galbraith to the Earl of Rosse.

If these numbers be added to the foregoing, we get the following table, showing the state of the population at the end of each period.

TABLE III.

[illegible]	[illegible]	[illegible]	[illegible]	[illegible]	[illegible]	[illegible]	[illegible]	[illegible]	[illegible]
24,000	33,[illegible]	33,480	32,[illegible]	[illegible]	[illegible]	31,[illegible]	[illegible]	[illegible]	[illegible]

Dividing these numbers by 1,000, we get the following, as representing the probable number of Fellows in the body, supposing two, and one only, of the average age of 24 years [illegible] elected each year in and after 1879.

TABLE IV.

[illegible]	[illegible]	[illegible]	[illegible]	[illegible]	[illegible]	[illegible]	[illegible]	[illegible]	[illegible]
24	33·666	33·[illegible]	32·[illegible]	[illegible]	31·919	31·407	30·[illegible]	[illegible]	[illegible]

The usual interpretation is to be put on these numbers, which seem to include fractions of an individual; for example, the figure 33·480 signifies [illegible] the figures 31·919 and 31·407 show that it is almost certain that the number of Fellows in the body would be [illegible].

[illegible]

In sixty years the present body will be exhausted, after that the probable number of Fellows will be [illegible], that is to say, it will fluctuate evenly within small limits on either side of this number.

In order to adopt a Life Table which from past experience will best enable us to estimate the future number in the body on the proposed plan of election, I have endeavoured to obtain, with the aid of the College records, as near an approximation as possible to the mean after-life time, commonly called the "expectation of life," [illegible] a period of [illegible] years ([illegible]), during which [illegible] Fellows were elected; of these [illegible] the ages of [illegible] at death. [illegible] The ages of the remaining [illegible] at the time of election were as follows:—

TABLE V.

[illegible]

The general mean of these ages is 24·[illegible], say 24·[illegible]. The number of years lived by these [illegible] persons [illegible], from which it appears that the number of years enjoyed collectively after election was [illegible], giving a mean of 36·[illegible], with a probable error of [illegible]. I shall now give the mean after-life time for the ages 24 and 25, according to the following Life Tables:—

Northampton ([illegible]).
Carlisle (Milne).
Equitable Experience (Morgan).
Institute of Actuaries.
Clergy Experience ([illegible]).
Healthy Districts (Farr).
English Life (Farr).

And between the ages 24 and 25 interpolate the figures which correspond to 24·[illegible], the mean age of obtaining Fellowship during this period.

TABLE VI.

Age.	Northampton.	Carlisle.	Equitable Experience.	Institute of Actuaries.	Clergy Experience.	Healthy Districts.	English Life.
24	[illegible]	[illegible]	[illegible]	[illegible]	[illegible]	[illegible]	[illegible]
24·[illegible]	[illegible]	[illegible]	[illegible]	[illegible]	[illegible]	[illegible]	[illegible]
25	[illegible]	[illegible]	[illegible]	[illegible]	[illegible]	[illegible]	[illegible]

From these figures it appears that the law of mortality of the Fellows of Trinity College, so far as it can be judged of by this mode of estimation, agrees more nearly with the Government Table, and Farr's English Life Table than with any of the others.

In order to form an estimate of the probable mean age of obtaining Fellowship in future, we must take as a guide the experience of the last [illegible] years. During this period [illegible] Fellows were elected at the following ages, [illegible] [illegible] From these figures we obtain, as a general mean, [illegible], with a probable error of [illegible].

I have stated that in the calculation of the mean after-life time, [illegible], corresponding to the age 24·[illegible], as deduced from the observation of [illegible] lives, there is a probable error of [illegible]. [illegible] the mean after-life time will amount to [illegible], which is practically the same as that given by the Carlisle Table. I therefore think it right to give the result of a calculation, using this well known Table for the basis, similar to that which led to Table IV., computed on the Government rate of mortality.

TABLE VII.

[illegible]	[illegible]	[illegible]	[illegible]	[illegible]	[illegible]	[illegible]	[illegible]	[illegible]	[illegible]
24	[illegible]	[illegible]	[illegible]	[illegible]	[illegible]	[illegible]	[illegible]	[illegible]	[illegible]

It appears, then, that if the Carlisle rate be assumed to correspond more nearly with the College experience, the number in the body, on the plan proposed, will never exceed an average of [illegible], and that an interval of [illegible] to [illegible] years must elapse before it [illegible] [illegible] providing a permanent additional place. [illegible], it is plain that the adoption of the plan of election to Fellowship recommended by the Commissioners, can never produce a serious strain on the funds of the College.

I remain, my Lord, yours faithfully,

Joseph A. Galbraith.

SALARIES AND GENERAL PAYMENTS:—

Salaries of Provost, Fellows, and College Officers, . . .

Professors, except those in Professional Schools, . . .

Scholars and Non-Foundation Scholars, ...

Studentships, Exhibitions, and Medical Scholarships, . .

APPENDIX XXV.

University Tests (Dublin).

Chapter 21.

An Act to abolish Tests in Trinity College and the University of Dublin. [26th May, 1873].

Whereas it is expedient that the benefits of Trinity College and the University of Dublin, and of the colleges in the said University as places of religion and learning, should be rendered freely accessible to the nation:

And whereas by means of divers prohibitions, tests, and disabilities many of Her Majesty's subjects are debarred from the full enjoyment of the same;

And whereas it is expedient that such prohibitions, tests, and disabilities should be removed;

Be it therefore enacted by the Queen's most Excellent Majesty, by and with the advice and consent of the Lords Spiritual and Temporal, and Commons, in this present Parliament assembled, and by the authority of the same, as follows:

1. This Act may be cited as the University of Dublin Tests Act, 1873.

2. In the construction of this Act,—

The word "office" shall not, so long as the University of Dublin shall continue to confer degrees in the Faculty of Theology, apply to any Professor of or Lecturer in Divinity; but, save as aforesaid, the word shall include every professorship, assistant or deputy professorship, public lectureship, prelectorship, lectureship, assistant lectureship, readership, fellowship, studentship, scholarship, and exhibition, and also any other or emolument not in this section specified, the income of which is payable out of the revenues or income of the said university or college, or any of the schools thereof, or which is held and enjoyed by any member of the same.

3. From and after the passing of this Act no person shall be required upon exercising, or to enable him to exercise, any of the rights and privileges which may heretofore have been or may hereafter be conferred on students or graduates in the said university, or upon taking or holding, or to enable him to take or hold, any office in the said university or colleges as aforesaid, or upon teaching, or to enable him to teach, within the said university or colleges, to subscribe to any article or formulary of faith, or to make any declaration or take any oath respecting his religious belief or profession, or to conform to any form of public worship, or to do any act in connexion with any form of public worship, or to belong to any specified church, sect, or denomination; nor shall any person be compelled in the said university or college to attend the public worship of any church, sect, or denomination to which he does not belong; and no person elected to a fellowship or any other office shall be deprived of his office by reason that he is not or does not become ordained in holy orders.

4. Upon the passing of this Act the Act specified in the Schedule to this Act is hereby repealed to the extent in the third column of the said Schedule mentioned.

SCHEDULE.

Sess. of Act.	Title of Act.	Extent of repeal.
33 Geo. 3. c. 21. of the Parliament of Ireland.	An Act for the Relief of His Majesty's Popish, or Roman Catholic subjects of Ireland.	So much of section 7 as excepts from the operation of such section the College of the Holy and Undivided Trinity, near Dublin.

INDEX.

www.ingramcontent.com/pod-product-compliance
Lightning Source LLC
Chambersburg PA
CBHW020805020726
47495CB00008B/2599
* 9 7 8 3 7 4 2 8 1 2 7 6 6 *